T0354983

A
Gangsters
Dying
Request

A
Gangsters
Dying
Request

W. D. LOEWEN

A GANGSTERS DYING REQUEST

iUniverse books may be ordered through booksellers or by contacting:

iUniverse
1663 Liberty Drive
Bloomington, IN 47403
www.iuniverse.com
844-349-9409

Because of the dynamic nature of the Internet, any web addresses or links contained in this book may have changed since publication and may no longer be valid. The views expressed in this work are solely those of the author and do not necessarily reflect the views of the publisher, and the publisher hereby disclaims any responsibility for them.

Any people depicted in stock imagery provided by Getty Images are models, and such images are being used for illustrative purposes only. Certain stock imagery © Getty Images.

ISBN: 978-1-6632-7009-2 (sc)
ISBN: 978-1-6632-7011-5 (hc)
ISBN: 978-1-6632-7010-8 (e)

Library of Congress Control Number: 2025900507

Print information available on the last page.

iUniverse rev. date: 01/20/2025

Dedication

· ·

To my friends who encouraged this endeavor:
Dwight Heinrichs who thinks I should become more Bohemian
Doralyn Heinrichs a great friend a colleague
Eleanor Desjardins who got me into pickleball
And most importantly
J-Girl who shall be forever *anonymous*

Forward

This work is entirely fictitious. The names used are fabricated and do not represent anyone living or dead. However, that does not mean that certain concepts within this book are not possibly legitimate.

There is no reason to believe that a cartel with extensive financial resources would not use tunnelling machines, or that the bayou does not seclude places of debauchery.

There is every reason to believe that drug and human trafficking is prevalent along the borders and to some extent is aided, if not by people, then by misguided policies such as sanctuary cities that give refuge under the guise of refugee status or to a segment of immigrants that "pretend" or may come as migrant farm workers etc., but are, in essence, entering the country to do no good. The United States is the number one consumer of illicit drugs coming from Central and South America as escapism is almost necessary in this environment. And who, if given the opportunity, may not be corrupted by the promise of wealth and sex without consequences? All that is required is privacy and anonymity.

Perhaps, as well, one should not believe the narrative that the CIA and FBI do not work together to protect the national interest. Of course they do. And does it make sense that an agent could retire if any past cases are still possibly active?

Graziano

RUNNING IN THE DARK OF night has always been one of my past times. Music in my ears, a clear sky, moon, stars and a nice warm breeze makes keeping in some level of shape a little more palatable. Fort Lauderdale is generally a safe city, especially in any of the communities just a bit farther from the beach. The beach attracts the homeless, PTSD soldiers, and drug dealers as well as party people having all kinds of mind-altering experiences. It's best to stay a bit of distance from the beach in the wee small hours of the morning.

It was a night like any other, warm, a bit humid and muggy and I was therefore out a bit late, and clocked the time at 2:00 A.M. Okay, maybe that is a bit later than a bit late, but I often don't sleep well. I seem to have been born to toss and turn, my mind never able to rest, drawing me back into dangerous liaisons past lived. Rather, I toss and turn until I beg for sleep to come, or until I just give up and land back on my feet. As an ex-CIA agent, I have had many years of working well into the early hours. A late-night run was just something I developed a habit of doing after working the hours that were necessary to track down certain unsavory elements of society. Moreover, it was the only way to obtain a bit of relief from loneliness. Awake, alone in the night, day after day and night after night, partly an occupational hazard, but partly my own inability to form a lasting relationship.

It was just when distant popping sounds amused my ears that the corner appeared suddenly at my feet. The corner was on a bit of a rise, and I was able to turn my head to the right and look down a slight incline, where, coming out of the alley, a car had transgressed half the street, a T-street, and had come to a halt.

Behind it, two more like cars, all Escalades, the last one barely peering out of the alley, as if it was a mouse searching for the presence of a cat. The caravan's path was halted from turning in either direction by two large gravel trucks and men with m240s and a variety of handheld pistols. The windows of all the vehicles appeared to be shot out and broken glass was lying everywhere.

I pulled myself back behind the wall of the building and hoped I had not been spotted. Any normal person would have turned and run in the opposite direction, instead of peering around the corner a second time just to watch people being shot. But occasional weapon fire exchange was not necessarily a new thing for me. I had spent my early years with the agency as a field operative, had chased down a few nasty criminals, usually hired help that rich guys or corrupt government officials were able to contract.

Luckily, I was wearing dark clothes, a habit left over from my past as an operative. No shelling was coming my way, so I peered out to see men with weapons pour out of the vehicles behind the lead Escalade. In the gun fight that ensued, I saw several men on both sides hit, in the bodies, the heads, the legs, as if scarecrows outfitted for gun practice!

In time, the driver's side door of the lead escalade opened; the driver got out and opened fire on what appeared to be the last remaining attacker. As he dropped the last attacker, he reached back and opened the door to the back seat and said to a greying and quite elderly man: "Come, we have to get out of this vehicle, our tires are full of holes, and they shot up the front of our car, hitting the radiator. We'll take the vehicle at the back of the line; it may still be good to go".

As the older man exited, he reached back and grabbed a small suitcase. In that moment he was struck in the back left side by a bullet. The driver turned and exchanged fire with the man he thought he had already killed, and in a few seconds both laid quiet.

I waited for a few minutes as I gauged the scene. I knew the police would be here before too long. This kind of thing doesn't go down with at least someone making a call when it finally gets quiet. I would not have been able to live with myself, however, if I just left a wounded man to likely die while waiting for an ambulance to show up as a result of someone calling the affair in.

Knowing the risk, given my assumptions about the type of person he might be, I decided to risk saving the one remaining individual. Running down, I grabbed the man and helped him out of his jacket so I could examine his wound. There was a lot of blood. He turned to me and said: "You must take me to my house as quickly as possible. When Oreski learns that this event did not go as he had planned, he will be coming for me there. I cannot allow him to gain access to certain information that only I have, and in fact, some I have with me. The remainder is in my home".

"I think we should get you to a doctor as quickly as possible." I responded.

"No way. I need to do something for my daughter, who knows nothing of my life or my business. She was the outcome of a brief affair. Her mother and I chose to never tell her who I was, but they were with me until my daughter was two years old. To protect them both, I ensured that we never had any direct contact, but until recently I have always known where she was and what her life was like. She has represented the only good and honorable thing in my life. Her mother passed away several years ago, and I am her only living relative. If they gain access to my house before I can destroy certain files, or give them to you, they will assume she knows everything about me and that she is involved in my business. I need to ensure her association with me, my knowledge of her, does not fall into the hands of men who wish me dead. If they do it is unlikely that they will let her live."

"On top of everything else, the police will take me to the hospital, not let me leave there, and won't care if someone offs me in the hospital. The material in this briefcase must go to certain authorities, not the police, especially not the local police, and not just to anybody in the FBI, only to those couple of individuals for whom it is intended".

I considered this for a moment, realizing as I did, that whatever he wished to turn over must be significant. I helped him struggle to the last vehicle in line, still in the alley, and poured him into the back seat. "Where am I taking you"? was all I asked. He gave me a West Palm Beach address along the AIA. "You indicated that someone named Oreski would track you down at this address, is that correct?"

"Yes, we have a limited amount of time. He would have assumed his attack tonight would have been successful. He is too arrogant to think it would go wrong. I doubt very much that he would have sent anyone to my house at the outset, but he'll send an army as soon as he finds out things went wrong, and I am not amongst the dead."

"I suspect we have some time", I replied, the police will be on the scene soon and it will take some time for news to get out that you are not amongst the bodies".

"Oreski will have informants with the police, so it is only a matter of a couple of hours. Also, I don't have long, as I am growing weaker by the minute, and I have lost a lot of blood. To make things worse, I was recently advised that I had terminal spleen cancer. It made me rethink my legacy. The reason I had the data in this suitcase with me was because I was turning it over to a special organized crime unit within the FBI and Interpol. They were expecting me and will know something has gone wrong."

"If Oreski and his men arrive while I am still there, I assume my life will be at risk and all be for naught".

"No", he replied, "there is a secret passageway you can take to get out. It takes you out under the AIA and out onto the beach. If it's dark, you won't have a problem because there won't be anyone on the beach. If it's daylight, you'll have to do your best to blend in. They won't know who you are."

"Except that I will be carrying a suitcase. That will seem odd given it's a beach."

"Maybe we can find an alternative", was all he said. I shrugged and decided to give it an hour or so. However, I wanted to know who this Oreski was in relation to the man I was assisting. "What can you tell me about this Oreski character", I asked.

"Tony Oreski started out as a relatively small-time gangster and now runs low-end drug trade and street hookers in Fort Lauderdale and all the way through to Louisiana. He has been looking to expand and has always envied me based solely on my reputation. However, he knows very little about what I actually do, he just knows I have ways and means of getting what I want for my operation."

"And your operation consists of what exactly, and why are you are your staff being gunned down in the streets?"

"Name is Graziano. I have for years run a criminal syndicate originally started by my grandfather. For reasons that don't need to be shared with you right now, I had decided to turn significant information over to the FBI and Interpol, essentially giving them leverage over a great deal of corruption. I guess you could say I have had a rather significant pang of conscience in my later years. In part this is because I have reached a point in my life where I have established legitimate enterprises and can earn substantial income from them. However, I know that I have lieutenants and lawyers who have no compunction about doing evil in the world".

The Request

· ·

AS HE SPOKE, I FLAT footed the gas pedal down the AIA as best anyone could without getting pulled over or running into something. I knew the road well, having been up and down it several times. It took a good hour to reach an entry gate with the name Graziano, and he gave me the gate entry code as we proceeded. The property was surrounded by high fences, with thick hedge growth that made the yard area private, not unusual for West Palm Beach. Interestingly, the garage had a separate security code. We closed the garage door behind us. He punched another number into the door leading into the house from the attached garage. "Please make a note of all the entry codes in case you need them later", he suggested, and as he showed me the various codes, I plugged them into my cell phone under his name.

"There is a quick response security unit always nearby. They are legit and patrol the community at large. The gate and fence are electrified and there are security cameras in the open, but also in a variety of hidden locations throughout the property, on the roof line, in trees and shrubs. Also, there are trip wires and photoelectric cells. So, you'll have to stick with me," he warned, as he struggled to the door of an elevator. "This elevator is the only access to the second floor. It has a feature that allows it to be shut down, which we will do when we get upstairs. This is the code to the elevator; you will need to remember this as well, as you will need to go back to the car and remove any evidence that you were ever here. Oreski has people within the police that he bribes, and they would be more than willing to pin this on you if you leave DNA behind. That would take the heat from them, as they know, given what happened tonight, it's coming their way, so do not touch anything else. As well, this same code will let you exit the property, entirely. I'll explain as we go".

"Do you not have a doctor on call?" I asked.

"Yes, but we have to take care of this business first and you will need to exit before anyone comes. I want you to make every effort to see that my daughter inherits that which she should. You will have to do a lot of explaining."

"Yeah, no kidding"' I said, "But why me, why trust me, how do you know I am not working for Oreski"?

"Because he wants what's in this case, it's not just about money as the contents provide a great deal of information about how my syndicate operates. If you were working for him, you would have known that, and just ended my life. Instead, you chose to try to save me and despite your gallant effort, that isn't likely to be the outcome here. I have lost too much blood and am getting very weak and lightheaded. And cold."

"On the other hand, maybe you could tell me your name and who you really are".

"My name is Brock Tanton. I am a retired public servant, 56 years old, I worked in Finance, supply purchasing. Retired 7 years ago".

I chose to not say what my real background was with the CIA, largely chasing down international financial irregularities that affected or might affect the national security of the United States. While I started out as a field agent, my most recent role included organized crime elements that are still, or have been, involved in arms trafficking and drug trade where it impacts sales to terrorists. My territory was largely Spain, Portugal and Italy. I decided that my real story would likely have spooked him some and might have caused a lack of trust. Not that he had much choice at this moment.

The elevator opened directly into a large upper suite. At the far end a large desk occupied a large width of the room and behind that a walnut bookcase. A red Persian rug decorated an otherwise hardwood floor. We took a right turn and headed into an office where Graziano opened a large wall safe and extracted a 32 GB USB drive. He then turned back to the desk and opened the briefcase he brought with him from the car and opened the case with yet another code. It contained absolutely no money. Just several 6-terabyte hard drives.

"Under no circumstance must anyone with a criminal background or intent ever lay hands on this data. That would cement such a man as one of the most powerful crime syndicates in North America and Europe. Somehow Oreski must have found out that I was planning to take this to the Feds. I have no idea how, but I have to assume there was someone in the FBI or Interpol or perhaps in my own organization at a very senior level that had heard or recorded a phone call and put two and two together and brought it to Oreski".

"If you have this much portable data, surely this is backed up on major servers somewhere in your organization"?

"Yes, of course it was. There were two server rooms in different parts of the world, one here in Florida, the other in Belgium. However, I saw to it that these servers were both destroyed beyond repair."

"So, it seems to me, that destroying data banks would, by itself, have signaled to your competitors and your own lieutenants that something was amiss. As well, would not people in your own organization be suspicious that both databanks were destroyed about the same time? Believe me, if I worked for you, destroying the data banks would make you my first suspect. How sure are you that Oreski was even aware of this and is responsible for what went down tonight. Could it have been someone else"?

"To an extent it is possible that a competitor was involved", he replied, "but to my way of thinking, they would not have known I had gone to the authorities unless they had someone in my organization. They would have assumed I was simply consolidating power and was planning something else. As for Oreski, I have done some of my own investigation into his world and have reason to believe he is up to something huge, but I have no concrete evidence. I presumed I was the target of whatever he is planning because he has always talked about how much he envies what I have built and always boasted that someday it would be his".

"The portables? I assume they are encrypted?"

"Yes, I was getting to that". He typed a security code into the keypad on the wall safe, but it did not open the safe. Rather, a bookcase slid sideways, opening a new room, which housed another, albeit, well-hidden safe imbedded behind another bookcase. The first bookcase closed behind us as he opened the second safe and handed me a USB drive, and simply stated: "The encryption codes are contained on this. I intend to die here and have a vile of poison as I have no intent to live through the pain or be alive when others eventually find me".

"So, you are asking me to fulfill your dying wish, to cement your legacy as not being bad to the end"? "Tell me", I implored, "what is on these hard drives that you are asking me to protect, and I assume, take to the appropriate authorities"?

"The hard drive that is colored orange contains the names, the location of their offices, their home addresses, encrypted email addresses and phone numbers of one FBI agent and one Interpol agent on both sides of the continent whom I trust. You need to know that a significant amount of research and investigative work went into identifying agents that are not already corrupt, as some are. It is essential that you work only with these individuals. They are named Timm Hill, a special agent with the FBI and Casandra Garcia, with Interpol".

"The hard drive that is colored blue contains all the relevant information about my daughter, now in her mid-thirties. Her former address, her former bank account, her old email address, her former work history, all her history, basically her entire life, or at least as much as I still know about it. The remaining hard drives contain the data that I was about to turn over to the authorities. They are numbered and the first contains a video explaining who I am, and why I am doing this", he stated, as his voice trailed off.

"I am very weak and cannot keep my eyes open any longer, the safe contains an extensive amount of money, access to certain bank accounts which are not in my name, credit and client cards and pin numbers that will allow you to access whatever funds you need. There is a possibility that the authorities will eventually locate and suspend these accounts, so I suggest you access a great deal of funds before that happens. You will need extensive resources if Oreski and his crew find out about my daughter or about you".

"There are also names of individuals, here and in Europe, that will create new identities and documents for you if you need them. These people are expensive. Their contact details are included, and you will need certain password information, key words and codes that will allow them to trust that you will not betray them to the police".

"The exit you will take is behind this wall, just lift the panel two feet and crawl under. It will leave no mark, and it will be a long time before it is noticed by anyone entering the house. Also, there is a rainproof ScotteVest in the closet over there behind the door. You'll find multiple pockets, sufficient to hold the hard drives".

"The security firm I employ does not know about this room or the second safe behind this bookcase, nor about the tunnel access. If the police or Oreski find their way into this room, it's unlikely they would look behind yet another bookcase or find the tunnel. This is one of the first houses built along this stretch of the coast and was always used for smuggling. It is one of a few that have access to the beach, but not the only one. Most are now used for beach storage so an exit from here won't raise suspicion even if you are seen. Also, I live here alone and have no servants. Anyone entering should assume the first safe, which will likely be unlocked by the security firm at the request of the police, would be the only one. They will all assume that there is no other. In order to further protect this room, you need to wheel me back into the first office and make sure there are no blood traces leading into this room."

"Please give my love to my daughter", he quietly said as he closed his eyes for the final time, and he closed the safe.

The Exit

∙∙∙

I MADE MY WAY OVER to the closet and packed the ScotteVest with the hard drives, wheeled Graziano on his office chair into the other room. I then headed back downstairs to the Escalade, stopping in the kitchen along the way to get some bleach. I rubbed the car down as best as I could remember my touches, wanting to ensure that I left no personal trace. When I was satisfied that was the case I retraced my steps through the house, eliminating where my prints may be found. Of course, none of this is foolproof by any stretch of the imagination. A good forensic unit may just as easily find a lost hair, and all this is for naught. But I had to do what I could.

I thought briefly about going to the police, but I remember what Graziano had said, some are corrupt, and at this point, though I may have had the data to determine who, I did not have time to review any of it. When the police review the CCTV footage from the crime scene, if any exists, they could just as easily conclude that I was one of the killers that left multiple dead on the street. I simply could not afford to call the police, nor be caught still in Graziano's home.

I made my way back up the elevator, locked it down as he had shown, lifted the wall panel, and made my way into a dark corridor. It was pitch black and smelled musty! Along the way several spider webs stuck to my face causing me to leave a bent arm in front of me, eliminating them from hitting and sticking to my face, as I made my way through the tunnel. Nothing had been said about a flashlight, so I spent the next several minutes feeling my way along the wall.

I knew that I had to go down 20 or so feet to get to any tunnel that led to the beach. It was with great care and slow movement that I gingerly stepped forward foot over foot until I finally reached a stairway. Here in the dark, my fear of falling tensed my muscles and caused my stomach to squirm.

It was just then that I heard the alarms in the house going off, a seriously high-pitched and annoying sound that managed to find its way to where I was. I couldn't imagine the effect it had on those entering the premises, but I wasn't in any mood to find out. It could be Oreski or it could just be the police, although I wondered if the police would have been able to determine Graziano's involvement so quickly.

I felt my way down the staircase, not quickly by any means. At the bottom, the tunnel turned right and headed out under what I believed was the street as I could hear cars overhead for a few of those minutes. A few yards further on I confronted the end of the tunnel. I presumed there was a "door" of some sort and managed to find the frame that housed it.

Feeling around I discovered a lock and assumed the code would be the same as the one in the elevator based on previous comments. I felt around the lock for a moment and determined where each number was, eventually pressing the code in. The heavy metal door opened inwards, long enough for me to exit and then began immediately to close and re-lock. It was well looked after and made no sound. I turned back to see if it was hidden from sight, but it was not. I presumed that beachgoers assumed it was connected to beach supplies, or maybe associated with a private residence. In either case it was just there for everyone to see, in plain view. Clever! Being in plain view, when people entered or came out, no one would think anything of it. From the outside it looked like a large barn door with a rounded top.

It was still dark outdoors and there were no people on the beach, which suited me just fine. I checked my watch, 4:10 A.M. No crowd to blend into. I was on a beach where there were houses along the beach road and I needed to find public access back to the AIA. In so doing, I had to be careful not to run into Oreski's people who may be going up and down looking for someone just like me.

I meandered along behind the dunes until an access presented itself and I was able to walk the few hundred feet to the AIA. I was on Royal Palm Way and knew that I could cross to the mainland from this point. However, would I be seen? I decided to risk crossing the bridge on foot as a taxi would leave a record. The was a minor amount of traffic at this time of the morning, several food delivery trucks dropping off at hotels and grocery stores. I managed to get to the other side, I believe, without being seen by anyone that might be looking for a stranger. Of course, I still had on my running gear, so had a reasonable explanation for being out, as it was now about 5:00 A.M.

Sunrise was still a couple of hours away and that left me time to go to my own home and gather my thoughts. Get changed. Maybe check the hard drives. I would have to decide the extent to which I would need cash, especially in the event the accounts Graziano provided to me were suddenly suspended by the authorities. I had a little nest egg of my own, but decided I might eventually need that for emergency use, especially if they shut down access to these accounts.

I headed home and thought maybe I should plug in the disc associated with the daughter into my laptop. I needed to know where she was, who she was, and I needed a plan to get there, find her, explain things. Explain things??? What things was I going to explain? What was I to tell her? How much? How soon?

Do I do these things before I connect with the agents from the FBI and Interpol? Or after? And what was on these hard drives? About that time, I realized I badly needed some sleep and decided to hit the pillow for a four-hour stretch.

At 6:00 A.M. my head hit the pillow and I passed out. I awoke at 10:00 A.M. I badly needed a coffee, so I went down the street to the Starbucks (where else?) and picked up a large, whatever they call it, and headed back. I noticed the news stand along the way and stopped in my tracks.

Murder Street

THAT WAS THE HEADLINE, FRONT and center. The press reported that the police had arrived at the scene about 5 minutes after the car with Graziano and I had vacated the alley. Within seconds the press had managed to find their way to the crime scene and had published gruesome pictures of bodies and blood, with guns lying about. The story went to press in haste and stated that the police had no information about who the bodies were but that the police believed this was likely related to organized crime elements and likely the drug trade. The article went on to state that despite believing it was likely drug related, the police had no theories regarding what type of circumstances could have occurred between rival factions that might have triggered the event.

This was a major public shooting, and I was sure that the police would be under significant pressure to come up with charges emanating from an intense investigation. I had a few experiences as a field agent with "shots fired" and that a public event such as this would bring out the best the local and national police have to offer. A special investigative team would be created and although this was a local event, the FBI would be engaged. The authorities would quickly establish the identities of those lying dead in the street and their known associates and criminal records, places of residence, etc. That would be followed quickly with notifications to families, if any, and, without any doubt in my mind, visitations to Oreski and Graziano.

This was generally the path that would be followed. Although the CIA presumes to be clandestine in some respects, the fact is that they often operate in cooperation with authorities in both the United States and Europe. There were three or four occasions where, as a CIA operative, I provided evidence and insights into situations very similar to this.

It is unlikely that any direct connection would be found to Oreski himself and significant uncertainty as to how long it would take to find Graziano's body as the elevator leading to the second floor was locked off. However, upon further reflection, I realized that the aggressive and violent alarm at Graziano's would have alerted the security firm, and their response would be almost immediate. That would have left Oreski, or whoever else was the culprit that ordered the hit, little time to find the body, look for the hard drives and, as well, little time to resolve the elevator problem, if such a person was able to find their way there before the police.

The alarm meant the security firm would have entered the building soon after I left, accessed the elevator code and searched the house and premises. I was reasonably sure the security firm would not be able to assist in accessing the code to the saferoom behind the office, given Graziano said they were unaware of the room. Nor would the security firm know about the tunnel access. However, once the body was found they would do a sweep of the building and grounds. A sweep can be jammed with the right equipment and, although Graziano had not mentioned something like that existed, I suspected he protected that secret room and tunnel access very diligently. The security firm may have found the body, alerted the ambulance and the police, if they didn't bring the police in before even entering the building. Given the gunshot wound, the forensic unit would have, by now, already been in the house for a few hours. If I had left any trace DNA they would find it, but it would take time for the lab to process it. Given my agency background I would be in the CIA database, questions and theories about my involvement would proliferate.

It also meant that Oreski would wonder if the information on the hard drives was still in Graziano's house. However, it is unlikely that he would be able to access the house while the police tape was there. In addition, Graziano would likely have left instructions to his lawyers and maybe others with instructions as to what to do in the event of his death. They would be wanting into the house and likely would have some legal reason to gain access.

I decided I probably had time to look at the hard drives before formulating any type of plan. I wanted to know what I was getting myself into. I knew from past experience that once I turned this material over, I was to be under a microscope. Who was I? How was I connected? What would they believe? At the very least I expected to be "a person of interest", maybe be placed, at minimum, under house arrest.

Before accessing the hard drives, I flipped on the TV to see the news. Pictures of the scene were shown, warning that the material was graphic. The police had also released a video from the street cam showing who they now knew as Graziano being assisted out of his vehicle by a man as of yet of an unknown identity-me!!

The two of us disappeared from the camera's sight as we entered the alley, and as we had backed the Escalade out, there would not likely be pictures of me from that point. The police identified Graziano, explained that they had already been to the house, found his body, and that a forensic unit had been dispatched and was still processing the scene. In addition, they stated that they had identified some of the deceased but were not releasing names or associations until such time as the families had been notified.

That meant they already assumed Oreski was involved, and he would be visited shortly. He would, of course, have been at some public event as this went down, visible to the press and cameras. His personal alibi would be solid, and as the boys at the crime scene were all dead, there was no one left to tell of his personal involvement unless there was an informant inside his organization. If there had been, or there had been an undercover operative, this would never have gone down, so it is safe to assume Oreski is on a solid legal footing-alibi wise, at least.

Oreski, or whoever else was responsible would now have two issues. First, he would be wondering if the hard drives were at Graziano's house, assuming he knew about them, or had something else happened to them? Second, did Graziano trust them to me and who then was I? Was I an FBI operative or one of Graziano's inside men? The FBI, knowing that Graziano was planning to turn things over, would have the exact same questions.

I was concerned that the police forensic unit may find evidence of my involvement. If that occurred, and I have gone in the wind, they may identify me and ask for the public to be on the lookout for me. "If you see this man, do not approach, he is to be considered armed and dangerous, call the police immediately". Further, if that occurred, then Oreski, or someone else, would be more determined in locating me than the police were.

I realized I had in my possession information relating to Graziano's daughter. It was clear that if this information fell into the wrong hands it could lead to her being identified publicly as a person of interest, and/or worse, put her at risk from one or more criminal elements. I figured I had made a promise to a dying man who, at the end of his days, had decided to do the right thing, something a good citizen ought to do. In order to fulfill my commitment, I needed, at least for the time being, to keep all the data in my possession and away from other interests.

The Data, Part 1

. . . .

I CONNECTED THE HARD DRIVE related to the daughter and loaded the first file. It was a video presentation by Graziano, explaining who he was to his daughter, the history, why he kept his distance from her and why he had now, after all these years, chosen to go to the authorities and also reach out to her. He went on to say that there was an inheritance that would eventually be made known to her, that would leave her with substantial wealth. Wealth derived from legitimate businesses, with law-abiding employees. Yes, the original monies to start these businesses may have come from ill-conceived gains, but they were now run by good citizens with good intentions.

The next file on the hard drive revealed what Graziano knew about her personal life. She had lived, or was living, in New Orleans, near, but not in, the French Quarter. Her name was Michelle Savonne and she was 35 years old. There were multiple pictures of her growing up, a soccer player, student achievement awards, past boyfriends, university degree-a master's in criminology, a job as a jail guard, a job as a parole counsellor, and then for some reason, this ended at age 32. Three missing years. I had no idea if the address provided by Graziano was still current. I could not imagine why Graziano would not have had more recent information. New Orleans was my starting point to locate her. By my standards it is a short drive from Lauderdale. Easily done in a day.

I figured I had very little time, as the forensic lab, if I had left any evidence, would identify me before noon hour the next day. I had maybe an hour to pack and then head out. The thing was, if they do identify me, what good would my car be? They would put out a bulletin and I would be picked up before I even began the quest. I may as well turn myself in and go from there. I would need to get to New Orleans another way if I wasn't going to the police first.

I packed one change of clothes, my laptop, the hard drives in the ScotteVest and added my trusty handheld, as Florida was open carry. I decided an ankle holster and another weapon might become valuable. As well, I decided to leave my former CIA credentials behind, in case Oreski found me first. The next question was money and identity.

It was then that I realized I did not take the fake IDs, credit cards and passports that Graziano had left for me in his safe. I had a choice to make, go it on my own with my own identity and with what limited funds I personally had, or go back to Graziano's. I knew the forensic team would be finished during the day at some point and I knew I could access the house through the underground tunnel without the authorities knowing. The blank passports would, of course, be useless to me until the passports could be completed with my picture. Same for a driver's licenses. I wasn't going to be able to rent a car without these documents and would then be using my own name. Of course, none of that mattered if there was no evidence that I had been at Graziano's or had not been recognized from street camera footage.

The police will have a guard outside and the usual "do not cross" crime scene yellow tape, which only keeps the good guys out. Everyone else can figure a way in after the police leave. I figured Oreski would be amongst the first to want to gain access and the elevator would now take him straight to Graziano's first safe. But now he would have to wait until the police had vacated the property.

I figured I had about a two-hour window to access the house and get to the second safe before someone figured out it was there. I picked up a flashlight and left my apartment, got into my car and headed back to West Palm Beach and across highway 704 to cross gain beach access. I parked my car in a beach parking area and headed out onto the sand. I easily found the access door and punched in the code. The door opened inwards, and I took one last look back to see if anyone had been around to see me enter. The beach was dotted with a few people here and there as it was mid-morning, and the sun was just warming up. Their attention, of course, was either buried in a paperback, a warm nap or focused on the diamond sparkling ocean waters.

I retraced my steps and headed up the stairs to the wall access. It made very little sound as it opened. I punched in the numbers for the bookcase and second safe and was relieved to find everything was still in place. I emptied the contents entirely and was surprised to find a last will and testament. "This should make for interesting reading", I mused as I closed the safe and bookcase. As I did so, I heard the elevator being engaged.

I was in the second room which I presumed had not yet been located. I moved over to the door, hoping that there was more than one person coming up and perhaps I would be able to overhear some relevant conversation. As the elevator opened, I could make out the conversation. Based on what I could hear, I was able to ascertain they were investigators. Person one was a woman and she seemed to be the lead investigator.

Person 1: "There must be a wealth of information hidden here someplace, unless he stored it all in a safety deposit box in a bank somewhere. We need to be very thorough in this search to see what we can find."

Person 2: "He would never keep criminal data in a safety deposit box. He would know that if anything happened to him, the police, given his reputation and the way he died, would obtain an access warrant and find it almost immediately. At the very least, maybe he left a will".

Person 1: "Or not. He could have just decided to let everyone fight over the remains. As I understand it, he had no family of any kind, so it's possible there is no will. On the other hand, there has to be a warehouse full of information regarding his criminal empire. I am hoping we can find that here. He had a state-of-the-art security system to have everything watched at all times and would need means to hide criminal data. It may be here".

Person 2: "Well, we have a search warrant, so we can take the place apart wall by wall if we need to."

Person 1: "I don't think we can actually cause structural damage. What I don't understand is why we have a dead FBI operative in the group attempting to take out Graziano. We all thought it would be Oreski, and although it appears that he was never involved, we don't know that for certain".

Person 2: "Well, it seems clear now that the FBI agent was acting without authority, and it doesn't seem like he had any authority to even come close to the type of action they were carrying out. We have been given special authority to investigate the FBI and there are lots of things about doing so I don't really like".

Person 1: "Okay, same here. But let's get to work, there has to be more to this place. Let's see what we can find".

I didn't wait for their work to begin. If they were going to search the place from top to bottom, it was possible they were going to find the room I was in before too long, and then very likely, sometime after that, the access tunnel. I headed out to the beach as noon was approaching, got in my car and began to head home.

On the way I reflected on the conversation. A rogue FBI agent was part of the group that attempted to take out Graziano. Maybe that made some sense. Graziano had said that he was on his way to turn over all sorts of data on his criminal empire to the FBI. Perhaps someone, or several someones, in the FBI, did not want that to occur. I knew then that I had to be very careful, not knowing who within the FBI or the local police, to trust.

The deceased agent at the crime scene would, perhaps, have been operating on orders from a more senior person. If that was the case the more senior person was obviously corrupt, or he would not agree to participate in a murder. Perhaps the agent was operating on his own and trying to protect his involvement in a criminal organization. Alternately the agent was undercover but that would mean he was unaware of what he headed into that night. This theory seemed not the least bit logical. As of now, irrespective of what the situation was, there would have already been serious internal questions raised as to how this occurred, who gave the order, if there was one, and what information he was acting on. And now, as I gathered from the conversation I overheard, some type of special investigation had been created to investigate FBI involvement. And what of Oreski? Was he not involved at all, or was the agent working for him or someone within Graziano's own organization?

The Identity Man

I HAD NO IDEA HOW much cash I would need to pay his contacts for establishing fake driver's licenses and passport. The cash in the vault totaled over $150,000 but I had left it all at my house. On the way, I decided to stop at a bank and access cash from my account. I decided to take $15,000, visit the local contact he had provided to me and make arrangements. I checked the address given to me and soon realized I had to head into the northern Miamai area called Hollywood to meet the contact. On the outside the place seemed to be a small electronics repair place. I went in and a guy came out from the back. The building was quite long and one wall was adorned with Mardi Gras style masks along with busts where various works were unfinished.

"Are you Jimron", I asked. Obviously, a made-up name I thought to myself. And what is with all the mask work?

"Yes, I am. The masks for Mardi Gras and certain tv and theatrical events is my basic income. Are you looking for a costume or do you need something repaired"?

I simply gave him the code that Graziano had provided. He checked it out, looked me up and down, and said "You don't seem the type?"

"What type would that be?" I asked.

"Most guys don't come in here dressed like they are out for a jog with a dead dog", he replied. He went over to the front door and hung a sign that said out for a half hour, pulled down the blind and locked the door. I realized that I had woken up in the same clothes I had been wearing and had just gone back to Graziano's in the same outfit I had found him in. I had dried blood stains on my shirt and shorts.

"Come into the back room and we can get started. My Instructions from Graziano were to provide you with three identities-two U.S. and one German. You'll pay me $5000. 00 up front and another $10,000 when you come back to pick things up. That is for each new identity you would like."

I figured from my old days that he likely had a video camera on me in any event and maybe played both sides, helping the police in certain cases. I couldn't take any chances and agreed to his terms.

"When I come back"? I asked, "When will that be?"

"Just about two hours. Let's take your picture, get your age correct, pick some places of birth and make sure it holds together. You will be given names of people that actually existed, so the birthplaces and ages will hold up. This works for most things, but if the police ever start to really investigate the backgrounds associated with these names, they will know you are using fake ID. For that reason, you are going to slightly alter your appearance for each of these so if one fails, the next one will work for a time. For example, a slight change in hair color, use of eyeglasses etc.".

"So how does this work"? I asked.

"I keep a database of deceased people and would normally access those that are your age, height, and general physical features. We then photoshop your picture slightly to make your ID pictures appear more like the person we have chosen". He pulled three pictures from a database. One was from Phoenix, one from Atlanta and one from Munich. "In this case, however, matching the pictures of the three men won't be necessary since they have no criminal records and are all from some distance away".

The Atlanta identity was of a man named John Sterling, who was born and raised in New Orleans but had moved to Atlanta at some point. He had lived and worked as a private investigator and had retired to France to live out his remaining days. He had passed two years ago while in France and the United States would therefore have no record of his death. His hair was grey, like my own, facial features were similar enough for the ID to be effective.

The Phoenix man was named Jeff Atkinson, also retired, my age. He had retired in Puerto Vallarta and passed away four years previous. He had worked as a lawyer primarily representing small businesses.

The last ID was Hans Goebel, a German bar owner from Munich. He had retired in his home in Munich to be exact and had lived out his days there.

"I have done some homework on each and you'll have some information about their real lives, enough to get by in a short conversation, or if you're asked a few of those simple questions we all get asked at border crossings, booking cars and flights, etc. Unless you have enough cash with you, I'll see you back here in about 2 hours".

I left and decided to go to each of the banks that Graziano had provided me with and went to different branches as I had the pin numbers for the various accounts. This used up about three hours before I was able to return to Jimron and pick up my stuff. I now had IDs that matched the credit cards and client cards.

"Just one last request", I asked of him, "before I leave here, I want you to erase your video files that you have of me when I walked in here".

"Smart man", he replied, and I accompanied him to the back once again and watched as he eliminated the file, ensuring it was the one of me.

"That's great, I said, now remove the CD and break it into pieces, because it can still be accessed. As well, let's go destroy the back up and erase the backup hard drive as well".

Jimron complied, adding, "I see you have been down this road before. "Been stung?"

"Yes", I replied, lying. "Served three years for fraud". Another lie.

I turned and left, went over to my car and looked back, doing a very thorough survey of the external part of the property to ensure there were no external cameras. I then went behind my car and muddied out the license plate. Someone could still ID my car by type and age, but it was a sufficiently non-descript old Toyota, and there are hundreds like it in the Miami and Fort Lauderdale area. I drove home, parked my car in the garage and finished packing. I wasn't sure where things were at in the investigation, so I turned on the TV news with the hope of picking up some useful information.

It was now late afternoon the day after, and the news was on. There were still pictures of Graziano and, as of yet, some unidentified man helping him out of the car. The reporter went on to say that the police believed they were the last two remaining persons involved in the shootout.

I knew the forensic stuff must be nearly finished. I again considered using my own ID and car to drive to New Orleans, but then thought better of it. Instead, I made some supper, took a bite out of the sandwich and then left it all sitting there, with the TV still on. If anyone came into my house, they would, at least at first, assume that I was still nearby. I figured that, along with my new identities would buy me some time.

I considered leaving my real ID behind, along with my wallet and car keys as well. But on further reflection, decided to keep my wallet with me. I figured they, whoever they might end up being, would look at the not eaten meal and deduce that if I had for some reason quickly left, I would have taken my wallet. Taking it with me would likely assist in deceiving someone into believing that I was still nearby. I decided that I would get to New Orleans before my personal involvement became known, if that indeed did happen.

By 5:30 P.M. I was in a cab and on my way to a short flight to New Orleans and had booked a hotel near the French Quarter, oddly called the Quarter House.

Oreski

· ·

TONY ORESKI PICKED UP THE burner phone in his sports jacket the instant in rang. "Was this your doing," asked the voice on the other end. "I thought we had an agreement to keep ourselves away from anything Graziano until we were ready for a takeover, and one that is likely to be a little violent. At this point, we don't have sufficient information from within his organization to make a move of this magnitude."

"I assure you, Mr. Alvarez, I had nothing to do with this. No one at the crime scene was not on my payroll, and I have adhered to our agreement. I can only assume that someone within Graziano's own organization arranged the hit. I have no idea why this event took place and rest assured, I am aware of how much heat I will be under from the DEA and FBI. Our friends within the border patrol will be keeping their noses super clean until this is all sorted out. It slows down our movement of workers into the country if my people are being closely watched. I get that, but I have to admit, someone appears to be doing us a favor".

"Look Oreski, I have every intention of checking into this in my own way. You have a reputation for acting without thinking of consequences and then smoothing things over. You have a reputation with the press, the police, the FBI, everyone watches you these days. I am beginning to think I made a mistake entering into this arrangement with you. If I find out that you, or anyone within your own organization is involved you, my cabron, are a dead man".

"I would never have taken this risk at this time. Yeah, maybe in my past, but since entering into an agreement with your cartel, I have been extremely careful to keep my nose as clean as it can be, as secretive as it can be. As you know, we have a major shipment of coke coming into Shreveport this week, and are bringing in more workers, men and women in shipping containers and some through the tunnel at Laredo. Some of our clients have lost some of their workers and need to have those filled. I get the risk".

"The most important thing we have to do is expand the tunnel network, as it is the safest and least expensive way to bring people and drugs into the country. We need to do this all the way from New Orleans to Laredo and we need to do this as our first development priority. Laredo, in particular gives us access to San Antonio and interstate 10, which is becoming the highway of lost souls, largely due to the cartels. We should be proud as someday soon the southern United States will be embroiled in as much violence as Mexico. This will enable us to control the territory through which we can distribute our product. It will significantly enhance our distribution capacity and it is far less expensive than paying shipping companies and paying bribes to port authorities, and far less risky than air transport. I have just gone out of my way to purchase a tunnel boring machine because that way there is no blasting and they don't cause as much damage to the surrounding rock, thus making the tunnel far safer and enabling us to line the tunnel walls. The soil surfaces throughout the border areas we work with is soft and conducive to supports. Texas soil and sub-surfaces are particularly good for this. Of course, we will continue to also use waterways until these are done".

"Look, Alvarez, I am fully on board with your plan. I swear I would do nothing to jeopardize this. I have millions of dollars to gain, and we can ultimately move into the kind of syndicate that Graziano has been operating forever. You need to hear that there is no one in my organization that has the wherewithal or courage to pull off something like the very public murder of Graziano. My contact with the Fort Lauderdale police service has informed me a deceased FBI agent was involved in the attack. Given that I know my informant's information to always be accurate, it means the FBI was either involved in the attack or there is someone with the capacity to corrupt FBI agents to the point they would be willing to participate in a hit of this magnitude. I was thinking that it might be a rival cartel and was wondering if maybe you knew what was going on behind the scenes on your side of the border".

"Our cartels within Mexico are well connected with each other through territorial treaties. We don't see any value in attempting to take over our competitor cartels territories, especially in the U.S. To ease your mind, at least with respect to Central America, there is no one here that would attempt to pull such a stunt and risk our plans. All of us have agreed to be in this together. We have everything to gain with all of us being on the same page. We have carved out our agreed territories with respect to the U.S. and these decisions are also viewed and protected as treaties. You have nothing to worry about from our side on this, but we need to find out, as much as the authorities do, why this went down. If there is no one other than you and us, then something else is going on."

"Your role in all this, my dear Antonio, is to look after your share of the packaging and cutting the coke as well as arranging and controlling the distribution network. And, also to pick up the refugees we are forcing into the states by destabilizing and taking control of national and regional governments in Central America. Ultimately, we will own the United States. You need to reach out to Graziano's lieutenants and find out what they know and are willing to tell you, because Graziano's syndicate is still powerful and has the ability to destabilize us and even take over our own stock and trade. Can I count on you to analyze what they say, try to ascertain the real meaning and if there is any threat behind their words"?

"Of course, Amigo", offered Oreski, "I will reach out and ensure they know that I was not involved in any way and arrange a meeting to see what they know. I can start by attending the funeral, nothing will go down at the funeral, and if they think I was behind this, it is not a place they will risk doing anything. There is likely to be a ton of FBI and police presence there, so it is a good place to make the connection. I will call you when I have had that meeting".

The Data: Part 2

· ·

WHEN I ARRIVED IN NOLA, I took a taxi to the hotel and was lucky enough to be able to check in a bit early. I set up my laptop and plugged in the next hard drive.

There was, once again, a short introduction by Graziano, explaining what one was about to find, content wise.

The hard drive contained comprehensive information about the legitimate businesses he had established and the people managing them. He went on to say that he had built these businesses for his daughter and that they were not now, and had never been, involved in any criminal activity. In some cases, they were franchise operations, a portion of the proceeds of which went to Michelle through accounts Graziano had established in her name, managed through a trust. They were itemized, with records of current owners, managers, staff records, tax records, financial statements, employee benefit plans, providers, insurance etc. The whole ball of wax going back years.

As I sat reviewing the data it became clear to me that Graziano's intent had always been to leave a legitimate legacy for the daughter that had never known him. As well, he clearly itemized the profits, portions used for growth or maintenance and month by month, amounts transferred to three different trust accounts all of which were in his daughter's name: Michelle Savonne.

The accounts showed that no withdrawals had ever been made, and that Michelle was due to inherit about sixty million of which she had no knowledge. I considered this for a moment. The accounts were in her name, not Graziano's. A will is not required to leave her this inheritance because everything is already in her name. Anyone involved in any of these businesses might already know her, by name, at least, and believe that she was their boss or silent owner of some type.

How was she supposed to find out about her inheritance if he died, and I had not come along? Someone else must exist that had some instruction or knowledge. But who? Did that mean that there was someone else, other than me, looking for her? Did another person have access to this information or was the hard drive now in my possession the only place this information existed.

Based on events to date, I had to assume I was the only one in possession of this information. Nevertheless, the question remained. And, what therefore, was in the will that I now had in my possession? A will has to be a legal document. It cannot detail elements of a criminal empire to be left to someone else. The will, itself, was likely not referring to anything that could be confiscated by the authorities.

And who would have drawn up such a document? One can assume that a man such as Graziano would use a lawyer for his criminal activities, maybe more than one. But would he involve the same lawyer for a legitimate will? Maybe. If all the businesses were already going to the daughter, what was in the will? I closed the hard drive without watching the remainder and went and got the document and opened the sealed envelope. Unlike most wills, where itemized statements begin with "And to my....I leave...", this will began by itemizing properties owned. At the end the end it stated: "to be transferred to the holder of this will".

This was like bearer bonds, he who has the document gets the proceeds. It made no sense to me that I was to be the lottery winner in Graziano's story. I presumed the original intent had to have been that the will was to be given to someone else. It seemed improbable to me that his daughter was to be that person, or she would have been named in the will.

The will was signed by a lawyer and there were two witness signatures. The lawyer's name was Jeff Atkinson, the witnesses were Hans Goebel and John Sterling. And I now had identification-passports, driver's licenses, etc. that identified me as all three of these people, a living representative of those now all deceased!!

It was clear and obvious that the man who forged these IDs had known for some time that Graziano would be requiring these exact identities to be used for someone. That, by itself, was no real surprise. What worried me was how they had matched my description so closely. I began to feel that I was somehow set up, that this was no coincidence. But to my knowledge, there was no way that Graziano would have knowingly wandered into an ambush knowing at the same time that I was on the street corner. My presence at that point in time had to be a coincidence. I did not always run the same route, sometimes I headed to the beach, the route taken that day was unusual. My features were similar to three men who signed a will and were now deceased. This somehow all had to be an accident of fate. There was no other explanation that I could see at the moment. It is possible that Graziano just happened to see the similarity when I came along and made a snap judgment.

I could give this document to anyone, including Michele Savonne, but it seemed to me Graziano must have had some other reason for not naming her. I decided to put the will aside for a few moments and check the news. When I turned on the TV at 9:00 p.m. the reporter was explaining that the man at the crime scene had been identified through DNA analysis from Graziano's escalade. I had likely touched the seat or door handles getting Graziano out of the car and helping him back to the other vehicle.

My picture was front and center on the screen, with my name just below. The reporting went on to say I was a retired government employee...it was policy not to release previous CIA employment, so the employment information ended there. The press would assume I was somehow now in the employee of Graziano.

The FBI on the other hand would know and would now have notified my former agency head of my involvement and would be seeking information from them as to why I might be involved.

However, the reporter gave way to a clip from the Chief of Police in Fort Lauderdale asking anyone who may have seen this man... me... to contact the local police or FBI offices, and to keep their distance as I was to be considered armed and dangerous. To me that sounded, at this point, at least, that no one in my agency had been contacted, or they would likely have kept this quiet. Great! I thought.

I went back to the will. The properties itemized included a villa in Southern Spain, Malaga to be exact, a penthouse apartment in Puerto Vallarta, and a flat in Munich Germany. There was no coincidence here! As well there were bank accounts identified in their names, leaving the proceeds to these three individuals, or alternately the holder of the will.

Was Graziano planning to assume these identities after going to the authorities? It was possible, especially through plastic surgery. It may have been that he was in possession of this will for that exact reason. And, he had not given me the will, it had been in his safe when I returned to pick up the credit cards. Of course, at that time he knew he was about to die and may have assumed I would take the will along with the other items.

But none of this explained where his daughter was or why there was no information about her whereabouts on Graziano's files for the past three years. Clearly, I had agreed to undertake this task and felt some obligation. Retirement had been boring to a large extent and at least this had my adrenaline back up and running. I decided to call it a day and went out for a bite to eat, keeping my ball cap pulled down over my eyes. By 10:00 p.m. I was back in my hotel, walking through the little interior courtyard at the Quarter House. I took note of the people sitting around the tiny swimming pool, more of a dipping pool really, went up the elevator, admired the fleur-de lis carpet in the hallway, opened my door, and hit the shower before wandering off to bed.

Searching for
Michelle Savonne

. . . .

THE NEXT MORNING, I BEGAN with the last known address on Michelle Savonne's file. The house was an older two story in the Garden District of New Orleans with excellent door security, and I had to buzz to have someone come to the intercom. A man answered, I assume a security guard: "Can I help you?" was all he said.

"I hope so, I am a private investigator contracted to find a former resident of this house, a woman by the name of Michelle Savonne. She was named in a will and is due to inherit some substantial wealth. I wonder if you would mind talking to me a bit about her?"

"You'll have to show me some ID, with your name and occupation." I held the John Sterling driver's license to the camera for him to see. He buzzed me in. "Has her room been rented out again or has it been empty", I asked, knowing the answer given three years. He replied with a slight smirk that it should be obvious to me that the building is highly secure and sought after for client's looking for a safe place in this part of town.

"What was she like as a person? Quiet? Music? Come and go at all hours? Male friends?"

"She was a very quiet person, had a few girlfriends and male friends over from time to time, but nothing serious I don't think. Her work as a parole officer wore her down quite a bit, she often expressed it made her tired. Often, she would get called out to deal with a violator and end up coming back very late hours. Long days sometimes, she put in."

My next thought was about her departure. "Do you know when she left here, was it about three years ago, longer, shorter?"

"My recollection, he replied after some thought, "is that she left about four years ago, right after she got a new job".

"Do you know with whom?" I asked.

"The FBI, Criminal Investigation Division". The reply was a bit of a stunner. Her father kept watch for a year after she joined the FBI. I couldn't imagine what he might have been thinking at the time he discovered this and there was no information in what I had seen of Graziano's materials that suggested he knew. Perhaps I should have watched the full hard drive.

"Do you know if she stayed in New Orleans, or was she transferred somewhere else?"

"I don't know he replied. But I can say she was becoming uncomfortable here. She felt she was being followed and there was occasionally a blue Camry parked across the street. I can't really see the street all that well from in here, but once or twice I thought I saw someone taking pictures of her coming and going. I think it may have led to her moving".

"Maybe", I said, "but she would have gone to Quantico for training in any event, so I suspect she was just posted somewhere, and it could have been anywhere in the U.S."

I thanked the security guard for the information and went to the library.

I started with the phone book to no avail; then the white pages name search and reverse look up-all to no avail. Not one mention of her name anywhere. I thought maybe the address registry at the library might have a past record if she had owned property. No luck there either. As the day wore on, I thought maybe I should check obituaries and the graveyard, but realized I could do that as a last resort. If she was deceased, what would happen to the businesses in her name already. I suspected there might be some documentation somewhere in Graziano's files in that event.

Then I thought maybe she had gotten married, so I checked the local registries there as well. Again, she seemed to not exist, at least not here in New Orleans.

Finally, it occurred to me-yes-I was a little slow on the pickup here-to check with the employer she was with when she was living at the address I had just been to. I made an appointment with parole services, using Jeff Atkinson, the lawyer, as my ID. I indicated my reasons were related to a will and her inheritance and again, showed ID to meet her supervisor.

Jerry was a large man with a big round beer gut. Again, not much of a surprise there, it's almost a given in the parole world.

"So Jerry", I began, "I really appreciate any light you can shed on Michelle's possible whereabouts. Maybe start with her reason for leaving if you know what that was about and why she joined the feds. Do you know where she went"?

"Well"' he started, "she lost her mother about that time. It was her only family connection. No brothers or sisters and her mom never married. She expressed a desire to track down her father, but she understood that meant misuse of government resources. Nevertheless, I believe that was part of her motivation. As well she was burning out in this job, like lots of us do. Too many crazy people to deal with".

"Have you ever heard from her since"?

"No, she left and never looked back".

Given that there were photographs detailing much of her life, someone other than Graziano must have taken them and it sounded like that had been occurring at her past residence. Someone on contract. It was a safe bet that the Private Investigator would have been involved.

I assumed that Graziano would have used the PI to ensure he had ongoing pictures and information regarding Michelle's life. I knew that Sterling was deceased, but someone may have taken over his practice and perhaps his records were intact. Failing that it was possible his old records were kept by a wife or family member.

Certainly, the contract with Graziano would have been a lucrative one. An ongoing contract for 30 plus years is a gold mine for a private investigator that is often unemployed between jobs. Perhaps someone continued the work after he passed.

I went back to my hotel, went out for supper-after all it's New Orleans. I found some great, and hot, Cajun food. There is nothing like a hot spice to give a hot burn on your tongue, the sides of your cheeks and the back of your throat!

Back at the hotel I phoned the front desk and asked if I could send a picture or two to the office printer, and asked if it printed in color. I should have thought of this earlier and downloaded two high-quality pictures to show people. After having $15 added to my bill, it was back to my room and a good night's sleep. But first, I turned on the local news to see what was new. New Orleans was showing very little of the event in Fort Lauderdale. There was no mention of Graziano, murder street or that the police were looking for me. I knew that was going to last about one more day at maximum. Then the search would go country wide.

Sheila Sterling

THE NEXT MORNING, I RENTED a car and drove the 7 hours to Atlanta. I was able to find an office address for Sterling and Associates, Private Investigators, with no trouble. It seemed that they were still in business. Obviously, I could not use any of the IDs with the agency if the 3 individuals were all known to each other. As well, I could not use my own. If I was asked to show ID I was going to have to come up with a suitable explanation. At this point I hoped that those in the office knew about Graziano's payments, but I was also concerned that they would be sworn to secrecy. They were not about to violate that confidence.

On the other hand, if they had learned about his death, that may have changed. The other consideration was whether they would be concerned that I might be the man the authorities were looking for? I walked into the office and asked to see the manager regarding a former account that was being investigated. In a few minutes I was ushered into an office. Behind the desk and just standing up was a very attractive, somewhat elderly woman, about my age perhaps. She introduced herself as Sheila Sterling, and asked what she could do for me. I was immediately drawn to her crystal blue eyes, fine wisdom lines and a striking smile that caused that immediate stomach flutter. Not that I trusted the feeling anymore, since it had betrayed me several times in the past.

She was slim, wearing a blue business suit and blue-trimmed eyewear. Short red hair that perfectly accentuated her face and slim frame. I dropped my guard briefly as my eyes fell to her lips and I wondered what she would be like...I recovered in time to get back into character as she smiled, having noticed my reaction.

I decided to be bold: "I understand that your agency was monitoring Michelle Savonne on behalf of Graziano. I have in my possession his will which left substantial property to three individuals, including a villa in Southern Spain, Malaga to be specific, in the name of John Sterling, your father, I believe".

Sheila was a little taken aback, which was a good thing. She replied almost immediately: "Malaga, really!" She never asked me for any ID. "I did see the footage of Murder Street, as they dubbed it, and was somewhat sorry to see this happen to him. As far as we were concerned, we felt it was sweet that he took such an interest in his daughter despite who he was, but I guess that is more common amongst members of the mafia, especially where they are catholic to begin with".

I said: "Yes, Malaga. And you are correct in that assumption. However, there was a condition that I undertook, at Graziano's request, a search for his daughter Michelle, to ensure she is made aware that he has established a number of businesses in her name, held in trusts and I am assuming they are likely currently under the auspices of a CEO he must have appointed. It seems she has simply disappeared after joining the FBI and is completely unaware of any of this".

Sheila sagged slightly and said: "Yes, my dad had several contracts, so when I turned 20, he asked if I would like to fulfill this contract for Graziano, all very confidential. I either took or arranged almost all the pictures that went to Graziano. But the contract expired when Graziano could no longer determine where she was. He asked us to try to locate her, but it was to no avail. Like you say, she joined the FBI and simply dropped out of sight".

"I was wondering if you knew why your father would take a contract from someone like Graziano and perhaps anything you can tell me about the arrangement."

"Graziano was adamant that we never disclose that we were keeping him apprised of his daughter and her whereabouts. I suppose now that he has passed our commitment to him can be broken, especially if, as it seems, that he has left her a substantial inheritance. And, for that matter, me as well! But I will need to know more about you to ensure you are who you say you are".

"Have you ever heard of a man named Hans Goebel"? I asked. "He was also named in the will along with your father". I wanted to know if Sheila was aware of the lawyer's name, but I did not want to use it if she knew him.

"Not someone I know", she said, "Is that you"?

Given that she was unaware of the name Hans Goebel, although her father had co-signed the will, I assumed then that she would not know Jeff Atkinson, the lawyer, so I introduced myself as Mr. Jeff Atkinson, the lawyer.

"Sheila, if you still have the files and pictures would you mind if I could have a look through them? Sometimes there are clues tucked away that one doesn't know are there until you have a reason to be looking".

"I guess it would be alright", she replied, "the files are in a secure storage but the pictures are saved to an encrypted hard drive in my home. Perhaps if you buy me supper, I could invite you over to browse through them?"

"Well, that sounds like a wonderful idea"! I replied.

"Great then you can meet me at Nikolai's Roof about 7:00 P.M."

"Will do", I replied, and left to go book a hotel in downtown Atlanta, somewhere near the restaurant. I had a shower and changed into a blue sports jacket, grey slacks and blue suede shoes. I arrived at the restaurant 15 minutes early, excited. A beautiful roof top with views of Atlanta. I sat down, ordered some Klinker Brick Zinfandel and sat back to wait for Sheila. I figured if I was paying, I may as well have a wine I enjoy. Shelia arrived a few minutes past 7 o'clock.

As she walked in the front door, I noticed she was wearing red leather boots, and a black dress that ended just above her knees. I paused a moment and noticed her legs were in fine shape, well defined muscles, but not overly. My eyes slowly moved up and stopped for another moment at her breasts, perky for a 55-year-old woman, (sports bra I guessed) as she was wearing a body tight sweater. My eyes rested again at her full lips. When my eyes finally met hers, she had a little smirky grin, obviously having noticed my interests. She had short red hair and bangs, just my style.

"I see you've already ordered the wine. Presumptuous!" She said as I pulled out the chair for her, "nice jacket."

As I pushed the chair in, I noticed she was wearing a very nice perfume.

"Not necessarily, the wine is a reasonably good red and given you suggested a steak place, I figured red was in. Besides, if you want your own bottle, feel free."

"That won't be necessary. I am a Zinfandel fan myself. I decided to come in a taxi, I am guessing you did the same?"

"No," I replied, "I walked over from the hotel. I had made that choice in case we were stopped somewhere along the way for a breathalyzer. The last thing I needed was to be picked up and identified. I was also hoping that supper would be short, and she would ask me back to her place that evening instead of the next day, to look at the photos.

The waiter came by as soon as she was seated and poured her some wine, rattled off the specials and saying he would be back in about 10 minutes, unless we were in a rush.

Shelia immediately replied that no we were in no hurry, and I made the assumption that I would find my way to her place in the morning. But as I was thinking exactly that, she leaned over and quietly said: "Look, we don't know where Michelle disappeared to, and you might want to take some time looking through our files and the photos. I have a guest suite in my home, and you may as well spend the night. We can get an early start going through things in the morning, maybe over a cup of coffee, and breakfast if you like".

I was more than a little taken aback at how forward and pleasant she was, and how nicely she was dressed. I won't deny I had my hopes up. It had been a long time since I was intimate with anyone. "That sounds like a wonderful idea", I replied.

"Well Jeff, you know what I do for a living. I employ about 15 investigators and make a great living, mostly off other people's hardships, I admit. But the way I look at it, we generally make their lives better by resolving the mysteries they bring our way. A lot of our work comes thought lawyers with whom we maintain loose partnerships, as in no contracts, but regular work in some cases. You said you were a lawyer, and a lawyer coming by our offices is never a surprise. But working for a deceased Graziano, now that's a surprise".

"Well, I guess you could say I was working for a deceased man, given he has now passed. But I look at it as working for Michelle Savonne. I understand she never knew her father and would not be aware of or expect anything to be coming her way. And certainly not something of the magnitude he has arranged for her".

"That is comforting", replied Sheila. "If you had said you were still working for Graziano and his organization, I would be more hesitant. But I am usually a very intuitive and quick judge of a person's character. I make a lot of snap judgements and am seldom surprised".

The waiter came by, and we asked for a few more minutes, deciding to finally look at the menu. When he returned, Sheila ordered a steak, medium rare, and I ordered medium well done, same meal otherwise. After we virtually devoured our meals, Sheila asked if I had practiced law in West Palm Beach, since that is where Graziano was from.

Carrying on with my fake identity, I explained that I had a practice in Phoenix Arizona but that I had retired to Mexico and met Graziano at a Hard Rock Hotel, in Puerto Vallarta, in the bar. I did not know who he was, but in conversation he suggested that he had a private residence in Phoenix, was in the process of selling it, and would feel better if he had a lawyer on site. After that transaction went through, he hired me to represent him on a few other business arrangements, every single one of which was legal and above board, and these were the interests to be left to Michelle, his daughter. In addition, he then asked me to draw up a will. Your father was a witness to the will, and I now understand why Graziano would have chosen him".

I hoped that Sheila would not ask to see the actual will as it stated that the properties were to be given to the holder of the will. Of course, there was an easy out in this regard, as all I had to say was that Graziano had left me with the instruction to render the necessary transactions to transfer the Malaga property to Sheila. With all my lies seemingly intact, I suggested we think about heading out and flagged down our waiter and paid the bill.

Sheila had called an Uber and put it on her account, and we headed for her home. We arrived at her place about 9:30 and she showed me the guest room. She then suggested a nightcap. "Maybe a brandy? Or a coffee"?

I replied that a brandy would be a great way to end a very pleasant evening. I wandered into the living room and sat down on a chesterfield. A few minutes later she came in with two snifters, heated, and they were not single pours. She had changed into a pair of skintight running shorts and a loose top that came down to just above her belly button. Her tummy was amazingly flat for her age, and she had lost her bra. Her breasts were clearly still firm and just the right size. I fantasized them fitting perfectly into my hands. She sat on the couch beside me, turned her body to face me and pulled her legs up underneath her on the couch. Sitting, as she was, her head was slightly higher than mine.

I could smell the perfume and it was seductive, as was the brandy. She reached over and twirled the hair behind my ear. That was all it took!!

I reached up and pulled her face closer, kissing her gently on the lips for what seemed like an hour as I was running out of breath. She was a great kisser, only parting her lips a slight amount, which I find very seductive. All women should kiss like this, men do not like to feel swallowed or be left having to wipe saliva off their face after a kiss.

My hand slid around her back, under her shirt, and as we continued to kiss, I slowly moved it around to her front, just grazing the bottom of her breast, then continued down her rib cage out to the side and then back across her tummy. I lingered there for a moment while I moved my lips down to her neck and slid my hand over her breast under her shirt. Her hand was on the back of my neck, and she pulled my head into her neck and tipped her head back.

"Let's move this to my bedroom", she quietly said, and see what happens next."

She took my hand, stood up and led the way, closing the door behind her. "It's just a thing I have about privacy, even though there's no one else in the house."

I sat on the bed while she stood in front of me. She took off her top, reached down and unbuttoned my shirt, and pushed me back on the bed, reaching down to unbuckle my belt. When my clothes were gone, I pulled her close and rolled her over on her back, placing one leg between hers and my lips found her lips once again.....

Her neck appeared against my lips next, then I followed my tongue down, across her tummy, just under the top of her shorts and I sat up and began to pull them down. She raised her legs up and I slid them off.

I came back up to kiss her lips while I moved both of my legs between hers. She tipped her hips up so the angle would be more conducive. Our movements together were slow and gentle which heightened my desire, and I moved a little faster, taking care not to be too aggressive and shortly thereafter and rolled sideways to lie beside her.

"I don't usually do this when I first meet someone", she said a little sheepishly. "I hope you don't think less of me"?

I recognized that she had raised her voice at the end, as if asking a question.

"I am guessing you just didn't want me poking around inside your stuff tonight", I replied, referring to the photographs.

"Well, I think we have established that you've already done that".

We both laughed and spent the next few minutes chatting about getting up early and getting the job done. She committed to staying home for the day and helping.

We both woke up about 6:00 A.M. It was now day 4. She rolled towards me and put her head on my shoulder. We stayed like that for about half an hour before she got out of bed and went to the bathroom and then on to the kitchen to make coffee. She came back while the coffee was brewing, invited me to go take a shower and asked what I would like for breakfast. I replied that I did not eat breakfast until I had been up for a few hours, usually only eating two meals a day but the shower I accepted.

After I cleaned up we sat on the couch for 15 minutes and she went to make herself a small bite. After, she went downstairs to a storeroom where the older files were kept and also brought her laptop to the dining room table. She had the photos stored on a backup drive as well as having hard copies. We sat down together and began the process. As I was looking for possible clues about Michelle's current whereabouts, we started three and a half years ago about the time she was employed by the FBI. She had been missing for three.

Sheila pulled up the photos from just prior to the time period and we began moving forward slowly from there. A thought struck me as we were looking at the pictures: "My goodness", I said, "it just occurred to me that you were really stalking this poor girl. These pictures are taken day and night, you must have employed another photographer for some of the time"?

"Yes", she said, "I suppose it appears like stalking, and yes, we have a few people on staff that I ask to do this sort of work. After all, it is pretty common for private investigators. Our contracts contain clauses to prevent disclosure unless we authorize it. These pictures only went to Graziano."

"I am curious, Shelia. Did you ever meet and talk to Michelle"?

"I did. I made an effort to talk to her a few times from the time she was about a teenager until she was graduated from high school. I spent a fair amount of time in New Orleans as we lived there until Michelle turned about 25. It was then my dad opened up the office in Atlanta. I was following her sporting activities and the first occasion on which she asked about who I was, she was about 13 years old.

She finally recognized that I was taking pictures and it occurred to her that maybe she was the subject. I explained that I was a small-time freelance sports photographer and that I had been assigned to follow high school sports".

"We struck up a bit of a friendship after that and she asked if she could see anything that got printed. I said I would do my best but made no promises. I decided to create a "Teen Sports Beat" newsletter covering New Orleans, so I had a so-called legitimate reason to include her. I started doing a feature athlete once a month and the newsletter became quite popular in some of the high schools, especially if one of their own was highlighted. It was a good cover".

I asked Sheila what kind of impressions she had of Michelle at the time.

"We talked off and on. I couldn't be caught by her or her mother shooting her all the time, especially when no sports were involved, so we ended up with 5 different photographers fulfilling the commitment. Graziano paid very well to keep us involved. I got the impression she had very few friends for a teenage girl, but I think there were two she had a bond with. When she went to University, I continued with an occasional visit to her but could no longer say I was following her athletic endeavors, so others took over. I continued to supervise the photo and video collection and made the decisions as to what to provide Graziano."

"When I looked through the pictures it was clear that she kept close contact with her former high school friends and that continued into her adult life. I got the impression that she was lonely. No surprise there, as that generation is one of the loneliest on record. When we lost track of her, I had worried about whether she may have committed suicide. On the other hand, women secrete the bonding hormone, oxytocin and tend to seek out about 8 female friendships, on average. Michelle never got past two that I could tell. Her work wasn't exactly conducive to forming and keeping friends. She was called out all hours of the night and seemed to be on call a great deal".

"I do know from the photographs that the two friends in question also went to the University of Louisiana and that they maintained a bit of contact at least until after Michelle seemed to vanish."

I thought about possibilities for locating Michelle and asked Sheila if there were pictures of the two friends and if she had any idea of their whereabouts.

"Of course," she replied. "As we go through the year before she went off the grid, so to speak, I'll pull the most recent pictures of the women and what I know of their careers, although that data will now be a bit dated. To my recollection they both stayed in New Orleans after graduation from university. Both were married as per my most recent information."

About 2 hours into the morning, we came across very good pictures of both girls: Louise Landry and Jesse LeBlanc, common last names in New Orleans. I was hoping they had current and not unlisted phone numbers. But it did mean I had to head back to New Orleans.

"Did you ever get a chance to meet either of these women?"

"Yes", replied Sheila, "on a few times that I talked with Michelle they were present. Their knowledge of me, however, is that I had a little sports column. They have no idea who I really am, but they may remember the name I used, Liz".

I thanked Shelia for all her help and promised I would return to Atlanta when I could to begin the promise of transferring the villa in Malaga to her name. As I was leaving, she accompanied me out to the taxi. We shared a nice long kiss and she said, "Make it soon, I'd like to see you again, villa or no villa". I headed back to my hotel around 9:00 A.M. and checked the message board. Oh yes, the message board.

Always Available

· ·

YEAH, I KNOW, CONSTANT CONTACT-ALMOST sounds like an alien adventure. Of course, there are human aliens as well as those from space. The thing is, the CIA never loses contact with former agents or retired agents. It's not as though it's like the movie, "Retired Extremely Dangerous", however. The purpose relates to possible information needs, sometimes developing a prosecution effort based on past work, sometimes assisting or advising agents currently in the field.

Retired or resigned agents maintain a responsibility to make themselves available, or whereabouts known, in certain circumstances as needed by the agency. The contact occurs through a message board that we are required to monitor on a frequent basis. Such was suddenly the case for me. The call was urgent and was to discuss a matter with a senior in person, in Fort Lauderdale. No other information given. It was always just that way, no traces!

I called in, and set a time, knowing that it would take me about nine hours to get back to Fort Lauderdale from Atlanta. Meeting up, finding Michelle's friends would have to wait. I arrived about 6:00 P.M. and went straight to the appointment. I walked into the local field office and made my way to the agent in charge, John Szabos. I had met John previously, as I was about to retire from the agency. He was an experienced handler, about my age, greying, full head of wavy hair and 6 foot 4 inches in height.

The admin assistant stood as I entered, apparently working late and recognizing me as I entered. He immediately ushered me into John's office and closed the door as he left. John, despite being a consummate professional, never wore a suit and never asked that of his agents unless in court or meeting with members of the senate or other ranking officials. Today he wore khaki slacks, a dark blue t-shirt and sketchers. He was second assistant to the head of the CIA, as Southern n Florida was a key location for international activities. He welcomed me in with his deep baritone voice.

"Good evening," John said, "I am glad you made it here today, there are some things unfolding as a result of an FBI investigation into the death of Carlos Graziano, apparently the FBI's favorite mob boss. It appears they are looking for a man that assisted Graziano out of his car and ultimately into his home. When they put the picture out and it ran through the system, as in our system, the facial and body posture recognition program identified you as a possibility. We have reached out to the FBI and suggested the possibility that the picture might be of one of our agents. We have asked the FBI for a few days to determine the validity of that possibility. So, what I want to know, is that you, and if so, what is the story"?

The thing about the CIA and the federal government, they protect those who have provided clandestine services. The old adage that you're on your own if you get caught, just simply isn't true. The agencies, all of them, have a host of legal counsel that support the staff of the various agencies. It's all part and parcel of being who they are.

"Yes", I said, without hesitation, knowing John already knew the answer, "I was out for an early morning run when I happened upon the crime scene. I caught the very end of the gunfight and when it seemed over, I noticed that Graziano, car door open, was still alive and hurting. Of course, at the time, I had no idea who he was and just decided to step in and help him. The thing is, he told me he was on his way to provide major information to the FBI and asked if I would ensure certain data was so provided. Moreover, he requested I take him to his residence and asked that I provide certain

A Gangsters Dying Request

information to his daughter as well. It appeared to me, and as was stated by Graziano, he didn't feel that he was about to survive. As a result, I agreed to fulfill a dying man's wishes as they seemed honorable, despite who he might be".

John accepted my explanation without question. That was the way within the confines of the agency itself. "Here's the problem," he began, "this was a very public event, and the FBI are under some pressure from a public perspective to explain the event. However, they have settled on a warfare between factions of the underworld, in terms of a public explanation. However, they are most concerned about the fact that at least one current FBI agent was involved in the attack on Graziano. It seems possible that there is a faction within the FBI that did not want Graziano to come forward with whatever incriminating evidence he possesses about whatever it was he was about to reveal. The assumption, and maybe a sound one, is that the FBI agent lying dead on the street, and maybe others within the organization, did not want the information coming to light".

"That may seem to be the case", I responded, "but you have called me in because there was a possibility that the face and body recognition program might lead to me. So here I am telling you that it is me, in the camera's eye. What steps do you want to take at this point".

"We have developed a story line to provide the FBI in the event we confirm that it is you. It will state that you were in the process of investigating financial crimes that were followed across international boundaries and were in the process of following Graziano as part of the investigation. What we are telling the FBI is that you had just left your car as you had noticed the vehicles stopped in the alley and moved forward on foot. We are asking them to publicly announce that they have found the person of interest in the video and that it was clear that his involvement was simply as a passerby helping out a wounded man".

"Of course, this isn't entirely believable, no one believes in coincidences of this nature and the press may pursue this for a time. However, we all know they will be stonewalled and will move on

51

to the next story as this dies down. So basically, the FBI gets one version, and the public gets another".

I knew that this was a moment in which to come as clean as possible. If there was one thing I accepted, it was that I could trust my own people within my own agency. I told the entire story to John to this point.

"Okay, so you have in your possession a number of hard drives that contain information that was going to the FBI as well as information about Graziano's daughter who stands to inherit legitimate businesses and dollars. But you have not yet looked at the remaining hard drives to determine what the issue is. Yet, at least one and maybe other rogue agents within the FBI were doing everything in their power to prevent this coming forward. With respect to the FBI and Interpol, and the agents that were working with Graziano, their identity has now been secreted as best as is possible with both agencies, for their protection, assuming it's not too late for that".

"Those specific agents have reached out to us based on the international nature of the crimes involved, and I will share your name with them. The only real solution here is to have you back on the payroll. Of course, they do not know you have these hard drives and the information Graziano was about to give them. It seems that not only are you trying to fulfill a dying man's wishes to come clean, but now you are the only person in possession of data that could bring down an international crime syndicate. One thing I suggest is that you find out what is in your possession on those hard drives. In the meantime, there are external agents also appointed to look into the FBI rogue agent issue. I have arranged a meeting for you with the agents appointed to investigate the FBI".

"How certain are we that these agents are not involved with Murder Street as it has become known as"?

"The Senate Oversight Committee reached out to me as a senior official outside of the FBI. I had the agents suggested investigated, a deep dive into their past, going back to junior high school and all the way up to their current roles. They are squeaky clean. I spent two hours interviewing them, had them on the polygraph and so forth. But we also know that there is a possibility that a senior agent in the FBI that may have been involved with the hit on Graziano. The FBI has also initiated an internal investigation, tracking the relationships between the downed rogue FBI agents and other officials within the FBI. That investigation is being overseen by a special prosecutor appointed to do the investigation".

"The meeting with those external investigators, for tomorrow morning, is in your home".

I took the hint that the meeting was over and went back to my home, assuming it was adequately safe from anyone searching for me at this time. Not so. As I unlocked the door to my home, I was met by a man and a woman enjoying a drink from what little bar I kept. I had no idea who they were or what they wanted. The fact that they helped themselves to my bar suggested that they were not likely authorities.

I was wrong!

I reached behind me for my 45 as the woman held up her hand and said that would not be necessary. I suggested to her that I would make that decision after they told me who they were and how they got into my house.

"My name is Hazel and this here young strapping piece of manhood is Jimmy. We were appointed, if you will excuse the term, to investigate the recent wrongful doings by what appear to be rogue agents within the FBI. In that context, we understand who you are and would like to know what transpired between you and Graziano".

Hazel was obviously very fit, super slim, 6 feet tall, perfect posture, and moved with grace as she stood to shake my hand. Jimmy, similarly was not a man one would choose to tangle with.

I recognized their voices from listening through the wall at Graziano's house. "So show me some ID", I responded. They did, seemed about right and I holstered my weapon.

"It is my understanding that at least one rogue FBI agent was involved in the attack on Graziano. Why should I assume that you are not also involved in some way with what went down on Murder Street"?

"We were given your name by John Szabos. He ensured that we were adequately cleared through CIA intelligence channels. He was given access to our personal information and our work history. He spent a great deal of effort looking into who we are, our records are spotless, and our personal identities are not known to FBI agents or senior staff. The way it works is once an internal investigation is authorized, usually by the head of the agency, the investigators are outsourced from one or more other agencies. Further to this, we are clandestine in the sense that we do not and cannot use our real names. We have, based on John Szabo's recommendation to us, made an exception in your case. I guess the only reason for you to trust us is that John set up this meeting".

"What is it you want from me", I asked politely, as the explanation made sense, and rogue agents would not know of my association with John as it currently exists.

"Well," she began, "we would like to know what it was that Graziano told you. In particular, was he aware of any negative factions within the FBI that he was worried about"?

"There were a few phrases that transpired between us that gave me an impression of that. However, he was more concerned that it might have been someone named Oreski and perhaps someone internal to his own syndicate. What did he really want from me? He asked me to find his daughter and gave me information regarding legal businesses that he had developed, already in her name, of which she is unaware. He seemed only interested in her".

I had chosen not to provide any information re the hard drives in my possession. Besides which, they were in New Orleans, resting in my hotel room safe.

There was a long pause while Hazel and Jimmy considered whether I was being as forthcoming as they would want. I figured they might not believe me in any event and likely try to keep tabs on my whereabouts. Good luck with that, I thought. If I turned the hard drives over, I would have no way of knowing what had been really going on in Graziano's head. I decided then and there to make copies of the hard drives in my possession and then, perhaps turn what I had over to them, whoever "them" would end up being. I was sure that not all the information on the hard drives had anything to do with Graziano's death, such as that specific to his daughter.

Hazel went on to state that this may have been a gang war and that they were also investigating the possibility of Oreski being involved and whether he had any relationship with the FBI. That portion of the investigation was, in fact, exactly what the FBI itself was doing, along with also investigating themselves. I asked what they could tell me about Oreski.

Hazel filled me in. "The so-called Oreski, was born Antonio Oreski. Notorio was a nickname apparently chosen by Tony Oreski himself as he was trying to climb the ladder, and it was further cemented by the press years later. It was largely assumed that Tony wanted to take over control of Graziano's empire and there have been recent rumors that's something was afoot in that regard".

In truth, according to Hazel, this explanation made little sense. Oreski's criminal activities were low level drug trade and prostitution on street corners, Hazel did not see Oreski having the smarts or the organization to take on a syndicate as sophisticated as Graziano's.

"It is more likely", she suggested, "that Graziano's real competition was European-based, likely out of Spain, Italy or even an eastern country such as Serbia, places with large criminal organizations that had been in business with Graziano at points in the past and had knowledge of his organization from within. Whoever was involved in the shootings, she went on, had to have adequate resources to recruit FBI agents to the dark side".

"The point is", she went on, "the Notorio story in the press simply gives the general public a bit of confidence that the investigation is proceeding successfully, but the truth is not known at this point."

I thought about this for a while, but the question remained as to why Graziano himself thought that Oreski was likely involved. I debated as to whether I should share this with Hazel and Jimmy.

"When I was helping Graziano, he specifically mentioned Oreski as the likely person to have carried out the shooting and suggested as well, that it had something to do with the information that he, Graziano, was about to turn over to the FBI. He said whoever had the data would become a very powerful crime lord".

Jimmy leaned in and suggested, "It is possible that Oreski had formed associations with overseas crime syndicates, maybe by some organization that wanted to use him in this way. However, the question remains as to why anyone other than Graziano would know what information he had. It does seem more likely to me that someone Graziano was close to, or someone within the FBI did not want that data to surface.

"That is the only thing that makes sense from my perspective", I added. "So you are investigating possibilities within the FBI. Who is investigating sources within Graziano's empire itself"?

It was Hazel who responded. "That would be the FBI itself, as well as investigating Oreski's possible involvement. Even if Oreski had knowledge of what Graziano was about to reveal, it is a safe avenue to assume he would have gotten that information from inside Graziano's organization. Someone within his organization knew Graziano was about to reveal too much and put the lives of people within his organization at risk of long-term prison sentences or worse. For that to be the case it has to be someone high up, likely a confidant. Maybe someone inside the FBI itself, or someone with the power to sway FBI agents over to the dark side".

"And just so you know, we are not entirely certain you are squeaky clean in this matter. We have this question as to whether Graziano actually had data in his possession at the crime scene given he was on his way to become a key informant. If so, it seems you are the person who may have that data. It is just too much of a coincidence that you were on the scene and Graziano chose a stranger, if that is what you are to him, to assist him. Maybe you are really more than that to him. Maybe you even arranged the hit to get inside his house. The thing is, at the moment, we have been told you are hands off to us, but don't think you are scott free despite what your boss thinks and has told us".

Her comments reinforced my desire to keep data to myself where these two were concerned. I responded by saying that I did not have anything of that nature and it was likely that Graziano was on his way to meet with agents to assize up the situation more thoroughly before turning things over. I guess that just constituted lying to special investigators. Yikes! But that would have to change in time, maybe! "So, I am assuming that you are done with me for now"?

"For now." Hazel confirmed, and they excused themselves, leaving me home alone at last.

The new, and fake, FBI story broke that night and did not identify me in any way other than to say that the man at the scene of Murder Street was an agent involved in investigating financial irregularities for a sister agency and that it was possible that his investigation led him to be present at the crime scene. Nevertheless, they were still interested in finding this person of interest to determine if he was in possession of any knowledge that might have led to the killings on what is now becoming known as Murder Street. Clearly Hazel had not shared our conversation within the FBI.

A Time for Truth?

....

ONE OF THE GREAT SPOTS to take a break, Café du Monde, the original French market stand, originally established in 1862, is open 24 hours a day and ships their hickory flavored coffee anywhere you ask. The place is always packed as it has become very famous. I made a stop and picked up some of that famous hickory coffee as I was going to need a lot of it over the next few days. To make matters more interesting the season of Mardi Gras was just beginning.

I had two relatively immediate tasks ahead of me. One was to find and interview Michelle's two friends and the other was to see what other information was on the hard drives in my possession. In regard to the latter, I intended to make copies and needed to purchase the hardware. I also knew I would have to hand these over to the correct FBI/Interpol investigators with whom Graziano had been planning to share and essentially destroy the empire he had built. If someone within his organization had learned of this, it is now likely to be more than one internal source. I had been identified as a person of interest, no doubt they would be looking for me., given that hazel and Jimmy had not shared with them. I thought about cancelling my existing reservation and book into a different location, using the Jeff Atkinson identity, but ultimately decided to stay where I was.

It was unusual to find an open time share in the French Quarter of New Orleans. The Quarter House had been a good choice, the suites were small but very private and separate elevators were required to access different upper floors of the hotel. The carpet on the fourth floor in the back quarter had fleur-de- lis carpeting and the room had a brick wall running from the kitchen and bedroom walls. Coming in, one had to step down a few stairs and make a left turn. There was no getting in really quick. In addition, the back bedroom window, the only window, was 4 stories off the back alley. All in all, it offered some protection in case someone tried to break in. After checking in, I headed out and purchased a few hard drives and a few groceries. I reasoned that copying might take some time and needed to get that process started. It was relatively safe from prying eyes for the time being, so I decided to load one up and then go search for Michelle's friends while it was copying.

Both Jesse LeBlanc and Louise Landry lived in the non-flood district of Lakeview, New Orleans. The area was upper middle class, nice community. I found their addresses and phone numbers with relative ease as both were listed. It seemed odd to me that both families had land lines in this day and age of cell phones. I called Jesse LeBlanc first and explained that I had been hired by Michelle's estranged father, that I had been told that Michelle had never known him, and that he had left her property in a will which is why I needed to find her. At this point there was no reason to explain that the properties were already in her name. I also explained that I got their names from a former sportswriter named Liz that Jesse might remember from their high school days.

Jesse expressed a certain level of apprehension about my story and said she would like to talk it over with her husband before meeting with me. I suspected at that point she would also call Louise and they would come to some kind of decision to meet. Jesse indicated that she would get back to me in a couple of days. Given the delay, I decided to return to my hotel and continue copying the hard drives in case I had to turn them over sooner rather than later.

As I started the process my phone rang. I answered expecting it to be John Szabo and was surprised to hear Sheila's voice on the other end. "Good day", Jeff, she began, "You do realize I am a very good investigator, do you not?"

I replied in the affirmative. "Yes, it is really good to hear your voice. How did you get my number?"

"Is that a problem for you?" She asked, "I got it from the office from when you originally phoned in to see me. It is standard procedure in my line of work".

"No, of course not it's not a problem. What seems to be on your mind"?

"Well," she began, I was watching the news feed from the Murder Street, and they have this picture and video of a man assisting Graziano. He looks a lot like you, same gait, same way he holds is head. Soooo, I did some research because I really liked you. You said you were from Phoenix and retired to Mexico where you met Graziano. And yes, I did locate a Jeff Atkinson's with history of a law firm in Phoenix and was able to determine that he did retire to Puerto Vallarta. When I looked for his name in Puerto Vallarta, there was no phone listed, but when I checked into the property register, I found a Penthouse still registered in his name".

As I listened, I knew where the conversation was going. I liked Sheila and was considering telling her the truth. But telling anyone that I worked for the CIA just sounded like a fairy tale. I decided to wait out her explanation instead.

"I called an investigator in PV and asked him to visit the property, hoping to find you. It was in a wealthy part of town, near Playa Los Arcos, a nice building with a doorman. He was asked if he knew you. I was a little taken aback by the information I got back. He said you had died a couple of years back, but that the property had been left to his daughter. I asked if she ever visited and he said yes, a couple of times to his knowledge".

"Of course, it took a little time, but deaths are registered in Mexico. I called the Civil Registration Records office and simply explained that he had been my lawyer and that certain work was left undone and I needed to get in touch with him or his office, if he had one in Mexico. They confirmed his death, which leaves me wondering who you really are and why you were not honest with me, especially after the great evening we had together and all the help I gave you. So, was that you at the crime scene and if so, how is it that you are roaming about as free as a bird"?

I considered for a moment before I answered. "Yes, that was me. In the beginning I knew your father was not still alive and what his connection was to Graziano. In retrospect, the next morning I considered filling you in, but thought better of involving you any further. To a certain extent the less you know, perhaps the safer you are. There are several possible sets of people looking for the person who helped Graziano, a mobster named Tony Oreski, who like the press to call him Notorio, perhaps people within Graziano's own organization and perhaps certain unsavory elements within the FBI itself. At the time I just felt better keeping your involvement at some distance".

"That doesn't really explain to me who you are. There is no information in the news that suggests the FBI is still not looking for you as a suspect. It's not as though I haven't been exposed to dangerous situations several times in my life given the nature of some of the investigative work my agency has undertaken".

"Okay, Sheila. I am not sure telling you the story is all that believable, but this is the truth. I am a retired CIA agent and was simply out for a run. I have trouble sleeping at night and often go for a run when it's nice and cool. I stumbled into the scene now called Murder Street, and saw most of the action, including seeing Graziano wounded and the last man standing. I chose to help him as he was dying and refusing to go to a hospital or see a doctor. His dying wish was for me to find his daughter and inform her of her inheritance, so he took me back to his house to provide me with the details. But there is more. Graziano was on his way to provide agents within the FBI and Interpol comprehensive details of his criminal organization, both here in the U. S. and in Europe. It is unclear to me why he had a sudden pang of conscience, but he did, it would appear. I have assumed it relates to his legacy relative to Michelle."

Sheila's response heartened me. "I have a pretty good idea that what you have told me so far is at least largely true. A person is unlikely to enter into a crime scene and spirit the remaining survivor away without some specialized training within an agency or the military. Most people would just have turned and ran the other way. You chose to stay around. As well, years of investigative work have taught me a few things about when people are lying. They fidget, their eyes dart around or look down, they fold their arms when telling half-truths, their voice changes, they say too much, they cover their face or mouth, and so on. You don't do any of those, but then again, you know all this and know how to lie. And I also know you are still not fully disclosing. I know Graziano, things to do with Michelle would have been open and above board. He didn't take you back to his house without some other agenda, so I am guessing he had something with him, or at his house that he gave you in trust"?

"Yes", I replied, "but I think it is best I keep that to myself for the time being. I have access and know the whereabouts of certain material but have not yet had time to examine it."

"In the meantime, you search for Michelle Savonne, which seems to be more of a priority for you. What I want to know is how is it that you haven't been picked up by the FBI for questioning".

"But I have. Because the FBI had at least one rogue agent involved with Murder Street, an agent now deceased, facial recognition within both the CIA and FBI identified me early on. The news as to who I was is secreted, thanks to the intervention of my former CIA section head. I have met with the external investigators appointed to investigate the FBI and my former boss arranged a meeting with those investigators. In the meantime, the regular FBI is still searching for me, but have not been informed who I am. Graziano supplied me with alternate identities, finances, and a will signed by a lawyer whose name you know, your father as a witness and a third person, Hans Goebel in Germany, all deceased. He provided me with access to a person to forge passport documents, driver's licenses and gave me credit cards and access to bank accounts with those names. I am using those identities in the course of investigation. In the meantime, I am also back on the CIA payroll as at some point in time there is an international financial bent to this, and my skills may be needed in an audit sense".

"So I assume there is no villa in Malaga to be my inheritance? Interestingly, Graziano seems to have arranged this without my father's knowledge, as otherwise it would have been in my Dad's will".

"Well," I replied, "the will does happen to specify names for the properties identified and the villa is specified for your father. It is possible that if you were in possession of the will, you could have the property transferred to you. I will commit to having the property transferred to you at some point. And maybe I could visit?"

Sheila chuckled. "Okay, I intend to hold you to that, both the transfer and the visits. In the meantime, you still haven't said what other information Graziano gave you. I assume therefore, it has something to do with the material he was about to give to the FBI, otherwise why give you, a stranger by your account at least, access to alternate identities and finances"?

"Yes, that is the case. But I have not had an opportunity to look at it as of yet. There appears to be a lot of data and there is another issue. Whoever killed Graziano and his people must have known he was going to the come clean. That person or organization is still looking for me as well. There is some thought that it is Tony Oreski, a mob guy by his own design. However, there are those that don't think he or his organization is sophisticated enough to pull that off. He runs low end drug trade and street prostitutes, so he is an unlikely suspect in certain circles. In the meantime, the press has been fed that story to appease public concern".

"Okay, then are you willing to let me help? We could be good together. It seems to me that, although you've likely worked alone a great many times, in this case, you could use some help. I could go with you to meet Michelle's two friends. It may be more likely that will talk to me than you, since they will likely remember me from the past. And a sports reporter may be more trusted. As well, I could help you go through the data that you have it in your possession".

I thought about the hard drives and extent of information they contained. It would take me hours on end to go through it all, so I agreed. "I guess that means you'll be coming to New Orleans"?

"Yes", she replied, "right in the middle of Mardi Gras. Maybe we can have some fun while we're together. But I would really like to know your real name".

"My name is Brock, Brock Tanton", I replied, with a grin, mimicking the James Bond style.

"Okay, then, Brock Brock", she teased, I'll get in my car and meet you. I would prefer to have my car there as any investigation may require us to occasionally go in separate ways, and we need convenience. Just where might I find you"?

I gave her the address to the Quarter House and asked her to text me upon her arrival so that I could meet her in the lobby.

Mardi Gras!

I HAD STOPPED AT THE tourist office on the way into Louisiana and picked up the 2023 edition of the Mardi Gras guide, given it was the time of the year for the festivities. The magazine had a great deal of historical information about the Mardi Gras. I took the time to read up a bit.

It outlined that the celebration of Mardi Gras came to North America from France where it had been popular since the Middle Ages. In 1699 a French explorer and his men explored the Mississippi River from the Gulf of Mexico and set up camp on a spot 60 miles from the current location of New Orleans, on March the 3rd, as Madi Gras was celebrated on that day, and they named the site Pont du Mardi Gras.

The articles went on to state that in the late 1700S pre-Lenten balls were held in New Orleans, and under French rule masked balls flourished but were later banned by Spanish governors. The prohibition continued until New Orleans became an American city in 1803. By 1823, the Creole populace prevailed upon the American governor and balls were once again permitted. In 1837, a costumed group walked in the first documented parade but the violent behavior of the maskers during the next two decades caused the press to call for an end to Mardi Gras. However, in 1857, six New Orleanians who were formerly members of a group called the Cowbellians, saved the event by forming the Comus organization.

The men beautified the celebration and proved that it could be enjoyed in a safe and festive manner.

It also stated that many visitors to New Orleans are surprised to discover that Mardi Gras is not a single parade over a single day, but spread out over several weeks, beginning on January 6th, the Feast of the Epiphany and ending on the day before Ash Wednesday, a moveable easter date and the start of Lent. The carnival season may see in excess of 50 parades in 3 counties, over 1000 floats, close to 600 marching bands, over 3500 parade units and over 135,000 participants.

I was content to know that my hotel was in the French Quarter, just two blocks from Bourbon Street and there would be limited revelry on the street or the back alley behind me. In addition, the activities associated with the festive season would provide an extra layer of anonymity for a period of time. With the larger number of tourists blending in without being recognized will be more likely. It is noted, however, that street masking is only legal on one day, Fat Tuesday, and only from dawn to dusk.

While I was waiting for Shelia, I popped in another hard drive to copy and decided to go for a run. I turned right and wandered down Bourbon Street, passed a few music venues and turned right and headed to the River Walk. A bit of a run along the River Walk is possible, but all in all the French Quarter in downtown New Orleans doesn't really lend itself to a good run. Nevertheless, a little jog up on the bank of the Mississippi offers some good scenery. I decided to drop back into a walk and have a beer at the Coyote Club, but timing was off as there were no dancers on the bar. Maybe next time! Along the way I wandered into a few shops, checked out the Mardi Gras souvenirs and beads, along with some Cajun cookbooks and thought a bit about what Sheila and I might do together. I headed back to my room and popped in another hard drive and hit the sack.

Jesse and Louise

· ·

SHEILA ARRIVED THE NEXT MORNING, now day 5, and we decided to call Jesse LeBlanc. I advised Jesse that I was bringing someone with me that she might remember and told her about Sheila who she had known as Liz. She said that she did remember her seeing and commenting on what a good athlete Michelle had been in high school. She said that she had spoken to Louise and that they would meet us together, in a place of their choosing. Jesse worked as a real estate lawyer and had a private office not far from her neighborhood and asked us to meet her and Louise there. Louise worked as a financial consultant investing funds on behalf of both commercial and private clients.

Jesse had an air of professionalism as is fitting a real estate agent. She dressed in a beige pant suit with a black sweater underneath and wore high heels. In all she stood at my height, about 5 foot 10 inches with heels. Louise on the other hand was short, like Sheila, and came dressed in blue jeans, a white blouse and running shoes. After we all introduced ourselves, Sheila opened the conversation.

"I am not sure you remember me, I used to edit a small newspaper report for high school athletes under the assumed name of Liz Thorpe. One of the people I followed for a time was Michelle Savonne. She was quite the athlete in high school".

"University as well", replied Louise, "she was a stellar basketball player and long distance runner. She used to get up at 5 a.m. and run 6 miles before breakfast, then go to practice. It was like she never tired out".

"You were no different", Jesse said to Louise, "you and Michelle both had a thing for winning as well. I had two of the most competitive friends and their attitude towards life helped me understand what it means to be competitive in business as well".

"I definitely got the impression that Michelle did not like to give up", said Sheila, "did that carry over into her work life or did she calm down after she started working in the prison system"?

Louise exchanged glances with Jesse. "Just how much do the two of you know about our friend, and what do you really want from us?"

It was time for me to jump into the conversation. "As I said on the phone, I met Michelle's father and in his dying moments he explained that he was estranged from his wife and daughter Michelle for since the age of two, but he had Sheila's father's agency, a private investigation firm, follow her life from time to time. In essence, Liz here was working for her own father at the time and is an accomplished photographer. She supplied the photos that Michelle's father received from time to time".

"In essence then", Jesse stated, "you were basically spying on our friend and stalking her on behalf of a man she never met. Michelle grew up without a father in her life and she attempted on several occasions to get her mom to respond to the need she had. If she had known who Liz here was and who she was working for, her life may have been different, better somehow. Both Louise and I think she went into social work because she felt she was missing part of her history and maybe she would be able to help others like herself. Liz, you made an effort to talk to Michelle a few times as I recall. Did it never dawn on you that you were in a position to relieve some of the heartbreak she was feeling"?

I responded for Sheila. "Liz was working for her father at the time and investigators entering into a long-term contract of this nature are sworn to secrecy or face the prospect of serious lawsuits and forfeiture of their license and livelihood. She could not disclose without risking her own father's livelihood".

"I guess that makes some sense", suggested Jesse, "Michelle told us that she went into correctional services hoping to eventually find some clues as to who her father may have been. That then led her into parole services where she had the opportunity to counsel many clients being released into halfway houses or into temporary jobs in New Orleans. Unfortunately, none of that ever panned out for her. About three years ago she decided to apply to the FBI and was accepted".

"What we would like to know from you", asked Jesse, "is who Michelle's father was. It would seem to me that there is no longer any reason for Liz to maintain her silence. Any contract that was signed is now defunct by law as the principles to the agreement are both deceased".

"I cannot in all good consciousness provide you with that information". I responded. "Her father was in possession of some highly sensitive information and was in the process of meeting with both FBI and Interpol agents when he passed away. We have been made aware that there are at least two factions that would do just about anything to prevent the law from knowing what the data is. There is a possibility that the detective agency as well as my involvement may come to their attention, if it already hasn't. If there is any possibility that you know anything about any of this, you could be in danger. We want to gather as much intel from you as possible about how to locate Michelle, and then keep you away from this from then on".

"Okay, I understand where you are coming from", replied Jesse, but you indicated the FBI and Interpol are aware of certain data. Is it not possible that Michelle already knows all of this from within the FBI"?

"We don't know for certain", I replied, but the investigation was very secretive even within the FBI, so it is unlikely she would have been brought into it".

"It seems unlikely to me", offered Louise, "that she would not have come forward to her bosses within the FBI if she had discovered who her father was and that he was in possession of information important to the FBI. In addition, she would be all over the 'inheritance' and would want to be part of any investigation that involved her family connection. Knowing her, it would be impossible for her to be kept out of at least part of the loop, given her legal status as a living relative. I assume, the only living relative, otherwise you would not be here looking for her, correct"?

"Those are likely correct assumptions", I replied. "What can you tell us about her whereabouts"?

Jesse responded first. "Very little at the moment. In addition, we are not sure we would share that information with you in any event. We don't really know if you are who you say you are and could very well be the people that could put her in danger".

I noticed a shift in Jesse's behavior as she said these last words. She shrugged, turned her eyes away, looking at the floor and began fidgeting with her fingers locked together. Most people lie some of the time, and it is not really possible to be sure someone is lying. The situation one is in, might just be causing nervousness and it is not unlikely someone would lie to protect an important friend in their life. I assumed, from her reactions, however, that she was well aware that she had something more to share than she was offering.

I looked over at Sheila and suggested we leave, knowing that Sheila must also be aware of the same behaviors I had observed. We both knew that it was unlikely that we would be given much more information at this time. However, Sheila decided to ask one last question, "My agency lost track of Michelle after she joined the FBI. If you can't tell us where she is at the moment and have no way of getting it touch, can you tell us anything about her year in the FBI before we lost track of her"?

Jesse and Louise exchanged glances and Louise spoke up. "Prior to joining the FBI, Michelle had been working with parolees, one of whom had these horrific stories to tell about things he had seen, and to some extent, experienced himself. Supposedly he had 'gotten religion' was part of the story, and felt he had to unburden himself of some of his guilt. Among other things, Michelle advised him to seek counselling from the church as well as going to the authorities. He said there were too many corrupt people in the police and some in the FBI of which he was aware. About a week after his last session with her, he was found hung in his room. Michelle said she found it difficult to live with the things she was told, keep them to herself and not also believe he was murdered, that it was not suicide. It was that series of events and stories that led her to join the FBI".

"After she joined the FBI, did she pursue these events to your knowledge", asked Sheila.

"It was her desire to do so", said Jesse, "during the months she kept in contact with us, before going dark, shall we say. Because we want to believe she is alive and well, and maybe undercover somewhere, she hasn't been able to convince her bosses to investigate, or at least they have not allowed her to get involved".

"She must have shared some stories with you", I suggested, "when she was still with parole services. Are you willing to share any of those with us, any sense of what they were about"?

Jesse responded. "She was quite worried that we would know much of anything. However, they related to illegal immigrants and how they were being treated and used by any number of people in this country. She said a lot were related to violence elsewhere in the world, such as Haiti and Central America. But she would not share details with us because she said they were appalling and giving her nightmares."

I felt at that point Louise and Jesse were unlikely to give us any more information, but I had the sense that they knew something about Michelle's whereabouts or her assignments. Besides that, I had another avenue through John Szabo, my boss at the CIA. If other countries were involved in something this dark, the FBI, and the border agency, likely had some knowledge and the CIA could have legitimate involvement, or already was involved. I excused ourselves and Sheila and I headed back to my room. On the way, we discussed whether we were both on the same page with respect to the two women. It was clear to both of us that they were withholding some information about Michelle, but they had not given us any clues as to what that may entail.

"We need some leverage to get them to open up a bit. Some way of getting them to trust us. What if I shared most, if not all of the pictures I have of Michelle and them together"?

"I agree" I responded. "We need to break through their secrecy. If Michelle is working for the FBI and they claim to not know here she is, it means her assignment is to be kept closely guarded. It is most likely that she is undercover. If that is the case, it has to be deep cover, alternate identities, the whole bit. Undercover means her assignment is high risk but it also requires a warrant to be issued for anything undercover for more than 24 hours. I can ask my boss to see if he can get the FBI to share that information. I was told by Graziano that one of the hard drives explains who he is and why he had chosen to assist the FBI. I wonder if we could edit it sufficiently to share elements with Jesse and Louise. The thing is, if you want to change someone's behavior, the best approach is to appeal to their self-interest, and clearly, protecting Michelle is in their interest. However, knowing her family history is also in Michelle's interest. They have to believe that sharing what they know is in Michelle's interest as well as their own".

"But editing the drive would mean hiding Graziano's identity. Do you know if he appears on the drive, identifies himself, or how he explains everything"?

"No, I have not looked at or listened to the entire hard drive related to Michelle. We will have to have a look at it and determine if it is feasible to share in part, at least. Let's grab a bite, see if I can arrange an appointment with John for a very private conversation, which means I have to head back to Fort Lauderdale. Do you want to come with me, or would you prefer to stay here in New Orleans"?

"Not here. I am going to head back to Atlanta and pick up all the photos as not all are any longer on my laptop. I want to have them handy for when we next chat with those two women who obviously would go to some length to protect their friend. I would like to spend the night together, maybe wander down Bourbon Street and into a blues bar along the way, have a drink or two and catch some blues. We could continue our meander down some side street towards Jackson Square and find a nice restaurant. Then go back to your room and spend the night together. No sex though, I am exhausted and would love to just lay together tonight."

"Sounds like a perfect evening", I responded with a smile. We parked the car in the parkade provided by the Quarter House and headed the two blocks or so to Bourbon Street. We heard the music, a great Saxophone sound and stopped at Saints and Sinners for a beer to watch and listen. We wandered around a bit, and I noticed that New Orleans had kind of cleaned up Bourbon Street somewhat. There were teen and pre-teen African American kids drumming on upside down plastic pails for loose change.

One change I noticed from a previous visit was that there were no longer scantily clad women on the front of the Penthouse or Playboy clubs beckoning men to come in to join the party, so to speak. This was now behind closed doors and the establishments had to be licensed in some aspect. It was a pleasant change. As dusk closed in and the heat of the day dissipated, a slight breeze came in off the Mississippi. We turned south and stopped at New Orleans Creole Cookery for a salad and some gator bites, washed down with a little wine and some nice soft jazz, after which we headed back to the hotel and passed out for the night.

What seemed like shortly thereafter, morning arrived. We headed out, picking up our separate cars and agreed to meet three days hence with whatever came our way.

Enter the CIA

. . . .

FORT LAUDERDALE IS ONE OF the best cities in the U.S. in my opinion, limited crime, an ocean and beaches, great restaurants and constant warm weather. Most of all no snow and no heights for me to fall from. I grew up in Minnesota and can do without subzero windy days of minus 30. As you age, cold hits you more. It just seems to seep through whatever clothing you wear right into your very bones!

The drive from New Orleans is a good 12 hours on the Florida Turnpike and the road requires your constant attention. I left at 6 a.m. and arrived at my home 13 hours later. I called John along the way and arranged to meet the next morning. I explained that I was still on the hunt for Graziano's daughter. I also explained her move to the FBI, Sheila's agency's interest in Graziano and his daughter and that I had confided in her to some extent, including my real name and agency connection. I added that what I really wanted to know was if there was any chance of determining if a warrant had been issued to enable Michelle to work undercover. I went on the explain the connection to the two women who had been Michelle's friends and that they had stated they had also lost connection with her but appeared to be hiding something from me.

"Good morning, John", I said as I walked into his office, "I picked up a coffee for you along the way, with one cream, as I remember it".

"Yes", he replied, and I am in bad need. Your call yesterday left me with some work to accomplish before you got here. I reached out to the investigators that met with you to determine if they were any closer to knowing the involvement of the agent within the FBI that had died on Murder Street. Hazel responded in the affirmative. Apparently, he worked in different parts of the agency, so the current thinking is that he was acting on his own, without senior FBI officials knowing he was somehow involved. It could be he was conducting his own investigation, but it is more likely that he had somehow been compromised and corrupted. They have started an investigation into his life from top to bottom, money issues, family issues, gambling, anything that pops up on their radar from here on. As a result, I felt okay reaching out to senior officials in the FBI to explain our desire to know more about Graziano's interests overseas and explained who you were as well as your financial investigative background. I added that it might be useful to know the whereabouts of Graziano's daughter as an FBI agent and asked if there was more information about the Murder Street investigation".

"What was the response to your request regarding Michelle"?

"The head of the Criminal Investigation Division for Florida, a large branch as far as branches go within the FBI, was able to confirm that Michelle had gone undercover two and one-half years ago. She had come to senior agency officials with a story about the apparent suicide of one of her parolees. The stories this man had told her were rather horrific and involved human trafficking in all its forms. He had given Michelle enough information for the FBI to believe its authenticity. The agency and DEA has many field agents working in the southern borders dealing with this issue. Unfortunately threats of death or death of family members keeps the victims from coming forward. She went undercover about two- and one-half years ago and is expected to report in on a fairly regular basis. They informed me that, like all undercover operatives, the reporting cannot follow an established pattern which could be noticed by the bosses".

"That is a long time to be undercover", I responded, why leave her there, wherever there is, for so long?"

"She has had some success, has been arrested as part of her own sting operations so she can continue, but is always placed in a new location. She carries the phony criminal record with her as she goes, thereby enhancing her chances of success. The risk is significant, but her handler confirmed that her role doesn't require her to be involved in the worst activities such as personally being exploited sexually or involved in selling drugs or working as a drug mule supplying clients. She works in different roles, as a chamber maid, kitchen staff, server, etc.".

"So her assignment has to lie with events not as yet uncovered. Is she working towards a higher, more dangerous criminal aspect, something more directly related to what the parolee said to her"?

"It appears that way to me. At present the FBI simply stated that her assignments had been progressing to higher value targets by plea arrangements with those already being charged. He stated that they were on the verge of identifying significant kingpins, one in Mexico, one in Haiti and one in New Orleans. They went on to say that the Mexican connection operates from Miami through to San Antonio and El Paso, along the border; and that the New Orleans connection is involved throughout Louisiana, southern Mississippi and Alabama. It was suggested that the latter area is all Tony Oreski and doesn't seem to have any connection to Graziano's syndicate. It is felt that getting those three kingpins would bring an end to substantial criminal operations from Miami all the way to western Texas. Of course, we all know there will be new lords on the horizon to replace them, but notwithstanding, every win counts. Given the sensitive nature and current progress, they are not currently willing to share her whereabouts".

"I assume she is one of several agents involved in these operations. The more the better on one hand, but if the crooks have already subverted at least one FBI agent, who's to say they haven't managed the same with these agents? They have, after all, a lot of money to spread around."

"That brings me to Graziano. In a review of Graziano's finances they discovered a series of payments going into two bank accounts that are in the name of two individuals. They have determined that these two individuals are now deceased, and the FBI has been watching the ATMs for access to those accounts. It seems to them that a man that looks very similar to the man rescuing Graziano on Murder Street has accessed those accounts, here in Fort Lauderdale. I assume that was you before I put you back on payroll. Given the amounts accessed I assume you used the funds to buy identities illegally, before I put you back on payroll. Hazel and Jimmie want to have another chat with you. You'll have to come up with your own explanation for those. While it's common practice for us outside the country to use ill-gotten gains for our own purposes, it isn't legal to do that here. I told them you were coming in today. I will give them a call and have them meet you tomorrow morning at your place. They will mostly want to know everything and aren't likely to be overly polite. They think you may have lied to them earlier, also a crime. I suspect that Hazel and Jimmy may include one or two other senior agents from within the FBI".

I thanked John for the heads up and decided to head straight home. I had a couple of hours to ensure there was no incriminating evidence in my home. However, I was more concerned that they may determine my location in New Orleans and get a search warrant to access the room. If they found all the hard drives, I would be looking for a good lawyer. I had no good explanation for not turning them over, other than perhaps saying that as a result of the FBI agent being found on Murder Street, I had no one to trust.

When I got home it occurred to me that my phone may be bugged so I went back out and got a burner phone, transferring the necessary phone data. I phoned Sheila, explained my dilemma and asked her to head to New Orleans, by air, as quickly as possible, collect the hard drives, and secure them in a safety deposit box. By now we have copied all the data and so I asked her to take my laptop as well. She agreed to leave right away and said she would pick up her own burner phone and call me back when all was secured. I phoned the hotel in Fort Lauderdale, advising that I had an urgent family problem to attend to, and that a person named Sheila Sterling would be dropping by to pick up some of my belongings. I asked the hotel to ensure they had her ID before letting her in.

Hazel and Jimmy showed up as expected at 1:00 p.m. on the dot. I let them in without any fanfare given John had set up the meeting.

Hazel started off. "We have a short little video to show you. It seems that a man of your description has been accessing accounts set up by Graziano in the name of two men who are deceased. He looks exactly like the man who rescued Graziano, which you confirmed was actually you. So you have accessed accounts of two people no longer living and must therefore have their credit cards and pin numbers at the very least. It seems that the best-case scenario for you is that you have been operating as a CIA agent on our home soil, not a good thing for you. Or perhaps you are far more involved with Graziano and his syndicate than it appears. Jimmy and I think you need to come clean with us, or perhaps we should just arrest you here. Got anything to say"?

"I was in a position where Graziano asked me to locate his daughter as he was dying. He thought that I would need to alter my identity to protect myself as he thought that Tony Oreski was responsible for the shoot-out and may be looking for the man that rescued him. He felt that I would need the money to carry out the search, perhaps for travel, perhaps for bribes for all I know. You are correct, I did use the money to purchase new Identification, in the names of both individuals. However, I have used the Jeff Atkinson identity to find the private investigation firm of John Sterling, now run by his daughter. She was smart enough to figure out that the Jeff Atkinson identity was a fake and confronted me about it. As a result, where she is concerned neither identity has any value. However, it still may have value where the search for Graziano's daughter is concerned".

"We examined the accounts and know that you only accessed funds and didn't bother to look up account balances. The accounts have a significant amount of money in them, in excess of a few million, and there are still deposits going in from Graziano's legitimate businesses. Were you aware that was the case"?

"I had no idea that money was still going into them. However, it doesn't concern me too much if the proceeds are from a legitimate business. Further to that I am in possession of a will which I can provide to you that essentially leaves the proceeds to the holder of the will document, which is in my possession. That means the accounts are legally mine, despite their deaths".

"And how did you come into possession of such a document and given its unlikely veracity. Why would we believe you have it? Interesting that Graziano would give it to you and say it was to help find his daughter".

"He did give it to me. I explained earlier that he asked me to find his daughter to inform her, and to provide her with the necessary information for her to assume control of the businesses he established in her name. He felt I would need funds and that I would need to keep my real identity secret as I travelled around. That is even more important now that I was named as the person that helped Graziano in all the news media. I have no idea what I will do with the money in these accounts. By my way of thinking one-half belongs to Sheila Sterling".

I had no intention of telling the FBI there was a third person involved, overseas. Someone I knew nothing about. I knew that I was likely going to have to find out about Hans Goebel for myself.

"If what you say is true, then we should have a look at the so-called will document, to verify your story. We are still of the opinion that it is just too much of a coincidence that you just happened by and that Graziano would solicit your assistance, the assistance of a man he did not know, to find a daughter no one knew he had".

"I think that is the point", I replied, "he has always kept his daughter a secret from the world he lived and operated in. He did not want to jeopardize her or have to have her protected 24/7 from a kidnapping or other event concocted to get at him. And, yes, I will arrange for you to see the will and testament. Right now, it's in New Orleans, in a safe place".

"We will want to see it ASAP", replied Jimmy, I think I'll go with you back to New Orleans. We don't want you creating a document on your own to clear us away for a few days".

"Fine by me", I replied. "Now, perhaps you can share a little with me. I am struggling with my own coincidences. You know who I work for and what my skills are, at least to some extent. You are obviously being kept fully informed about the FBI investigation or you wouldn't be able to do your job effectively. First, there is the issue of why the cars were in an alley which essentially trapped Graziano's escape route, given there was a car behind his car. Secondly, what can you share about Tony Oreski, I assume the FBI has interviewed him by now and you are privy to the content of those conversations. And thirdly, who takes over Graziano's empire in the event of his death"?

Hazel responded. "Street cams show that a delivery truck had parked sideways along Graziano's route. They were forced to take the alley to try to get to the rendezvous with the FBI. We assume that whoever wanted Graziano out of the way knew the route. It seems that it would have to have been an insider or someone planted inside the organization for that to occur. Also, one would expect there to be someone in the truck to prevent the escape route that you took. We just don't know why the escape route you took wasn't covered unless it was assumed that there would be no escape. As for Oreski, no one has been able to find him. We assume he has gone underground somewhere until this blows over, but his M.O. would suggest otherwise. He normally is in some public place to establish a personal alibi. This is the case in this situation. He was seen at a public event as the shootings took place. There is no reason for him to hide himself away. As for Graziano's empire, we had assumed a power struggle might occur, or at least there would be some noise, or retaliation of some kind. But nothing has occurred".

"There is a reason for Oreski to go underground if he felt that he was a target as well", I replied. "As for who takes over, they may be waiting for the funeral to take place and some time to pass before any moves are made. But I agree, it is eerily silent. It almost seems as though no one on any side knows who targeted Graziano and no one is making a further move. I am thinking that the hit was internal, that someone inside his organization discovered he was coughing up operational secrets and names. It might explain why there was no one left in the truck altering the route. Someone had to know to place the truck there, and that leaves a source within Graziano's own organization, a rogue agent of supervisor within the FBI itself. Graziano operated a criminal empire for a long time without ever being caught and convicted. He should have been too smart to allow himself to be overheard within, so I am thinking FBI. As well when is the funeral for Graziano? It would be interesting to see who attends, both at the church and the gravesite".

"It is three days away", replied Jimmy. "The autopsy has been completed. There is lots of time for you and I to make it to New Orleans and have you produce a copy of that will. Even if it temporarily clears your access to those funds, in our minds, it may have other relevance".

I realized, in that moment, I had not been totally honest with respect to the third person named in the will. I considered texting Sheila to forge a legitimate looking copy, excluding Hans Goebel. I thought about the risk of withholding evidence from special investigators and decided to do it anyway. It wasn't as though it would be the first time. The CIA isn't supposed to operate on U.S. soil, but we did it all the time. And forging documents is not that difficult. We employ lawyers and other specialists to do exactly that.

I excused myself for a bathroom break and texted Sheila, explaining the dilemma, and provided her with names of those lawyers with whom she would have to get in touch. We had less than a day to do this, but that is nothing new. She agreed, and we arranged a time and place to meet with Jimmy and provide him with the altered document.

When I got back into the room, Hazel offered me one more piece of information. "Based on your I guess we are okay with sharing one piece of information with you Brock. The FBI agent deceased at the crime scene has a striking similarity to you in age and appearance. While it is still early days, our working theory is that he was 'reached', shall we say, by Graziano and placed him within whatever organization had arranged for his assassination. Our best guess is that this agent was discovered and therefore killed by his own team. We think the will you mentioned and fake identifications were likely intended for him".

Sheila texted back at 4:30 to advise that she had secured all the hard drives. While the FBI didn't know of my involvement with Sheila or the purpose, it wouldn't take them long to connect the name I had used at the Quarter House to her agency in Atlanta, and the ID that had been used in Atlanta.

When all was said and done, Jimmy and I headed out. He agreed we would drive, in part because he intended to stay in New Orleans for a day or two, depending on what they both thought after seeing the document. Hazel wanted to know where the funds coming into those accounts were from and intended to use FBI resources to make that determination. She had already pursued the warrant and had an appointment for Jimmy with the banks involved.

Jesse and Louise
Second Time Around

THE NEXT DAY, NOW DAY 7, Jimmy and I met Sheila, and she produced a new original copy of the altered will for Jimmy to peruse. He looked it over, was satisfied that I had told the truth, which I had not, and he called Hazel to let her know that all was well. In the meantime, when he got off the phone, he advised that Hazel had not yet determined the source of funds, her meeting was still an hour away. He excused himself, saying he had to visit the local office for a chat.

After he left, I brought Sheila up to date with respect to the funeral, the missing Oreski and the silence within the Graziano empire.

"You know", started Sheila, "as a private investigative firm, we are asked to find missing persons on a regular basis. Sometimes teens, sometimes abducted children, sometimes missing spouses. I read somewhere that more than 2000 people go missing in the United States every day and that there are almost 100,000 active missing person cases...100,000!!! Some, of course, are individuals trying to escape an unhappy life. Some though, are murderers, or criminals going to ground, some get resolved, some remain forever unknown. Oreski could be any of these, most likely gone into hiding somewhere. In the meantime, what are your thoughts about meeting with Michelle's two friends? I did bring the photos of Michelle as she was growing up over the years. I think they could help to establish some level of trust".

"We had talked about winning their confidence by showing them as much of the Graziano disc as possible. There is a risk though in sharing that information with them. The more they know about who Graziano was, the more they are at risk. We will be able to edit the disc if Graziano identifies himself and remove his name and photos if there are any. However, that detracts from trust. We will need to review the disc and decide what to leave for Jesse and Louise and what to provide to Michelle. Given her current assignment, this might come as a distraction for her. On the other hand, she's a big girl, with a big job and capable of making her own decisions about all of this. It's mainly Jesse and Louise we need to keep certain information from".

"I think I agree with that assessment", responded Sheila, "let's get the disc and see what needs to be done. In the meantime, there are likely some parade routes we need to check out so we can add a little fun to the day, and maybe find a street band or two to watch for a while. Game"?

"Of course, and I was also reading from the Mardi Gras guide. Did you know that no one organization or the city coordinates Mardi Gras? The police issue parade permits for the nearly 60 parades in the 12 days that precede Fat Tuesday, and each parading organization is completely autonomous. For 117 years the parades went through the French Quarter but in the 1970s the larger floats and larger crowds on the narrow streets rendered the routes unsafe, so the city banned parades in that area".

"The combined parade routes are said to cover over 300 miles, and processions are on the street for over 200 hours over several weeks. In 1973 the city issued a ban on parades through the French Quarter due to the size of floats and width of the streets. What is fascinating as well, the city does not spend a dime promoting Mardi Gras and there is no such thing as anything officially licensed, such as posters, and there is no general theme, which basically means that businesses are free to create different themes, posters, etc.".

Sheila piped in with a few of her own facts. "Did you know that the organizations you are talking about are called Krewes. Many are named after various mythologies from the Greek, Roman and Egyptian eras, some are named for their neighborhoods through which they travel and some after historical figures or places. One of the "games" I like to play is to ask people which is their favorite Krewe name. When I was young, I always thought I would like a member of IRIS which is the oldest female Krewe in New Orleans. They were the first Krewe to have their carnival ball televised, giving publicity to the pageantry. The IRIS riders wear white gloves, masks, and colorful wigs to maintain their anonymity".

"It has always struck me that the concept gives rise to a bit of debauchery. You know, masks, wigs, etc. I read in the annual Mardi Gras Guide that carnival balls are usually private and by invitation only. They apparently are held in the grand ballrooms of hotels where mock kings, queens, maids and dukes are presented in order. In some cases, theatrical scenes are staged by krewe members and favors are given to special guests. Apparently though, there are a few which throw large parties to which tickets are sold. Maybe we should try to find one of these and go. But you said IRIS *was* an early favorite. Since then, what appealed to you"?

"I think my new favorite is the Krewe of Eve, a ladies parading krewe, because they have themes like *famous lovers, or we go together* which is expressed like as in *Batman and Robin, Peanut Butter and Jelly, and Rock and Roll etc.* They have over 700 members, over 25 floats. What about you? You said you picked up the Mardi Gras Guide, any krewe appealed to you"?

"At the risk of being too obvious, I think King Arthur appeals to me. It was started by a 17-year-old and now has 2,400 coed members. Of course, I like the coed versions, you know, being a guy. They throw Karmal Corn, Fedoras, Merlin Hats, princess cone hats, and decorated grails. If their tandem floats were disconnected, they would number over 71 individual floats".

"I guess I'm not surprised that you would pick King Arthur", responded Sheila, "but I also thought maybe you would pick one of the floats involving trucks rolling through the city. I heard that some have over 100 trucks and 4000 riders. I also like that many of these krewes sponsor charities. And, by the way, I like the idea of scoring some tickets to a carnival ball. Maybe there is one on Fat Tuesday so we can wear masks on the street during the day so we can wander around before the ball".

By the time we had gone through the Mardi Gras conversation, it was time to head back to the hotel. I was thinking along the walk how much I enjoyed spending time with Sheila away from the troubles of the day. I sensed we both felt the same and that led to a nice night of loving. I placed a pillow under her hips so she could tip upwards a bit. We were on the fourth floor and the drapes were open with the streetlight casting our shadows on the bedroom wall. I could turn my head and watch our shadows as her perfectly-shaped legs were straight up in the air. Images and sounds I'll never forget.

The next morning, we were lying close together in a nice warm snuggle.

"So Brock, tell me about your love life, past and present, any significant others in your life now, have you ever been married"?

"You are pretty significant to me; in case you haven't noticed. No, there is no one else or I wouldn't be spending this kind of time with you. I tried marriage twice, after I was no longer a field operative and also had a few liaisons, I guess I would call them, between and after both marriages. In retrospect, I wasn't very good at it. I didn't understand the importance of affirmations at the time, and it took me a long time to realize that every person is very different from the one before. As well you form friendships connected to your partnership and when you separate or get divorced, it's like you divorce your friends as well. Eventually you end up being alone a lot of the time. On top of that I was constantly travelling. My first wife thought I was out and about having affairs when in fact it was all work all the time. But the trust wasn't there. I suppose in retrospect we didn't really love each other and in part, at least, for me the marriages were about alleviating loneliness instead of working on a partnership. What about you, have you been married"?

"Never", responded Sheila. I have had a few longer-term relationships, but I never really felt I wanted to get tied down and I certainly didn't want the whole family thing. I loved the excitement of my job and agency and when I became the boss, well, who wants to date a private detective? But hey, you are not getting off that easily. Tell me the rest, one was jealous and not really for you? But you got married a second time, was it true love that time?"

"At first, I thought I was in love, actually we both thought we were in love. But she had serious anger issues, and we fought a lot. She was a highflyer career-wise and spent hours after hours if you will. In time I began to feel she was stepping out. She would say she was at work, but if I phoned there was no answer, you know, in the days before cell phones. She eventually told me that she was seeing someone else, so I moved out. In retrospect, she likely had manic depressive disorder, but it wasn't a thing that was diagnosed back then".

"What made things really difficult for me was the endless nights where you lie beside someone you really like, in the same bed, who doesn't want you to touch her. You eventually reach a dark place where you just dread that you are going to lose this person from your life and end up alone again. Dread isn't like anything else. It's not like fear which relates to things that haven't happened yet, or terror where you usually fear for your physical life. Dread comes at you like a shadow and shrouds you and takes over your soul. You get a pain, or pressure behind your eyes and it seeps down into your gut as it's both your emotional well-being and your entire soul that seems to be at risk. The only way out is to escape".

"So those were your marriages", said Sheila, "what about the other women you mentioned, the ones before and after"?

"I guess I have to say that I wasn't always the good guy. I know there were a couple of women with whom I had affairs that wanted to be with me, and I didn't want any commitment with them. For me it was just fun and sex, but they wanted more and were hurt. There were also a couple of cases where both of us just wanted to have a bit of fun together, but of course, those things do not last very long. Eventually, I just decided avoiding a long-term thing was best for me. And now, I have shared enough".

"Just one more question, said Sheila "what am I, just a little bit of fun, since you don't do relationships"?

"It seems to me that may just as well be my question. I really like you though, and I am retired, and you are wealthy enough to retire, so why don't we just stick together and see where this goes"?

"I like that idea", she responded, "and I like you too".

I rolled out of bed and went to the kitchen to make coffee, got out the laptop and opened up the hard drive that contained Graziano's messages to Michelle so we could decide what to share with Jesse and Louise, and maybe as well, with Michelle. Sheila joined me a few minutes later, and we got down to work.

"When we copied the hard drives, we kept the color coding the same as Graziano's originals, to avoid any future confusion. Graziano said the hard drive that is colored blue contains all the relevant information about his daughter, now in her mid-thirties. Her address, her bank account, email, her work, all her history, basically her entire life, or at least that is as much as I know about it what is on the drive. Let's review with this one and see what we can share and whether we need to edit anything out. I am not sure we want Jesse and Louise to know who Michelle's father was. It is also possible you can augment any conversation with pictures you have".

As we watched the information unfold several thoughts occurred to me. "It will come as a surprise, to all the women, but he doesn't identify himself in any way on the disc, it's just a voice, data and photographs of Michelle growing up, and no video of him. It does contain pictures of her over the years, so it is essential that we are honest with her as to where these photos came from".

"I don't think we have to share his identity we Jesse and Louise", replied Sheila, "we have already explained to them he was in possession of sensitive information he was handing over to Interpol and the FBI and if they contacted Michelle already, Michelle may have made several assumptions about who her father might have been, or at least what type of man he was. But they would still be assumptions, and she will press for answers. She may go as far as trying to find out from within the FBI who he was".

"I don't think she will do that in advance of meeting with us. She will want as much information as possible before she takes that step. I am certain, though she will want to meet with us, and I am willing to bet that if Jesse and Louise have a means of getting in touch with her, they will have done so by now. They know how important it is to her, but Michelle will be cautious, not knowing for sure who we are, and she will have imparted that concern to Louise and Jesse. Also, I don't think that we have to share any more information with these two women, this should be sufficient for them to feel that Michelle may feel it's in her best interests and therefore their own, as well. If they kept this from her after seeing this, knowing how she has searched for her father, they know she would be more than a little angry. And they know that it's up to Michelle to make her own decision about this".

"I agree", commented Sheila, "let's arrange a meeting and see if they are willing to admit they have a means of contacting her and are willing to reach out".

With that as the plan, I phoned Jesse and arranged another meeting. At first, she had responded by saying they had nothing more to share with us, but I decided to explain that their behavior in our first meeting, the fidgeting, casting eyes downward, etc. led me to believe they knew more than they were saying. I also went into my belief that they would be faced with a dilemma if Michelle ever discovered they had kept things from her. In addition, I shared that we had made overtures to the FBI, but they were unwilling to share any information about Michelle's whereabouts, given her current assignment. I explained they were our only hope, and Michelle's as well. Jesse ultimately agreed for us to meet the two of them at her house on the weekend. She explained that they did not want their spouses involved as they were unaware that the two women still had contact with Michelle.

We stepped in and Jesse invited us to the living room. Sheila had come with a full folder of photographs, newsletter clippings from the stories she had written about Michelle, as well as her laptop from which she had already downloaded photos onto a USB. We also showed the women the hard drive with Graziano speaking (without his image in the drive). The material was pretty convincing. They understood how unlikely it was that someone would have hired a private investigator to follow Michelle's life without some compelling reason to do so. Family connection was the only possibility to explain the detail about Michelle's life-her bank account, her work history, her school and university years, even her former email address.

"I have copied all of this onto this USB", explained Sheila, handing the drive over. "Given that you agreed to meet with us, we assume with some certainty that you have some means of contacting Michelle. We have more that can be shared with her, but it is more personal, and it involves fairly substantial business interests".

"We do have means", responded Louise, "it is secure, but we can only leave a message, and she gets back to us only when it is safe for her to do so. She is very seldom able to see us in person, but with Mardi Gras, and all the people coming into the city, it may be possible, even probable, that she would be coming here in any event. We will do what we can and if she agrees she will let us know how to go about this. Rest assured she will be very cautious. We can't send this material anywhere because we don't know where she is. For now, we will keep it safe. I expect she won't meet with you until after she has a chance to see this. She will need some means of ensuring you are who you say you are before she meets you, if she meets you".

"That is a given", said Jesse adding, and expect to have her stay in the shadows in some regard with respect you, even when and if she agrees to a meeting. She has said more than once that her current assignment is fraught with danger, and very dangerous people".

"That is okay with us', I replied, "there is no need for us to necessarily see her in person, or close up. The main idea is to get her the information".

Sheila and I excused ourselves. "You know", she started, "this inheritance thing still leaves me with a question. It's not about Michelle, but rather about me. At one point you said the will left a villa in Malaga to my father. Given that he has passed, it seems to me that the villa is mine. In fact, you said that. However, when you had me copy the will and alter it for the FBI, I noticed that there were bank accounts in the names of three men, including my father. So, it seems that should also be my inheritance. N'est pas? What are your plans for this, at least now that I know"?

I squirmed a little before responding. "I should have mentioned these things to you before I had you copy the will. The will leaves everything to the three men, but in the context that whosoever possesses the will can cash in. I know I can pretend, if you will, to be all three people, given some similarities to my own appearance. But at some point, that must end. As a result, it has always been my intention, and I think the lawyer's intention, to have the proceeds go to the rightful heirs".

"But it has to be enacted by someone in possession of the will itself. We know you are one of the rightful heirs, we have no idea who Hans Goebel is, but the lawyer does appear to have a daughter at minimum. In the meantime, the investigators, Hazel and Jimmy have an edited version of the document, know that you are a rightful heir, assuming these are not ill-gotten gains, and have advised me that there is still money going into these accounts. I think that is what Jimmy is doing at this moment here in New Orleans, trying to determine the source of funds still going into these accounts".

"I am happy to hear you say that", laughed Sheila, "given that you allowed me access to the document, I had assumed you trusted me and that you were trustworthy and honorable as well. Otherwise, the sex would not have been on the table".

"I can't recall ever being on a table with you, I'll salt that away for future reference. Or perhaps reference is the wrong word. Maybe further action"!!

"I don't think so", she responded, "tables would be too uncomfortable"!!

We headed back to the French Quarter, having handed everything we had taken with us to Jesse and Louise. There was no need to head back to the hotel. I called Jimmy and asked how he was doing with searching for the source of funds going into the accounts.

"I thought that was your superpower", teased Sheila, "just how much skill do you need to examine crooked books, hiding figures and such"?

"It depends on the sophistication; not all criminal records are done with great skill. Basically, though, I can look at a spreadsheet and almost instantly spot mathematical errors some of which are deliberately placed. They just pop out as if in bold sometimes. If spreadsheets go on for several pages of lines and columns, most people don't even bother to examine them. I expect when I get around to opening the other Graziano hard drives I may be intrigued enough to follow them through. For now, though, my main goal is to find Michelle. It isn't yet clear if there is anyone in the FBI who can be trusted to be given possession the other hard drives Graziano had in his possession. That is not the role for Hazel and Jimmy. Their job is to clear the individuals within the FBI, especially the more senior agents. These kinds of investigations into a syndicate like Graziano's can take years to build a case, so there is no immediate rush. In addition, I thought whoever killed Graziano would be trying to track me down, but I am certain we have not been watched nor followed as of yet, although my picture had been front and center on the screen, with my real name just below".

Follow the Money?

. . . .

JIMMY SAID HE HAD SOME information and had called Hazel to have me cleared to be kept up to date with that part of the journey, since it, as Graziano explained, identified resources left to her as his daughter. Jimmy agreed to meet with me on the condition that Shelia not be present, as she had no agency clearances. We met at the FBI offices in New Orleans.

Jimmy outlined that the monies flowing into the two accounts for Jeff Atkinson and John Sterling (I had not told the FBI about Hans Goebel) was being sourced from what on the surface appeared to be legitimate businesses, although likely the original investments are presumed to have come from his criminal activities. However, advised Jimmy, the accounts were in the names of Jeff Atkinson and John Sterling and therefore Sheila was the rightful heir to those belonging to her father. Jimmy went on to explain that the IRS had investigated Atkinson's holdings on two occasions with no tax issues found. Also, the same was true for John Sterling and without playing my hand I assumed the same would be the case for Hans Goebel.

What I still didn't understand was why the will with the three names existed at all. The will gave nothing to Graziano's daughter, all that was taken care of through the transfer of the legitimate businesses and profits directly into Michelle's name. If the identities, or at least one, were intended for the deceased agent, why not pay him directly instead of through a will. It occurred to me at that moment that Graziano may have considered the possibility of the agent being discovered and decided to provide for his family in the event of his demise.

And how was Michelle supposed to find out about her 'inheritance' if her father died, and I had not come along? Someone else must exist that had some instruction or knowledge. But who? Did that mean that there was someone else, other than me, looking for her? I had to assume that there was a different person intended for these identities and bank accounts and that whoever that person was might be looking for me. I expressed that possibility to Jimmy. In the end I suggested the deceased agent may have been that person.

"I agree that might be the case", Jimmy assented, "also, however, Oreski seems to have gone underground, but he could very well just be out and about looking for you. Of course, you hightailed it out of Fort Lauderdale almost immediately and since then have been using assumed names. However, it is very unlikely that Oreski would have known about this will, given that he and Graziano were basically in competition for much of the southern USA. It is also possible that this was for a close associate of Graziano, someone completely loyal who may have known of his plans to turn things over to the FBI and come clean. A golden parachute if you will".

"That makes some sense", I replied. "But it still leaves several possibles. The will could be intended for a completely not so loyal person who ordered the hit on Graziano, or there is a second person in his organization, that he trusted explicitly, who found out and ordered the hit. Either way, I have to assume one or two people are looking for me for different reasons. First, what did Graziano share with me, and second, what am I doing with these identities, bank accounts and businesses which clearly belong to the daughters or spouses of the people named on the will.

We also have to consider the reason for the hit. There is a possibility that someone like Oreski, but more powerful and more sly, wants to take over the territory. In any case, I have to assume that they believe I am a threat to them as the press has identified my name and that I was an agent involved in investigating financial irregularities for a sister agency. There is no doubt that someone in Graziano's syndicate will be looking for me to find out what I know. I am thinking that close associates will attend the funeral, so it is time to perhaps head back to West Palm Beach and see who is in attendance".

"There are also other avenues", offered Jimmy, "the FBI has to have a list of close and known associates of Graziano's. Hazel and I can obtain that information and we can film the funeral from a distance, identify persons of interest and share that with you. That will keep you away from prying eyes and buy more time".

In that moment I realized that I had to look into the hard drives that Graziano had provided as they may very well provide insight into for whom the will was actually intended and maybe identify the most likely suspects for his murder. If the drives contain substantial information about his operation the higher-ups in the organization are the most likely to be threatened by Graziano's plan to come clean and name names. Obviously Graziano's plan was discovered in time for someone to arrange his murder. As Graziano was travelling without an FBI escort he must have assumed he was not at risk internally. That then opened up endless possibilities from external sources who might want the territory.

I thanked Jimmy for the update, left the FBI offices, and phoned Sheila. The FBI may not agree to her involvement, but I certainly felt inclined to have another good mind looking at Graziano's hard drives. We met back up at the hotel, and I filled her in on Jimmy's findings.

"You know," she said, "Jimmy and Hazel are investigating your involvement as it relates to the death of the FBI agents on Murder Street and may be assuming your search for his daughter is not all you know about. Bringing you into their confidence is a bit of a technique with the hope you'll share what you may be keeping from them. To date, you have not updated them on your search for Michelle Savonne and that might suggest to them that you are not being fully open. Maybe it is also time for you to share that with

Hazel and Jimmy, since we are relatively sure they are on the side of the good in this case".

"It is true that my involvement and the not coming forward with respect to my, now our, search for Michelle must look a bit odd to them. It may lead them to believe, even more than they do now, that I have more than I am sharing. It would be a good idea to share with those two where our search for Michelle is taking us and go from there. It could also very well be that they have more knowledge than they are sharing with us. Their job is to investigate the FBI and the death of an apparent rogue agent at the crime scene, and now as well, they will have been read into the disappearance of Tony Oreski".

"I am a big believer in Occam's Razor, the simplest explanation is the most likely as it makes the fewest assumptions. Assuming Oreski was involved in Graziano's death requires a lot of assumptions about the strength of his ambitions and ability to challenge someone as powerful as Graziano. It is most likely an internal ambition as there had to be knowledge that something was about to transpire that was highly secretive and damaging to the criminal empire. The higher-ups in Graziano's syndicate had to be concerned about the loss of the servers containing all the data that is now on those heard drives. Let's take these drives for a spin around the block and see what pops out at us. But let's still begin with what we need to share with Michelle when we get that opportunity. We need to be ready at a moment's notice if we get that call".

We plugged in the drive that contained Graziano's more detailed message for Michelle. He began by introducing himself and stated that she may have heard of him, given that he had discovered that she had joined the FBI which, he assumed, led to her disappearance.

"I have always regretted not being in your life, Michelle, but your mother was adamant that I was not to be around. I was able to follow your life and hired a private firm to provide me with pictures and records of you growing up. If I had attempted to have contact with you, your mother would have moved, and I would not have been able to follow your life. I am very proud of your achievements and have now decided, as I approach old age, that I need to make peace with our God. I may not succeed in that endeavor given my sordid life, but I need to make the attempt. For that reason, I am turning data regarding my entire operation and all its criminal components over to the FBI and Interpol. You will no doubt hear about all this very soon. I came to this realization several years ago and have worked diligently to create legitimate businesses all of which are now in your name, along with bank accounts, profits, etc. Thes enterprises were not now, and had never been, involved in any criminal activity. In some cases, they are franchise operations, a portion of the proceeds of which go to your accounts every month".

"In addition," he started, "I have not managed these personally but rather have hired, on your behalf, a CEO to oversee your interests. He has had a free hand to grow and expand or modify operations as he sees fit as long as everything is ethical and legal. If you are seeing this, you now know that I have had you watched and photographed, filmed and so forth over the years so that I could watch you grow with some degree of pride. Now, you seem to have disappeared, shortly after joining the FBI. I am hoping that you are alive and well, that this all finds you, and that you are just undercover somewhere and hopefully not in my world somewhere. Maybe someday we can meet in person, though I know that you will not like the man I have been. However, there are two kinds of criminal overlords, one kind is the real dirty, running hookers, dealing bad drugs, selling people into slavery and so forth. I have never done that. The other is the kind of criminal I am, maybe you'll think I am just as bad, maybe worse. You'll likely read about me in the press soon enough and you can make up your own mind at that time. I am likely to serve time, maybe the rest of my life, time will tell. I have always loved you, though from a distance, and I hope this puts some things a little more right in your mind".

He went on to state that the hard drive contained spreadsheets with the name and itemization of every business, the names, addresses and records of current owners, managers, staff records, tax records, financial statements, He had started this process a few years ago when he discovered Michelle had joined the FBI.

"I am coming clean with respect to all the illegitimate and somewhat evil, I guess you could say, businesses that I have created. I am turning a significant amount of material over to both the FBI and Interpol. My syndicate has operated on both sides of the Atlantic, and that is why both agencies are involved. What I did, operated at a very high level, you might say. I was never involved in marketing street prostitutes or pushing hard drugs. A time will come when this all becomes public, and then you will know the type of crime for which I was responsible".

Graziano continued. "It is very disturbing to me that this country, which I love, is slowly being taken over by thugs from Central America who are forcing refugees across the border, shipping their cocaine, producing meth and fentanyl for street sale and generally killing people. And, rest assured, not all these refugees are refugees. A large and very unsavory criminal element comes along for the ride, and they are likely members of cartels with specific assignments and roles. I can no longer stand by and watch this happening. As a result, I started my own investigation into this. It is far easier to undertake, already being a criminal, than for the authorities whose hands are somewhat handcuffed by our laws. I know that Antonio Oreski is behind a large chunk of this type of crime as I have been able to subvert a couple of his seniors into sharing information, given that they think I might be a better boss and make them far wealthier than they are with Oreski. I have learned that there is an agreement between Oreski and a Mexican cartel and this information is included with the hard drives I am turning over to the authorities. I know that I am not likely to win your favor at any time in the future, but I needed to clear my soul as best I could at this time of life. If I never see you again, Michelle, I wish for you to have a good life, and as a good citizen".

"Interesting", observed Sheila, "especially the part about his attempting to get inside information from Oreski's camp. If Oreski found out about this he would most certainly have dealt severely with his own people. You know they have a saying in Louisiana with respect to people disappearing?"

"Yes", I replied. 'We have a swamp for that' is the expression when people need to disappear. However, given Graziano's opinion of Oreski, I wonder if maybe he made Oreski disappear. On the other hand, it could very well have been whatever cartel is involved, if they thought Oreski killed Graziano and was causing too much trouble. I think we have information on the hard drives that is important to the investigation into Graziano's murder, and we better not withhold it any longer from the FBI, Hazel and Jimmy. Let's give Jimmy a call and see if he's still in New Orleans".

"I agree it is important", replied Sheila, "but if we share this now, might they not think that we have other information we are not sharing? The FBI knows that Graziano was bringing data to their investigation on the day he was killed and likely are assuming you have it somewhere. We have made copies in case it was necessary to give up the hard drives, so we can continue our own search for Michelle. Nonetheless, I think we should hang onto the original hard drives until we can deliver them to the agents Graziano trusted. Hazel, Jimmy and the FBI know who you are and where you are as well as how to reach you. While it seems a safe bet that you are on safe ground with the FBI, given you are allowed to roam freely about, I suspect Hazel and Jimmy do know you have more information than you are sharing and are willing to let it slide for now."

I agreed with Sheila's analysis and picked up the phone and called Jimmy's number only to hear him say he had gone back to Fort Lauderdale. I asked him about his investigation into the source of funds going into the accounts for Atkinson and Sterling. He simply advised that he had hit a dead end and felt it best to hand it off to someone with actuarial capability within the FBI. He also said that he had kept my use of those identities away from the FBI proper as their investigation was still ongoing and these funds had come from Graziano in some context. He said that he and Hazel were still concerned about a leak within the FBI.

Sheila decided she would head back to Atlanta as we had not yet heard from Jesse and Louise, and I decided to head back to Fort Lauderdale to turn over the hard drive involving Graziano' information regarding his daughter. The next day was the day before Graziano's funeral. The FBI had previously advised that they intended to be present to see who was in attendance and possibly follow up. I decided to give my boss John another call to see if he had learned any more. I got back late and headed straight to my home.

Home With Oreski

I TURNED THE KEY AND walked in, directly into the somewhat fragrant aroma of a Cuban cigar and a vintage luger pointed at my chest. "Welcome home", said Tony Oreski, "I have been searching for you for a few days. It seems your home is easy to find, but you, on the other hand, seem to be able to disappear at will. Got any idea why I am here"?

I thought for a minute before responding. My first thought was that I needed better security, First Hazel and Jimmy, and now Oreski had found their way into my house without breaking the door down or climbing through a window. If Oreski had killed Graziano, perhaps he knew about the hand over to the FBI and wanted whatever was on the hard drives. But he may not be here for that reason, and I couldn't take the chance of spilling those beans. In any event if he did think I had the hard drives, he should have assumed I had already turned them over to the FBI. I assumed he did not know anything about Graziano's plans to come clean. That meant he was here for a reason I knew nothing about.

"I have no idea why you are in my home, and really don't have a clue why a gun would be necessary. You could have just asked to meet me for a coffee or a beer. Why don't you put the gun away and ask me a little more politely what it is you are looking for"?

"I want to know what every news reporter in Florida wants to know. Who are you, why were you at Murder Street, what do you know about Graziano and who the hell is responsible for his death.

The thing is, you see, everyone seems to think I had something to do with this and there is too much heat and attention for my associates".

Not smart criminals will always say way too much. It may not matter when they are talking to the average person, but to someone in law enforcement, or a psychologist, too many words give a lot away.

"Well, thanks for all that. If you have associates that worry about you bringing heat down on them, then you may as well put the gun away or this will just bring you more heat. You also told me in that little dialogue that you were not responsible for what happened to Graziano. I am exactly who the press reported I was, I just happened to be on an early morning run and happened upon the place at that time. I was just in time to see the end of the gunfight and a wounded man in need of help, after all the violence had ended. I did what he asked and drove him home. He said he would be fine and asked me to leave, that he could look after himself from that point. So I left. My turn now. Just who are these associates you are worried about and why would they be concerned about Graziano being dead? Of course, you could be here to throw suspicion off yourself, but that would only occur if I was able to report it". I waited for Oreski to say something.

A moment went by while he considered what I had said. He tucked the luger into a holster and said nothing. I waited. Most people hate silence, and Oreski, who liked to be called Notorio, was no exception. This was a man who wanted attention and went out of his way to find it. His associates, however, were asking him to stand down. Sooner or later, he was going to break his silence and say something.

"I apologize for the gun. I guess it's just that I broke in and wasn't sure what your reaction was going to be. I was just ensuring my own safety. I far as I was aware you may be one of Graziano's men or the person who killed him. I didn't believe you were who the press reported. What can I do to make this up to you, so you don't report me"?

"I'll make you a deal. Your associates make you, a seasoned bad guy by all accounts, very nervous, and they must have asked you to find out what went down with Graziano. If you had nothing to do with it, and they had nothing to do with it, then why not share with me who they are and let's see who else we can throw suspicion at. What thoughts do you have about this"?

"I don't like the idea that I would share with you who my associates are, that won't be happening here. Whoever killed Graziano has to be someone from within his own syndicate, unless it's the FBI itself, given that my sources within the police advised that a rogue agent was involved. There are one or two inside Graziano's organization I would put my money on. A guy named Martinez and another named Perez. I have met them both at various times and both are power players within Graziano's organization. I wouldn't be surprised if both were involved".

"Hmmm. If you are not involved why not turn yourself over to the police and let them know that? They told me you had disappeared or gone underground, which makes them very suspicious that you are guilty. I heard from sources that you have a solid alibi for yourself, so I don't see the point in you hiding yourself away. Of course, that still leaves the possibility you could have ordered a hit. On the other hand, how sure are you that your own associates didn't order the hit and are trying to have you throw suspicion in another direction, or throw you under the bus"?

"I am absolutely certain my friends were not involved, and the other thing is that as far as I know, I might be next if someone new was trying to horn in on our world", he replied, not realizing he was giving me too much information. "We don't want anyone looking our way right now".

"But you are a known, or thought to be, a criminal organization already. Suspicion is going to come your way no matter what. At least some of that goes away if you walk into the police station, maybe even with your lawyer and share whatever it is you know".

"It's a matter of degree", he replied, "I have learned that I can weather some storms and this needs to be one of them. I need to get back to my partners and let them know that I tracked you down, had this conversation and confirmed that you were involved in the way you said you were. Maybe we can work together to find out who did this"?

I quietly considered the means to end this meeting. Oreski needed to feel I would keep it a secret? Would he think I would report this to the police?

"No, I replied, I am just like you. I want to stay out of this. I don't feel good about working with you and having that come into the open down the road. Also, if I report you to the police, who still have me down as a suspect, it will cast more suspicion my way and a whole lot more doubts swirling around regarding my involvement. They would just assume I was trying to throw them off track. We both have something to gain by not sharing this meeting with the authorities".

Oreski agreed, as he stood, he reached out and shook my hand, saying thanks as he departed. What Oreski did not realize was that he basically admitted to being a criminal and that he had new associates, associates to be feared and who wanted things kept peaceful, at least for the time being.

The next morning, I called John to arrange a meeting at his office with Hazel and Jimmy. I told John I was turning over a hard drive given to me by Graziano. The meeting was set for 10:00 A.M. the morning of the funeral. When I walked into his office Hazel and Jimmy were already there. I noticed empty coffee mugs sitting in front of them. I presumed they had a pre-meeting, likely to discuss me. John suggested we go into a meeting room so we could spread out somewhat. When we all sat down, I reached into my jacket and handed the hard drive over to Hazel. I said it was time for me to hand over what Graziano had given me in my search for his daughter. Of importance, I explained, was the explanation Graziano provided with respect to his own investigation into Oreski and the nature of Oreski's criminal activity. In addition, although I had told Oreski that I wasn't about to share any information with the authorities, I also told them about my visit from Oreski and that I had no intention of pressing charges related to his break and enter, plus threatening me with a gun. I felt it was best if Oreski felt comfortable with my explanation and that he may very well present himself to authorities on his own volition.

The room was surprised that Oreski had surfaced to pay me a visit, and not surprised that Oreski had external associates involved in his criminal activities. We all agreed that this all meant that it was more than a little likely that Graziano had been offed by someone inside his own syndicate, which also meant that they would also be looking for me, as soon as the funeral was over.

Hazel explained that she also had an update regarding the funds going into Atkinson's and Sterling's bank accounts. Apparently, the actuary had also hit a dead end, but had been able to follow the funds only a short distance as a result of funds coming from shell corporations. As the funds were crossing international borders, the FBI actuary felt it was best left to the CIA to pursue. "Can someone explain to me what a shell corporation is and why is it illegal, I am no financial guru, I have trouble keeping my own bills straight", said Hazel.

I replied. "A shell corporation can be completely legal. They basically have no financial assets of their own, nor any significant business activity, in the sense that they produce no products and hire no employees. Rather they store monies and engage in financial transactions. They can possess real estate and copyright and are generally created in tax haven countries, like Switzerland, Bermuda, the Caymans, Luxembourg, etc.

As they knew my background, they asked what my views were on perhaps how to proceed. Of course, this left the door open for me to pull this back under my purview and I was not about to let that slip away.

"Just where in the world did the shell corporation lead, I queried, and was it assumed, or did he know if they were being used for money laundering. Depending on the country involved, they may or may not cooperate in an investigation and if they are being used for money laundering, we may be able to obtain a warrant to proceed".

"The actuary stated that the monies flowing into the Atkinson and Sterling accounts appeared to initiate from legitimate and fully legal businesses with no tax issues and no apparent fraudulent activity of any kind. He therefore assumed that there was no opportunity to obtain a warrant for further investigation. He said that he presumed, as a result, that they were not intended as a tax haven and were primarily intended to protect the identity of the person or persons providing the funds".

"What that really means", I suggested, "is that the accounts were receiving funds in a manner that ensured that Atkinson and Sterling would not come under suspicion by criminal elements that may be involved as the original funding source. I am going to go out on the limb here and suggest that these funds were coming from legitimate businesses that Graziano set up for his daughter, and that he was honoring Atkinson and Sterling for assisting him in establishing legitimate business ventures, both for himself and his daughter, maybe others as well. The hard drive I have given you has Graziano explaining that he created and hired a CEO to manage Michelle's assets until this time. He had known for several years that he was going to come clean and wanted to first set everything up for Michelle".

"That would explain a great deal", offered John, "but it also might suggest that Graziano, like every gangster with a financial brain or a good lawyer, would use shell corporations for money laundering as well".

"How would that work"? Asked Hazel.

"Shell corporations can be used to launder money", I replied. "Basically, illegally obtained cash is deposited in a bank, essentially turning it into a digital currency. It is then sent through a series of transactions, usually crossing international boundaries in order to hide the original source of funds. Generally, this is called laundering and the financial transactions may be of many different kinds. As the money can no longer be easily attributed to illegal activities, it is called 'clean' and can be used as if it were legitimate funds. Shell businesses are integral to the laundering process. The idea is

A Gangsters Dying Request

to create a chain of as many transactions as possible, so the source and destination of funds becomes confusing to investigators. These chains may contain dozens or more shell companies across multiple countries and the amounts of money transferred will be broken into smaller amounts across several countries and all of it is transferred digitally. As well, monies that are housed digitally may be housed on a hard drive in the bank and that hard drive may or may not be owned by the client. In some cases, the hard drive may be taken by the client or copied at the client's request. That would enable the owner to transfer monies, from his own computer, from and to anywhere. In that way these funds can flow back into the United States".

"Some countries will not assist with investigations or enable warrants to be obtained to even conduct an investigation. Authorities attempting to investigate will only have jurisdiction in their own country and thus cross border collaboration of law enforcement and judiciary is required to enable an investigation. As well, there are several countries that won't cooperate with such investigations. I presume that Graziano was using legal shell corporations in this manner to ensure that funds going to his daughter's businesses and those of Atkinson and Sterling were kept confidential. The only reason we have this information now is because he gave it to us".

"What is also interesting", added John, "is that he clearly wanted to ensure that Atkinson and Sterling were legal and above board in all respects. He just didn't want anyone to know the monies were coming from him, in order to protect their lives, at least while he was alive. It is critical that none of us in this room share any of this information with anyone else, including the FBI, until we know who is responsible for the murder. The murder was such a brazen and risky act; whoever arranged it is surely waiting in the wings until the timing is right. In addition, you should all know that the Interpol agent involved as well as the lead investigator with the FBI are in town, but in safe houses for now and under other identities. They are going to want to find the data that Graziano was bringing but have advised that they need to know the outcome of the investigation Hazel and Jimmy are conducting. Where is that at"?

"I can clear that up for you", Hazel responded, "we are currently looking into the lives of the FBI agent that died, or more accurately, was shot down. We have been able to determine from trajectories that he was not on Graziano's side of the gunfight. Also, he had something untoward going on in his life that made him vulnerable. He was depositing amounts of cash in his bank accounts, separate from his pay cheques and from unknown sources. We originally assumed he was killed by Graziano's men. However, what was startling information is that the ballistic report showed that he was gunned down, not by Graziano's men, but by individuals on his own side of the fight. It would seem that whoever he was working with must have discovered he was planted by Graziano and saw him as being a threat and a loose end that needed to disappear. It is safe to assume that he was also being paid by the same individual that ordered the killing as well as by Graziano. We have established what his role was within the FBI itself, and are going through the case files to determine, if possible, where connections could have been made".

"The other thing", I added, "is that Graziano was doing his own investigation of Oreski and had informants inside Oreski's organization as well as an informant inside the organization that was involved with the hit, which we now must at least consider, was not Oreski. While the people Graziano paid inside Oreski's organization thought they had a chance at more money and power with Graziano, they are now likely feeling vulnerable. They may be willing to come forward and give up information on Oreski, so maybe you should let the FBI proper know this. In the meantime, I need to resume my search for Michelle Savonne and will be heading back to New Orleans. I assume, John, that you'll let me know if I need to speak with the FBI agents that Graziano trusted"?

"I shall be in touch with them in short order and expect they will want to meet with you in the very near future. I will let you know when, and Hazel and Jimmy will watch the funeral and let us know who they can identify that attend".

With the meeting adjourned I was on my way back to New Orleans. I called Sheila and she agreed to meet me back in New Orleans about the same time as I was arriving back at the hotel. We were just a few days from the day of Mardi Gras where everyone is expected to wear a mask in public as well as at the various carnival balls. We had planned to be no exception. On the drive back, Hazel called to bring me up to date on the funeral.

"Jimmy and I attended the funeral from some distance, though there were a few regular FBI agents and supervisors in attendance as well. We had a chance to talk to them about others in attendance. Those agents advised us that two of Graziano's men were there and we shared our photographs of the funeral with them. They identified Martinez and Perez, both of whom were thought to report directly to Graziano. It is assumed that one or the other will take over where Graziano left off".

"As well, Oreski attended, a bit of a surprise, and he chatted for a few moments with Perez and Martinez. One of the FBI agents was close enough to pick up part of the conversation. Smart man, he had turned the recorder on his phone on and was able to catch the conversation. To make a long story short, Oreski was asking if the two of them knew what happened and why there was a rogue FBI agent at the murder scene. Perez responded by suggesting that Oreski should go find an alligator to play with. Oreski, on the other hand, pursued a little further. He asked if they knew who you were and why some guy would have just helped Graziano out of the blue. He went on to outline the conversation he had with you in your house. Instead of disregarding Oreski again, Martinez asked Oreski to fill him in on the conversation he had with you, which Oreski did, including telling Martinez that Graziano had asked you to find his daughter. He also tole Matrinez where you lived".

"Interesting that Martinez took an interest in me", I thought out loud. I made a note to enhance my security. "Did anyone think to follow Oreski, Perez or Martinez after the funeral"?

"Yes", replied Hazel, "I noted that the Special Agent in Charge of the West Palm Beach field office was in attendance and followed

Martinez. He was the supervisor of the rogue agent and when we had talked to him earlier in our investigation, he didn't seem surprised that his agent had financial difficulties, which means he should have been benching that agent. I followed him straight to Martinez's house where there was a gathering to "celebrate" Graziano's life. He didn't go in, but rather stayed in the car at a distance and took pictures of people coming and going. As I was sitting there watching him, Oreski showed up again. Oreski walked in but shortly after was escorted out somewhat roughly and asked to leave. I intend to have a further conversation with the Special Agent in Charge and see if he is up front about his intentions".

"It seems like Oreski is trying to find out who killed Graziano on his own, I offered, "which suggests that he is not at fault and is likely being pressured in some way by his own associates. Let us know what you find out".

And with that, we said goodbye. The first thing I did was phone Graziano's security company and arrange for my house to be monitored, as secretly as possible. I did not want alarms to go off, I just wanted the cameras to watch and film if there was any movement. I headed over to their office and dropped off a key and code to the door. They agreed, for a small amount of extra money, to go over immediately. With that done, I was back on the road to New Orleans.

Arrangements for Michelle

. . . .

SHEILA WAS ALREADY WAITING FOR me when I got to New Orleans. She said she had scored some tickets to a carnival ball and suggested we needed to find some costumes. We headed out for a bite to eat and a shopping trip. I figured that we also needed to call Jesse and see if she and Louise had been able to reach Michele. Jesse answered right away.

"I was just about to call, you must be psychic", she said teasingly, "I just got off the phone with Michelle. We had a very long chat as I filled her in on your two visits and briefed her on all the information you had provided. She wants to see what is on the hard drive. I was able to explain enough that she wants to pursue this. However, she is undercover and may not be able to come to New Orleans for any length of time".

"You may have to go where she is, but she wasn't willing to share that just yet. Before she spends a lot of time on this, she wants to meet you in person and do her own assessment of whether this is on the level."

"So is that two separate meetings", I asked, "one to size us up and one to meet with us in a more detailed fashion"?

"Yes, two meetings", replied Jesse. "She has the day of Mardi Gras off and will come here to meet you. But that's all she wants to do. After that, she will let you know through us, if she thinks you are on the level".

"That works for us," I replied. "We will wait for the call".

"A good step forward," said Sheila, "seems like we have a bit of time before the ball. Let's go get some costumes and some food. Did you know that there is a place or maybe more where you can have a mask of your choice made? We should go check that out, maybe we can be whoever we want to be. You can be a great quarterback and sign autographs, and I can be Marilyn Monroe. Then we need to start looking at the rest of the hard drives from Graziano and see what risk you are facing before you hand them over to the FBI".

We headed out, grabbed a bite at Couvant, gumbo for me and jambalaya for Sheila. Then it was off for a little costume search. Sheila piped up. "I guess the new word for this is 'cosplay' which stands, of course, for costume play. I think we should honor the traditional carnival colors-purple for justice, green for faith and gold for power. I'm going to opt for largely gold, because women should have the power, don't you think"?

"What I think is that women already have all the power in what we deem a healthy relationship. Therefore, what I think is largely irrelevant. I am going for justice, after all, purple suits what I am all about. I read somewhere that masking dates from the Roman carnivals when assuming false identities was a common practice. And, since I have been assuming false identities, I feel this plays right into my style".

We stopped in at a place called D&D Creations, but they were primarily a custom costume shop, and we did not have that kind of time. We finally found a place that enabled us to try out some costumes to buy, though we had just a few leftovers from which to choose. We then gathered up some beads, lightups and other paraphernalia. Masks are the best part of the whole dress-up gig and as we had tickets to the party at the superdome thrown by the Krewe of Orpheus, the son of Calliope, our costumes reflected that as best they could on short notice. After shopping was done, we headed back to the Quarter House for a night cap. Shopping was tiring and we both fell asleep instantly as we hit the sack.

I awoke the next morning to find Sheila across on the other side of the bed, lying on her stomach. I rolled over beside her and slid my hand under the t-shirt she was wearing, to caress her back. She moaned slightly as she woke up. In time, I let my hand slide down to her buttocks. She never wore anything except that T-shirt!! I let my hand move down to the back of her upper leg. I say 'let' because it was as if it had a mind of its own in these circumstances. As I reached under, she lifted her bum ever so slightly. I reached down with my lips and kissed that small part at the base of her back, she moaned with every movement and lifted herself a bit higher. I moved her t-shirt up so I could kiss her along her side until I reached her breast. She rolled over just enough that my lips and tongue could trace wherever she wanted it to go. I continued up and she turned her head to enable a kiss. She stretched her hands out in front of her to push back against the headboard. I was holding myself up with the back of my wrists until they were too painful to continue. I pulled my hands out and reached up, interlocking our fingers together.

20 minutes later we decided the room was too sweaty and decided to start the day. As I poured the coffee my burner phone rang. It was Jesse on the other end.

"I just heard from Michelle she said, she has the day of Mardi Gras off and will come to New Orleans. She will tell us later where to meet her, but she wants it to be clear that every one of us is to be fully masked. So, if we're out in public during the day, that is no problem. If it's at night, it will have to be indoors. She is coming into town to also brief her supervisor on certain matters, so it's two birds with one stone. As far as you guys are concerned, she is just sizing you up, so she said she wants eye-contact and wants to know who her father is. She was very clear that if you won't share that information with her, she won't allow a second interview to take place with the two of you. Once she knows his name, she wishes to do some of her own research into who he was. Are you okay with this arrangement"?

I agreed that Sheila and I were okay with that. After I closed off the call, Sheila asked, "Are you sure that sharing his name is a good idea? If she starts doing her own research and whoever killed Graziano gets wind of it, her life could be in danger".

"Yes, that is a possibility, but a slim one. The nature of the murder, it being so public, everyone is trolling the internet and television coverage like flies on the wall. Her interest might look just like anyone else's".

"How are we going to explain to Michelle who we really are? Or do you intend to? How can you explain your involvement at the murder scene? How are you going to explain how you are in receipt of this information? Chances are, it will all make her very nervous about both of us".

"Those are great questions. I'm not sure we have any options. The only path is to come clean about all of it. The other advantage is that she would then have access to everything, including his house, which I understand was in his name, although it's not clear that it wasn't obtained through ill-gotten gains. In any event it might be possible to meet Michelle there. A little walk on the beach is all that is required".

"I think you might be crazy", said Sheila, not joking, "although someone once said, maybe it was in a movie, Star Wars maybe, maybe not, "in a world gone mad, only the crazy are sane".

"I acknowledged the probability. But guys this bad are likely mad to some extent and being a little off the wall with your thoughts and plans can derail the best of them. Let's open up these hard drives and give them a little test run. Maybe it's time to see what there is to see. My recollection is that they are numbered".

We wandered over to the bank where Sheila had opened a safety deposit box to store the hard drives. The advantage of a safety deposit box is almost absolute security for the depositor. A warrant can be issued but the judge has to be convinced that there is incriminating evidence in the box, something very difficult to prove. I was pretty sure there was going to be such evidence, however, no one knew for sure that we were in possession of the hard drives.

Graziano's Evidence

· ·

WE POPPED NUMBER ONE INTO my laptop and started watching; that is correct, watching. This started with a video of Graziano.

"I wanted to do this as a video back up in case something happened to me. I don't want anyone to be in a position where someone can challenge verbal evidence on a tape and try to say it's all doctored. They may, anyway, but having me on camera will make that more difficult. As you may already know, my main source of wealth comes from several construction companies. I have won contracts for schools, highways including massive bridges, ports, hospitals, marinas, large high rises, etc. As you know, these structures contain a vast amount of different kinds of equipment, much of which is very expensive to purchase and install. What you also need to understand is that my operation extends to Europe, principally Spain, France and Germany so the income generated is significant. With respect to my business, I have split it into European and American operations, with a man name Jose Martinez heading up Europe, and Mateo Perez heading up the United States.

"There are some tricks to winning these contracts. The most important is to ensure there are no cost overruns for the majority. This may mean my bids are higher, but with the assurance of no cost overruns, most local and state-run purchasing agencies will opt for that assurance. But why take that chance? In order to ensure we can win such contracts, we do our research into the various personnel involved in approving, or even recommending approval of contracts. Often these are teams of individuals and almost always the final decision is made by someone appointed through a political avenue. We will have someone in our organization contact these individuals to determine the extent of their ambition and determine if they appear to be vulnerable. A rising politician likes to point to projects he helped approve and, if very ambitious, will break the rules when awarding contracts. We will aid such a person's campaign with funding, cash funding he or she can use as they like, even for personal use, which is even better from our point of view".

"How do we do this? We own several newspapers and some social media news outlets. We sponsor our target and control their editorial bent in the media. But, of course, there are others involved, always. We do our homework up and down the recommendation and approval line and eventually come to terms with how each individual may be compromised. In some cases, it becomes as simple as suggesting the right person makes alterations to the Request for Approval or RFP so that we have an inside track to winning the contract".

"And so, how do we make money if there are no cost overruns? We have a huge volume of work. We negotiate agreements with suppliers for cost reductions that others can't negotiate. They cannot, in part because they don't have the volume, but also in part because we enter into binding contractual agreements with these suppliers. This applies, to the extent we can make it apply, to the vast majority of every major piece of equipment that goes int a hospital or school. So far seems all legal, right? And it appears legal from the outside".

"However, we don't leave it at that because we cannot always find the right legal approach and we need more assurances. We get to know our targets as best possible. We determine where they hang out in their leisure time, find ways for our people to make contact with them, find out what their leisure activities are, what kinds of hobbies they pursue, what clubs they belong to, who their friends, are, what their personal circumstances are to the extent possible, and so forth.

When we think we know someone quite well, we develop a plan to corrupt them in the way we need, in order to enable bribes".

"Example 1:

One of our principal avenues is through gambling debts. A lot of men and women have addictive personalities, the trick is find out what is the most likely scenario. Some men, actually a lot of men, like to play the big shot role. They have certain tell-tale signs, like paying way too large a tip, or buying excessive rounds of drinks for their friends, and so on. The ones with lesser incomes find themselves in debt. We befriend them, reward their behavior through giving them lots of attention, thank yous, encouragement, 'boy are you ever a great guy' sort of thing. Eventually they find themselves deeper and deeper in debt. We suggest going to the casinos, several of which we own across the Gulf States. We get them into high stakes poker games, and they tend to lose more and more".

"At some point we pull them into an office, usually at a casino, and set up the type of bribe that works best for the specific individual. It has two components, first we threaten the person with legal action if they don't pay off the debt, but we already know they can't. The usual approach a person in debt will take is to see if he or she can borrow money to pay it off. In a few cases they may come back and pay off the debt, but when they come in to make the payment, we say thanks, and encourage them to go back to the tables or a poker game. Most will".

"Most people with such personalities will try to win back their losses with the borrowed funds before attempting to pay us back. The outcome is almost always deeper debt. It is at this point we pull them aside and offer to pay off their debt in exchange for certain favors, such as approving our extraordinarily high bid for a project. These conversations are always videotaped and then shown to the mark. He is threatened with exposure to his wife and place of employment if he doesn't cooperate. This hard drive will now show you an example of such a case, but rest assured, the remainder of the information on the hard drives will identify every person that has cooperated with us through this means".

The hard drive then showed one such person involved, and we watched from the beginning of identifying the mark, through to the conversation and showing the person the video of himself agreeing to the arrangement. One of many involving this method was on the drive. They covered not only the identification of the mark, but the projects for which he was involved in getting through the approval processes.

"Example 2:

A second major addiction avenue is through drugs. This one is more difficult to control because we don't want the person to necessarily become addicted. Just desirous. We are not talking about drugs sold on the street corner here. This is about wealthy people like lawyers, educators, etc. wanting cocaine, marijuana in the past at least, and sometimes prescription drugs that can get you high. The process is largely the same, getting to know the mark by befriending through his social network, buying a house in his community, participating in his leisure activities etc. We either identify people already using an illegal substance or we introduce it in some manner at a party or some other social event. We then work to make it worse, increasing the amount taken and making the high more unmanageable. Then it's really about filming the person using, ensuring the nature of the substance is visible and the resulting behaviors are filmed. And again, introducing the video to the person, arranging for an agreement to be filmed".

"Example 3:

The easiest form of corruption is through sex. Everybody wants it and everybody is always on the lookout. If your addictive personality is related to loneliness, sex is a huge desire. But that isn't the only avenue, the other is straight forward sexual deviation and the nature of such pursuits almost always have a need to be hidden. We own escort services, several of them in various cities across the south. Typically, but not 100 per cent so, this is about men. There are different methods of recruiting women to this business. It might be someone already working at an escort agency that wants to earn substantially higher income, which we will offer. It might start through already operating street people who are exceptionally attractive that we recruit. In the latter case, we employ women that are willing to train and educate a recruit of this nature just how to go about setting up the mark".

"The women know they are being filmed with the client. They get the income from the 'dates' because all we are really after is to corrupt the client using the service. The blackmail works in the same way, the client agrees to assist in the project and ultimately future projects. Also, we enable the relationships to be ongoing as long as we can ensure the safety of the women involved and the women continue to receive the income. If the project ends up making us a great deal of money, we sometimes give bonuses. These women represent an important asset, and we deal very severely with any mark that hurts one of the women.

"It's not always the person we mark, but sometimes it's a spouse or kid that the mark wishes to protect from prosecution, so we assist in that, for favors of course".

"With respect to all these projects, the cost of research, entertainment, etc. to set up a mark is built into the cost estimates as consulting fees, entertainment expenses, bonuses, and so on. Everything is accounted for through a book of codes. Every escort, for example, has a specific code that shows up in our accounting system as some type of what would normally be considered a legitimate expenditure. Once a project is approved there is ongoing follow-up, managed through a second set of accounts, which show how the funds did not all go where they were supposed to go. It shows or explains where corners were cut in the projects and where funds might be used for other purposes. In some cases, these funds go into building houses for our staff, purchasing items for staff and so on".

"I should mention that we make these people that we bribe, quite wealthy, much more so than if they stayed true to the side of the good, in part, as a means to keeping them under our control. We go so far as to build houses for them as part of the 'contract' for a school or a port as an example, and we might provide them with illegal immigrants in the form of servants, such as maids and gardeners. Those that are illegal immigrants remain so, as we confiscate their identification. While this might be considered a form of human trafficking, they, do however, live a much better life than they left in Central America as we ensure they are not subjected to abuse".

"In the case of politicians and certain wealthy people we own popular newspapers and magazines and also have a social media presence which we use for a "catch and kill" strategy. Essentially, we find out if any type of damaging story is about to become public and do our best to buy the story and copyright in order to ensure it never sees the light of day. In this way, we protect our investment in corrupted individuals in the longer term. We want them to see us as a benefactor, at least to some extent, on an ongoing basis and keep them performing deeds on our behalf. All corruption depends on a certain amount of fear, which requires the mark to be in our proximity. Keeping the mark close is essential to the process, the further one gets away from the thing you fear the less fear can be used as a form of control".

"Before providing more details, I also want to explain that the energies of my syndicate are sometimes compared to those of Antonio, or Tony Oreski who makes a living by recruiting street girls at very young ages, getting them hooked on drugs, running various dysfunctional people as drug miles in cheap bars and hotels. Lately, however, it has come to my attention that he is attempting to expand, and I heard rumors through my people that he has formed a partnership with a Mexican cartel. This is troubling to me because I love this country despite my past, and don't want death and destruction that comes with turf wars. As a result, we started investigating on our own, and have identified through our own wire taps etc., which I know were not legal, that the cartel is headed by a man named Alvarez. He bears scrutiny".

"Having said that, I am now offering up the details of my syndicate, from top to bottom, their individual roles, personal information and all the names and achievements accomplished illegally through our marks. I have also separated the projects we were successful in obtaining legally, without the use of bribes or corruption. You will find a comprehensive record of all the marks we corrupted, what they gained as a result, and the projects that they approved as a result. You will note that these projects cross the Gulf States, Britain, France, Germany and Spain. We were careful to stay away from Italy and eastern Europe as there are too many factions involved and the governments themselves are unstable and may be filled with corruption all without our influence".

That was the end of Graziano's introduction, essentially to what was on the hard drives. We had spot checked samples of the various hard drives and discovered they was a seemingly endless number of projects, staff involved, and marks. There were politicians, lawyers, housewives, celebrities, superintendents, professors, business owners, port authorities, subcontractors, and so on.

"I think it's time to turn this over", I suggested to Sheila. "On one hand, if I do this, I may be getting into deep trouble for withholding crucial evidence. I can't send it to John, because if he turned it over, that would potentially jeopardize him at this point in time. On the other hand we don't really know if we can, as of yet, trust anyone other than the FBI and Interpol agents that Graziano was trusting. John is planning to introduce them so we know who they are. Got any bright ideas as to how we handle the hand-off"?

"An option would be to wait until Hazel or John, advises us the Senior Agent in Charge has been cleared and then you would be able to turn it over with a reasonable explanation. If you hand it in too early, you cannot use the explanation that you were waiting for the agents Graziano said he trusted".

As we were discussing the possible choices, the burner phone rang. It was Jesse.

"Michelle has asked to meet with you during the day, tomorrow, which is Mardi Gras, in a public bar but fully costumed and masked which is kind of required in any event. Your mask should enable Michelle to see your eyes clearly and as well be able to speak, so the mask ought to not cover your mouth. Other than that, be as anonymous as possible. She wants the hard drive you showed Louise and I with her father's explanation. She has no intention of looking at it in your presence in such a public place. She'll come prepared to keep it somewhere she knows is safe. And, she wants you to explain who you really are. She says, she knows you are not who you say you are, so be prepared to answer those kinds of questions. Given her concern, Louise and I also want to know if you are someone different from who you say, but we won't be at the meeting. Michelle will let us know".

"I shall", I replied, assuming in that moment that Michelle may have checked with the FBI to ask about Atkinson, the lawyer from Phoenix, under the guise of her current investigation. If she had, the FBI would have provided the information that Atkinson had passed away. It was a safe bet for me to assume that she had done so, or Jesse would not have given that message. On the other hand, it could just be a bluff. In thinking it through it seems more than likely she got in touch with her handler within the FBI. In a few minutes after that call ended the phone rang again. This time it was John.

"Hazel wants to have another meeting with you. The Special Agent in Charge of the FBI field office has been cleared and that means the two individuals that Graziano trusted with turning over all his data will also be present at the meeting. We can meet in my boardroom the day after tomorrow, knowing that this is Mardi Gras and you and Sheila likely have plans. Plus, if those agents have anything they need to get together for the meeting, they may need time to do that. We are being careful not to meet in FBI offices because there is still the possibility of some inside risk".

"I shall be there", I replied. "I might have some news on my end as well, so the meeting should be interesting".

When I hung up the phone, I started to speak but interrupted my own thought: "It's interesting how I just thought I was hanging up the phone, but with cell phones you have nothing to hang up and nothing to hang it up on. Just strange how we continue with phrases that have lost their relevance. It's the night before revelry, let's go out for a bite and come back for a good night's rest. Tomorrow, we have to get all prettied up, wear sweaty masks all day and finally meet Michelle".

Sheila responded in the affirmative and we left the hotel to find a restaurant where we could get a great dinner, ate, headed back and hit the sack, out instantly as a result of all the wine we drank.

The next morning started with coffee and a solid breakfast of eggs and peanut butter toast. About 11:00 we got dressed and headed out to Bourbon Street which was just a couple of blocks over. It was like all of Louisiana was out in costumes and masks and there was music everywhere, blues and rock mostly.

"Did you know", Shelia began as we walked on by, "I read in the guide that the Royal Sonesta greases its balcony columns with petroleum jelly to keep people from shimmying their way up and onto the balcony to get a better street view? And later tonight we should try to catch the Bourbon Street Awards and see who wins for best costume, it's really a great event to watch".

As the day wore on, we finally received a call from Jesse with a location to meet you. "As indicated previously Michelle will meet with you without Louise and me. It's An out of the way small coffee shop, down a side street on the west side of canal street, away from the larger crowds. Michelle is there now and will wait for you. You will recognize her without any problem, she will be dressed as Ma'at, the Egyptian Goddess of Truth, Justice, Balance and Order. Quite fitting don't you think? You can look up Ma'at on the internet, she will have the traditional look, wings and ostrich feather included. You are not to use my name, you can say: 'Calliope said that we must see Ma'at'. Michelle may, if she has time, brief Louise and I sometime later, not today, and let you know if she wishes to pursue things any further".

Michelle

· ·

I THANKED JESSE FOR THE call and asked her to let Ma'at know I would be giving her a staff I carried as part of my costume (think Moses parting the waters). Sheila and I headed out immediately. We had downloaded a copy of Graziano's hard drive, with his message to Michelle, to a USB and had inserted it into the staff. When we arrived, Michelle was very easy to recognize. It was a small place and there were a few other people, but she had selected a booth at the back where she could see anyone coming and going and her costume was readily recognizable.

To my surprise, from the few facial features visible, Michelle was mixed race. Sheila had never mentioned that much to her credit. We sat down and I said, "Calliope had sent us to meet Ma'at, an Egyptian goddess, and you certainly look the part".

"We do our best", was the reply. "I love Mardi gras for all the pageantry and the chance to dress up and be part of a secret society. Did you know that there is a tradition of secrecy associated with Mardi Gras and that is why the masks and costumes, beyond the obvious fun part. I should let you know that our krewe is highly secretive and not listed in any venues. I'll explain that a bit later. I understand you brought a staff to complete my costume".

I handed the staff to Michelle, and she began to check us out. "Jesse and Louise did their homework, to the extent they could, between their first and second calls to me. But I have my own sources and sought you ought on my own. Where Sheila was concerned, that was an easy find, just the issue of using the name Liz and stalking me for two decades. My mom was always very careful, but I now question whether or not she actually knew. Then I checked into you, Mr. Atkinson. Apparently, you died a few years ago in Puerto Vallarta. So that makes me nervous, given I am well aware of the issues with drug cartels and so forth from Mexico. I think this might be a good time to be fully honest with me. After that, we shall see".

"I leaned into the table to speak quietly. "My name is Brock Tanton and I was a retired CIA operative and now, as a result of recent events, am back on the payroll. I am sure you have read about, or have been informed about, the event now dubbed Murder Street by the press. If you have, you will know a man came across the last survivor and assisted him to his home, where he was later found and pronounced deceased. The man who assisted him was me, and the man I aided, insisted he wanted no part of a doctor or hospital until he had given me some information and asked that I try to find you. As you know, he had Sheila's father watch and photograph you over the years. He kept his commitment to your mother to keep his distance to ensure your safety.

There are reasons for my use of an alias. The name of the lawyer I have been using had helped your father sell some real estate and he had, for reasons I still cannot explain, provided me with a legal document, access to bank accounts and access to a man that assisted me to obtain false identities to use. In part, this was to protect me from those who might find me, as he provided me with other documentation which he asked me to hold, basically until his murder was solved. The issue is who to trust. Because I had helped him, he assumed, rightly so, that I was not a threat as if I had been involved in his demise, I would have finished the job then and there and taken the data he had in his possession".

"I suppose you don't have to take my word alone for it. I can arrange for you to meet my boss and the two people from outside the FBI that are investigating why there was a rogue agent involved, as you may have read about. I know, however, that you are undercover and cannot readily just leave wherever your assignment takes you. I have lived that life and understand if you want more information, you will have to reach out the way you have here".

"Thank you for that. I said earlier that I needed to watch and determine if I can trust you as you explained yourself. However, everyone here is part of our krewe and all of us use Mardi Gras as a means of meeting when we can't otherwise do so. We are all agents of the FBI and DEA and I want you to meet someone, dressed here across the room from us, dressed as the Sun God Re, my supervisor, the Special Agent in Charge, West Palm Beach and Fort Lauderdale, Jeremy Hales.

Re, Sun God as he was, walked over to the table, I stood and shook his hand. He was a full 6 inches taller than me and towered over Sheila as well. As we all stood, I noticed Michelle was at least 5'10" as well. Jeremy Hales immediately put my worry to relief.

"Your John Szabo and I go back a long way. We have a meeting the day after tomorrow, I understand. You should be comfortable knowing that everyone present in this room has been cleared by Hazel and Jimmy, who just happen to be sitting right over there", as he gestured with his hand. "I will be interested in knowing what your theories are with respect to what appears to have been Michelle's flesh and blood, though I might say she isn't too thrilled about it", but he smiled as he said it and I could sense that there was a solid connection and trust between the two of them.

Michelle looked our way and said that they were about to go to a private gathering, which I assumed meant other law enforcement, but Jeremy piped in and said Michelle had to return to her assignment. As she was leaving, Michelle turned to me and said, "I suggest you and Sheila take in a couple of events, one is called the flambeaux, torches carried in the tradition of the Mistick Krewe of Comus representing enslaved African Americans and people of color. Make some friends".

We spent the rest of the day and evening enjoying everything that Mardi Gras had to offer, including attending a carnival evening where King, Queen, maids and dukes were presented, and a tableaux or theatrical scene was presented in the tradition of a medieval court. A late night, lots of food and drink and then back to the hotel. The next morning, we awoke, had the traditional morning coffee, otherwise known as the elixir of mornings. "You know", said Sheila, "I have yet to spend a day at your place in Fort Lauderdale. I am beginning to think I am just a fling. Not that I haven't enjoyed it up to now. In some ways it has been a lot of fun with intrigue to go along with it, but why haven't you invited me"?

I realized in that moment that I hadn't mentioned anything to her about the visit to my house from Oreski being a break and enter. I shared that with her and then added that I had upgraded my security with cameras and a silent alarm.

"You know, given the circumstances, I am not 100% sure that it is safe there. I suspect I am still being sought by the people who killed Graziano, and we now know that was not Oreski. As well, it is apparent to me that Oreski was not looking for the hard drives and likely knows nothing about them, or what Graziano was intending. I am going back to Fort Lauderdale for a meeting tomorrow. Jeremy Hales is stopping at his office in West Palm Beach on the way down and Hazel and Jimmy will also be at the meeting in Fort Lauderdale. Why don't you come along, and we can book into a hotel downtown, along the riverwalk or near the beach".

"Actually, that is a great idea. There is also another loose end that has been bothering me. My investigation into Jeff Atkinson turned up that he had a daughter, or at least someone claiming to be his daughter accessed his place down there. I think I want to do some further investigation into his life and see if there are other siblings, if she even is a daughter. If so, she, or they, are entitled to the inheritance in the accounts associated with your false identities".

"That is a good idea. We will have to fly back to get to the meeting on time if we spend the rest of the day here, which I think we should do. Let's also cap that off with a riverboat dinner cruise on the Mississippi. I heard they have a great Dixie Land jazz band. And I am not sure when we will be coming back to New Orleans. We may or may not meet Michelle here next time. I am not sure there is even a need to meet with her again. She has all the information she needs to meet with the CEO heading up all her business interests and it remains to be seen to what extent she plans to continue with her undercover work".

"I expect that she may want to finish her current assignment, especially if they are near to having enough evidence to bring charges against major players".

It was about then that my phone pinged. It was the alarm from my house. I opened the video file and Sheila and I both watched as two men, one of them Oreski, started going through everything, the couches, the fridge and freezer, under the mattresses. It was not clear to me that they were looking for the hard drives, as Oreski did not likely know I had them, which meant that the other person, unfamiliar to me, may have been someone that was involved in Graziano's murder. Having found nothing, they eventually left together. I dialed John and let him know that someone had broken into my house, yet again, and sent him a copy of the video.

"It's probably good that you weren't there, said John. "I'll let Jeremy know and send him a copy of the video as well. We can have a discussion about this tomorrow at the meeting. Maybe someone can identify the other individual".

"Well," said Sheila, "now I am happy I haven't been invited to your house. I assume that you will have to go back to put things in order, so after our little riverboat cruise tonight I am going to spend my time looking into Atkinson to see if there were kids, and if the daughter is real. I suspect that she knows nothing of the account that Graziano set up so it will be an eye-opener for her. If all goes well and she does exist, do you mind if I take the edition of the will minus one Hans Goebel"?

"That seems like a good idea. I don't see any reason why you can't take the document to provide evidence, to her, of the accounts. It seems she already has access to the penthouse in Puerto Vallarta though. I wonder then why it's mentioned in the will. If he has passed and she is his real daughter, then she gets the penthouse in any event. You may need to be cautious after all. There is something missing about the mention of the penthouse in the will if she has already inherited it".

"Yeah, that is odd, responded she thoughtfully. On the other hand, the same is true for me. The will must have been created when everyone was still alive. I think I'll check into her as closely as possible and check the land titles in Mexico. Maybe it's not odd at all. The will was created by Atkinson himself so he just legally was leaving himself the penthouse in Graziano's will, maybe looking out for his own flesh and blood in the process".

"Actually, that does make sense", I responded. If all is open and above board and you make contact with her or go to Phoenix to meet her, she will need to understand that the will has to be enacted and that there is still one other individual to contact. How about you start some checking into Hans as well. Let's see what we can learn. I would be very careful, maybe in both cases, to keep your actual identity out of the scene for the time being so maybe use an alias. We really don't have a lot of information on these people other than Graziano trusted them and looked after them in a will. For all we know given the surface information, they could be part of his syndicate".

"I shall be very careful", responded Sheila, "as a private investigator it's not uncommon to use alternate identities from time to time. Let's head out to the riverboat and enjoy our evening together. We may not see each other for a time".

Trusted Agents

I ARRIVED BACK IN THE late morning and made my way to John's office for a quick chat with him before going into the meeting. John said good morning and motioned me to have a chair. "Are you interested in a coffee after the flight, I know you were kind of rushed to get here today, and how is Sheila"?

"I'll pass on the coffee or anything else to drink for the moment. Is there anything I should know before I meet the agents involved with Graziano's case"?

"I just wanted to touch base with you before going into the board room. I understand you found and met Michelle as well as Jeremy Hales, so meeting him today and knowing he has been cleared will be no surprise to you. You told me a while back that Graziano had given you a number of hard drives with the information that was going over to the FBI agents that are now waiting in my boardroom. I presume you haven't released that to anyone yet. Is that the case, and if so, just where are they, and what have you gleaned from them"?

"I have not yet turned them over to anyone. Graziano was insistent that they go only to the agents he was personally working with, and only in person. The hard drives are in a safety deposit box in New Orleans. And I know your next question is going to be whether or not I copied them. The answer, of course, is yes, so it is time to turn the originals over. We can arrange that in the meeting, perhaps. What did I learn? A great deal about Graziano's illegal activities, enough to identify a number of corrupt politicians, civil servants, and others on both sides of the Atlantic and in several countries. As well, enough information to know why he chose the path he was on in terms of turning himself in; that he has provided handsomely for his daughter in a very legal manner such that she will be very wealthy, and as well, that he was of the belief that Oreski was likely, but not necessarily, the one who arranged the attack on him".

"Okay, said John, getting up from his chair, "let's go see what the future is going to bring us. It is waiting in the boardroom".

Jeremy Hales and two others were waiting, Hazel and Jimmy were not present. I presumed there had been a pre-meeting because there were empty coffee cups on the table still. Also in the room were two new faces who John began introducing by stating they were the two individuals that had been trusted by Graziano. Jeremy, however, did the formal introductions.

"Brock, I would now like you to meet two of our best agents. This person on your left is special agent Timm Hill who has been on the Graziano file from the first day Graziano made contact with my office and offered to provide significant evidence with respect to his syndicate on both sides of the Atlantic".

I shook hands with Tim and observed that he was about 6 feet tall, well built and about 35-40 years old. He wore blue jeans and a white shirt and, of all things, alligator cowboy boots. He noticed that I had checked him out all the way down to the shoes. "I see you are a fan of first impressions", he teased, "grew up in Baton Rouge where we like our boots".

Jeremy turned to the other agent, a youthful looking woman, I guessed to be about the same age as Timm. "And this is special agent Casandra Garcia of Interpol". She was dressed in a man's black pinstripe suit, no necktie but a rust-colored scarf that accentuated her brown eyes. Her jet-black hair was short cut with bangs. She reached out and shook my hand, a firm handshake! "Casandra has been part of this task force from the beginning as well", Jeremy offered, "as she is an actuary and has some of the same skills, as I understand from John, that you also have".

"A pleasure to meet you both", I said. I have been looking forward to having a discussion with you. However, I am not sure I can offer you much in the way of new information".

"Why don't we all take a chair and get started", said John, "there have been a few developments along the way. Jeremy, Casandra and Timm have been brought up to date as best I could, but they may still have a few questions for you. Beyond that, however, Brock, Jeremy has had some news regarding the investigation being conducted by another of his teams, the one Michelle is involved with. We want to read you into that and maybe immerse you. That particular investigation has turned up a possible connection between Graziano and Oreski, as well as a Mexican cartel headed by an individual know as Alvarez".

John's choice of words was telling. He was basically saying that Graziano was connected to Oreski and Alvarez as well. Nothing on the hard drives suggested that was the case. Just the opposite, in fact. I was more of the impression that Graziano had no use for Mexican cartels and thought Oreski was a light weight. I decided to let this pass for the moment, I could come back to it later.

Jeremy spoke first. "John has filled us in on your involvement, at least to the extent he is aware of it, which is not everything. We have lots to tell you to fill in a few gaps, however, we understand you are likely in possession of Graziano's hard drives. Now that I have been cleared and Timm and Casandra are here, maybe you could let us have them so we can get started on a massive number of warrants, and assuming you have been through them, at least in a surface way, you can give us a brief overview. No need for detail, Casandra and Timm can get into the nitty gritty after they have the drives".

"I do have the hard drives"' I replied, "and was reluctant to bring them with me until after I had met Timm and Casandra. Graziano was insistent that they be turned over to the two agents he was dealing with, and up until now the two of you have been squirreled away for your own protection. I assume you have a secure place to look at things"?

"We do", replied Timm. "It has been our worry that the FBI office in West Palm Beach, Fort Lauderdale and maybe Miami has been under surveillance by whoever killed Graziano, which is why we are meeting here at the CIA headquarters instead. We will be working out of the quarters of a private firm with ties to the U.S. military and Jeremy has arranged to provide us with round the clock security from that private company. They have no visible prevalence where we are located, but they occupy parts of the building and have installed very secure access where we are located".

"That sounds like something I might like to see, but unfortunately it is possible that while I am in Fort Lauderdale, the bad guys, whoever they are, could locate me and place a watch on me or just pick me up and try to force me to give things up. To my knowledge, to date they haven't been able to figure out that I am in New Orleans, but they know where I live. The hard drives are in New Orleans in a safety deposit box. I think the best bet is to send the hard drives by courier to a fake office that appears to have no connection to the authorities. The CIA can set that up in a clandestine way. Hazel and Jimmy can then pick them up, because it is highly unlikely that they are being watched or followed given they are investigating the FBI. How does that sit with you"?

"That seems to work from our perspective", replied Casandra. "We assume you have had a look at the hard drives, what can you tell us outside of the information relating to his daughter Michelle"?

"I think the first thing is that I don't think there is a connection between Graziano and Oreski. Graziano said that he wasn't a fan of the cartels and the level of violence. In the drive relating to his daughter, he appeared to me to be genuine in stating that he was a bad guy but had no use for Oreski or the kind of rackets he is involved with, which carried over to Alvarez. He also said that he had been able to lure three of Oreski's people into thinking they would have a better life with him than they would do with Oreski. He said these guys working for Oreski had told him about the connection between Oreski and Alvarez.

I looked at the content of the hard drives to the extent I could, and they code names, illegal projects, bribes, subversion, corruption to the extent you will be able to prosecute a great many people on both sides of the ocean. I am surprised to hear you say there may be a possible business relationship between Oreski and Graziano. Why do you think there is a closer connection to Oreski"?

Jeremy was about to speak when John's personal assistant, also a special agent within the CIA, knocked and entered.

"We have just been informed that a body was found at one of the motels used by the girls working the street. She had taken a John, ohhh, sorry John, to the room and found the body lying on the bed with his throat slit. There was a note pinned to his shirt, "this is just a reminder to those who think they can do their own thing; when I say I want things quiet, I mean quiet, stand down, don't call attention to us". The body has been identified as Tony Oreski."

The news was a little more than a little interesting. Jeremy called one of his agents directly and advised him to get over to the scene and call back as soon as he knew more. He started back into his explanation.

"Well, before that happened, I was about to explain the possible connection between Oreski and Graziano. Oreski is connected to Alvarez as Graziano has said, and Alvarez is the head of a Mexican cartel whose violence forces people to choose to be with him, be killed in some cases, or simply flee to get away from that life. As they come into Texas through an underground passage or find their way through a port, they have very little and are picked up by Oreski's men and their identification, passports if they even have one, are confiscated. The men, for the most part, are convinced to transport drugs into the country through various means and if they refuse to cooperate their families are threatened or they are killed and left in the desert. The women, many of them, are forced into prostitution or into work cutting the cocaine or working as drug mules. Many refugees and illegal immigrants live short lives and are hooked on drugs themselves".

"I am impressed by the amount of information you have about Oreski", said John, looking at Jeremy. That sounds like a lot of work over several years".

"It was, and is", agreed Jeremy, "and it was only possible because we had an agent buried deep inside Oreski's organization. He said that Oreski was constantly talking about how soon Graziano would have to form an alliance with him or be ousted".

We have a theory that Graziano already gets his pick of the women brought in by Oreski and employs them as escorts, trains them, and many end up living relatively wealthy lives as long as they toe the line. There are others that find their way into households as maids and gardeners or maybe chefs. Some find their way into the food service industry or the hotel industry in low level jobs where they can't leave because they are here illegally, and their passports have been taken".

"What this amounts to", said Timm, "is human trafficking. Human trafficking involves any situation where someone is being forced to engage in any activity where they cannot leave-whether it's commercial sex, housework, farmwork, or has had an ID or documents taken away or is being threatened by or is in debt to an employer or wants to leave a job but cannot freely do so".

"Maybe there is some connection", I commented, "in one of his hard drives Graziano was saying that one of the 'services' his syndicate provides as an after the fact, is household services to those who do his bidding, further cementing their control over the people they have bribed. I can see where a relationship, whereby Graziano gets his pick with respect to both men and women, works well for him. And I can see why he would not say to his daughter that he was involved in the less savory aspects of crime, if here is such a thing".

As Jeremy was about to continue his phone pinged again. After a short conversation, he disconnected and explained.

"The local police closed circuit tv, or CCTV, footage, picked up a man leaving the building, getting into a car and speeding away. More cameras further along picked up the car a couple of more times and the agent indicated they thought it might be Alvarez but there was no clear picture. The assumption was made based on the note left on Oreski's body which referred to keeping quiet until things were ready to unfold. However, we were not able to track exactly where he went after. The man in the car? I guess at this point, given the message left pinned to Oreski, that is no longer a surprise". Jeremy stated that his agent had already put out a bolo for the man identified as Alvarez in the security video in connection with the entry and possible murder.

"Actually", added Timm, "the bit about Oreski being responsible for Graziano's murder is just a theory, and we have another slightly different one. We also theorize it is possible that either Perez or Martinez found out about Graziano's plan to turn things over to the FBI and are responsible for murder street. Graziano had his own men inside Oreski's organization, or more accurately had convinced one or more they would be better off if they switched allegiances. I might be willing to bet that Martinez and Perez knew about those efforts from Graziano himself and may have found a way to let Alvarez know there were traitors on Oreski's team".

"I don't quite get what the motivation for what that would be" I asked. "Does Oreski's murder by Alvarez now throw greater suspicion that he was responsible for murder street? I suppose it's possible, but we know that it wasn't Oreski. Oreski would not have known about the hard drives, and neither would Alvarez. Also, it seems Alvarez is planning something more significant and therefore he wanted no trouble from law enforcement all the way from here to El Paso, but now this takes him away from that strategy. I am wondering, how clear do you think the CCTV footage is? What if it wasn't Alvarez at all, but Perez or Martinez in the car? If one of them killed Oreski to throw suspicion at Alvarez and at the same time make it seem like maybe Oreski killed Graziano, they take over the syndicate and have a good shot at squeezing Oreski's organization out entirely and also neutralizing Alvarez for a time".

"I like that theory", said Casandra, "it's sufficiently diabolical to be worthy of consideration. The question now is how to prove one or both of them was responsible for killing Graziano"?

"The FBI will have a close look at the footage and see if they can clearly identify the person in the car", said Jeremy.

"We may not have to prove they murdered him. We are likely to have enough evidence from the hard drives to put them away for a long time. Also, we can expect a fight from them on some level. We need to make sure that when it comes time to arrest them, they won't make bail".

"We have another concern", Timm started, "we know that Graziano and his syndicate have become expert at corrupting people to serve their interests. We can't put anything in front of a district attorney or a judge unless we know they are squeaky clean".

"When you review the hard drives in detail, I think you will find names of individuals and a record of their involvement which I suspect will identify corrupted officials at all levels. The data cuts across several states, Florida, Alabama, Mississippi, Louisiana, and Texas. Given this issue also crosses international boundaries, you should be able to identify locations where charges can be laid to stick, bail denied, D.A.s, prosecutors and judges that will support the efforts of the FBI".

""I think we are at the point where we can move onto the other part of our original agenda", said Jeremy. "Brock, we are thinking about a couple of things here. One is that you might be able to assist Casandra in going through all the information from Graziano, and while you can start that here, you are likely going to take a trip back to her home turf in Europe to check into aspects of the syndicate over there. The other issue is to assist with the FBI human trafficking investigation which Michelle is involved in. In part this takes you into Alvarez's world which crosses an international boundary, so CIA involvement is allowable, and it is in the interests of national security. What are your thoughts"?

I didn't have to think long about this. "I would think that Casandra will need to do a more detailed run through the hard drives than I did, and they are voluminous. That will take some time so while she is working her way through those, I can turn my attention to the other issue. I still need to meet with, or chat with Michelle one more time with respect to her inheritance, so that is the place to start. That takes me back to New Orleans where I can pick up the hard drives and courier them back here so Timm and Casandra can start reviewing them. Beyond that I would like a little more definition as to what the FBI wants me to do in regard to that investigation. Just exactly what does the FBI want my assistance with Jeremy"?

"This is all connected with the asylum and refugee issue, of course", he continued. We have worked with the office of Citizenship and Immigration to enable illegal entrants, who are willing to testify, obtain legal entry and a path to citizenship. It is a bold program because they have to face their own fears in order to do so and are under constant threat of being killed if they cooperate. Michelle's and the team work to identify individuals who might be willing to take the risk. They have to work undercover in order to identify candidates, and when an approach is made to someone, she and the other team members cannot be the ones to make contact, or their cover would be immediately blown by those who do not want to take the risk".

As Jeremy was explaining his phone pinged and he answered it immediately. When he disconnected, he asked John if there was any projection technology that allowed him to use his phone to show us the video he had just been sent. John went out, talked to his assistant and in a few minutes, the phone was projecting onto a drop-down screen. The video was sent by his agent who had attended to Oreski's murder and consisted of several clips captured by the CCTV cameras, on various streets, of the person escaping the scene. The first few were largely indistinguishable as the person had a ball cap pulled low over his eyes. "That isn't Alvarez", Jeremy said, looking at the last picture. "It's Perez"!

Jeremy called it in, and a bolo was put out for Perez to be picked up. At this point there is no evidence that he had committed the murder other than leaving the scene, however.

Jeremy began again. "I think we have gone far enough for today". I will let Michelle know that you will be in touch with her. Some of the individuals already on the list the team has put together are used to move drugs across the border, so they go back and forth. The way we see this working is that the individuals willing to give statements and testify will continue to work for the cartel until we are ready to bring charges. We need all the resources we can muster to safeguard these individuals when we are ready to make our move. John has provided us with a number of CIA and DEA resources to assist with this. Your role, and the others John has provided, will be to make contact with those Michelle and others on the team identify. You will arrange quiet passage for them across the border if they are in Mexico when all this goes down and help to ensure they get to safe houses on our side. We prefer the use of CIA agents on the other side of the border as the FBI cannot bring evidence to court if obtained on the other side, or through assisting people to cross over. I get the CIA cannot either, but we want to keep our FBI agents clean from the border perspective".

I think we are a month or so away, until we reach that point. In the meantime, I have asked John if it would be okay to use your skills to develop a financial plan to house, feed, and clothe those people over the approximate period of time from the laying of charges to getting their testimony. The Federal task force has a bucket of funds to enable this to occur, but we need an experienced field agent with financial planning skills that will understand the ins and outs of the cost of hiding people for a period of time. It's not new to you as you have developed such plans for secreting away witnesses throughout parts of Europe".

We will provide each agent with a safe house location somewhere from Texas through to New Orleans. You will be given the full list so that you can effectively develop a budget. That means we will be keeping tabs on their whereabouts through contact with the team. The team will, to the best of their ability and knowledge, have a good idea where they are at points in time and keep you up to speed.

And, as well, we have already identified and cleared prosecutors and District Attorneys who are committed to fast tracking the cases through the courts. That means we have to exchange evidence with the defense attorneys and prevent delay to the extent possible. We intend to lay charges in a way that keeps the first charge simple and hopefully is serious enough for the judges involved to not grant bail. Additional charges can be brought at a later date".

"The other thing John and I both feel you should do is get a feel for the territory if you don't already have it. This applies to all the agents John is providing. You are already familiar south Florida and New Orleans, so I suggest taking a road trip from here to San Antonio, maybe as far as El Paso, although the issue at El Paso is primarily coke being delivered by vehicle through the border crossing as El Paso and Juarez are really the same town. Our concentration, therefore, is Oreski's people which we believe involves human trafficking. We believe that in terms of drugs coming through Mexico, Alvarez was his principal supplier, and that route seems to be most prevalent around San Antonio. If we can take down Alvarez's cartel it will be a significant step forward".

"We are very close to being able to lay charges against a host of people associated with Oreski. If Perez and Martinez have taken control of Oreski's businesses, we may also have a case against them in short order. If not, we can keep that investigation separate as it will take us a long time to compile the all the data for the cases we need, but it is possible that we don't need to have every case sorted out. We just need to find the one that best indicates they would be a flight risk so we can keep them in the country".

"Keep in mind that it appears almost certain that Perez and Martinez are likely responsible for killing Graziano and may be likely in the final stages of consolidating Oreski's operation with their own, although that might require them to be in league with Alvarez. What I think I am going to do is leave the bolo out on Alvarez and create a press release regarding the murder of Oreski. The press release will identify Alvarez as a person of interest, which will please

Perez on one hand and should likely cause Perez and Martinez to stay away from Oreski's business for the near future, if they were, indeed, thinking about taking that on".

"As Perez appears to have killed Oreski", Jeremy continued, "if he and Martinez are aware of the existence of the hard drives, which they must be, they may very well think you have them in your possession. It would appear that makes you ever more of a target and they will be hunting you; they have your address and your picture. A little road trip out to Texas will keep them away from you for a time. The other thing is that I will call you or arrange for Michelle to get in touch with you. Just make sure you keep John and I informed about your whereabouts. It may be that someone else from the team gets in touch with you and not her. Also, you should know that we got quick warrants for Oreski's office and house as well as the brothel where he was killed. Oreski had extensive cd roms with videos of various very wealthy people committing various unspeakable acts, most under the influence of cocaine or some type of opioid. He was obviously using these for blackmail purposes, and we will therefore be able to charge the wealthy clients with several counts of criminal activity. Along with everything else, the data he possessed identified locations within the Louisiana bayous where such clients were taken to have their so-called fun. It is our plan to raid these the same day we enact our plan that Michelle is involved in. Michelle has inside information about these bayou brothels and may choose to explain more about that, but likely after the day we take a good part of Alvarez's cartel out. All in all, you'll have to be very careful when you meet with Michelle and the team she is on, to not blow their cover, in case you are followed".

"It's not my first rodeo like this", I reassured Jeremy, "and it seems to be in my best interest to head back to New Orleans when I leave here today and not head back to my house at all. I have a rented car, assumed other identities, and will take some liberty by altering my appearance. My first stop is to get the hard drives in New Orleans and courier them as we discussed".

With that we all shook hands and said goodbye. I figured Perez and Martinez might have people at the airport with my picture. As a result, I borrowed the keys to an unmarked CIA vehicle, and I was out the door and on the road in an instant. When I got onto the Florida turnpike, I called Sheila to see how she was doing.

Sheila's Investigation

. . . .

"**I HAVE TRACKED DOWN JEFF** Atkinson's daughter in Phoenix. Her name is Diane and she is married with two daughters in their early teens. She works as an administrative assistant in a retail store in a relatively well-off community and her husband works for a private firm that she did not identify, and she said he is currently away on a business trip. When I told her why I was calling, that there was a will, naming her father as a recipient, she was a little surprised, which doesn't surprise us though does it"? Sheila asked rhetorically.

"The reason for her surprise was that her father had left a will, so they were not expecting another one to appear. I reassured her that the nature of the document was such that it would not conflict with what had already transpired. She said she wanted to talk it over with her own lawyer, which she now has, and they have said they would like to see the actual document and could I send it to them. I said no, I could not do that, but I would be willing to go to Phoenix and bring the copy with me".

"That is a smart move", I complimented her. "Whoever is in possession of the will, at this point, at least, has access to all the funds and properties once the will is enacted. And anyone with the will could have it enacted the way it is worded".

"The question is", asked Sheila, "do you want to go on a road trip with me or would that be spending too much time together all at one time"? She teased.

"I think a road trip with you for an extended period of time will feel like a great vacation. I would love to do that, and I have a few thoughts of my own about trips which I think we will want to discuss".

"So that was my day, what went down at your meeting with John and the FBI"?

"A great deal", I responded. "During the meeting a call came in advising of a murder. As it turned out it was in one of the cheap motels owned by Oreski, and Oreski was the victim. Further to that the man who appears to be leaving the scene was identified as Perez".

"Oh my God" exclaimed Sheila. "That is terrible news and good news all in the same breath. Is the assumption that those left running Graziano's syndicate want to take over Oreski's operation"?

"You know, I thought about this as I was leaving the meeting, and I don't think that is the case or Perez would not have done that. I think it is meant as a message to Alvarez. And Jeremy, the FBI Special agent in Charge in West Palm Beach cleverly put out a bolo and a press release indicating Alvarez as a person of interest. Since he was in Fort Lauderdale at the time, he will now be scared back into Mexico and whatever major event he was planning with Oreski will surely see at least a slight delay as a result".

And so, what happened that was supposed to happen at the meeting"?

"Well, I met the two agents that Graziano was planning to work with as he had them thoroughly vetted -Timm Hill with the FBI and Casandra Garcia with Interpol. Casandra is a financial guru and I committed to sending her the hard drives with all the evidence, but not the one Graziano prepared for his daughter. So, while I am on my way to New Orleans, you could go pick them up and have them couriered to an address I can give you over the phone. We think it is highly probable that Perez and Martinez, one or both, knew about the hard drives and about Casandra and Timm, though they may or may not know their names. As a result, they are hidden away from sight and in a secure facility. As well, I am still at risk as they have my picture and name from the press reports on murder street. I intend to change my appearance some, but not so much I cannot use the identities".

"I have been tasked with a project to assist the team Michelle is working with. My role, as well as those of many others, is to bring those that team identifies as willing to testify across the border if they are in Mexico at the time all goes down. Part of my role as well as other agents, will be to get them to a safe house and the other aspect of my other role is to develop a financial plan to house and feed, those signed on as willing to testify, in a safe environment. If they agree to testify, they are also given an expedited path to citizenship, the probability of safe relocation, a new identity and a job. In order to do my job effectively, Jeremy and John thought I should take a road trip from New Orleans all the way to San Antonio. To my way of thinking I might dip down into Mexico a couple of times and just get the lay of the land, so to speak. We both have an objective relating to a road trip, and doing this together should be fun. By the way, did Phoenix have any other siblings"?

"No, she is an only child, and I got the impression they are not all that well off. They try to rent out the Penthouse in Puerto Vallarta to others, but they have to contract with a management company to look after it and that drains their income. I didn't tell her anything about what was in the will, but they will be presently surprised when they find out how much cash in the account".

"I agree. That takes care of two of the recipients in the will. The last one is Hans Goebel and we know nothing about him. Did you get a chance to do any research"?

"Not yet, it's only been a day, you know. I figured that that could wait until after we meet with Diane Atkinson. Is that okay with you"?

"Sure. Hey, something is going on just down the highway here. I have been down to crawl the entire time of our chat. Oh, looks like an accident on the other side of the freeway. I am just going by now. There is a small blue car that backed into the aluminum divider with the airbag deployed and out on the road. As well there is a semi,

L-shaped on the highway and a white SUV with the driver's door pushed in past the steering wheel. There are no ambulances, so I assume they have been and gone. There is no way anyone survived in that SUV. I am going to let you go and concentrate on driving the rest of the way, it is pretty sobering".

We agreed to meet at the Quarter House, about 8:00 P.M. and disconnected.

The I-10

. . . .

SHEILA AND I WENT OUT for supper, and she informed me that the hard drives were likely at their destination by now, and we spent the night just lying close to each other, not saying a word. There are times when that seems more intimate than sex, but then there are other times, like when we woke up and made love sweetly and gently, taking a long time to explore so that it felt more loving than lusting. Sometimes there is nothing more seductive than caressing the inside of a woman's bare thighs, unless it's her eyes...and plus, then the coffee together even tastes that much better.

We turned on the morning news and caught the press report of the murder of Oreski in Fort Lauderdale at one of the brothels he was said to own. The bolo was out, and the press showed a somewhat unclear picture of a man claimed to be the Mexican cartel boss, Alvarez. The report when on to state that Alvarez had been linked to Oreski as well as Graziano and may be responsible for both murders. A video and picture of the car he was driving was shown on the news and people were asked to immediately call the police if they saw the car or the man in the video, even though there was not a clear picture of the man's face in the video selected.

Sheila turned to me and suggested we pack a few things and get on the road to Phoenix and San Antonio. My agenda was different from hers. I intended to spend time in the not-so-great hotels or motels and maybe even homeless shelters along the way, maybe even dip across the border in places here and there. We agreed that she would stay in an upscale place but that we would get together from time to time and have some fun. The drive out of New Orleans was uneventful as we assumed it would be. Interstate 10 is in some ways an amazing feat of engineering in places. For periods of time and distance the highway is built over top of the bayou, constant water underneath with large pairs of cement pillars on both sides of the freeway, holding up the road, which is suspended maybe 15 or 20 feet above the water. Here one might assume snakes and alligators rule the roost, but the truth is that the true rulers here there are those dubbed the swamp people. If you want to hide, this is where you can get away from it all, you just have to stay alive.

As we were driving along, Sheila's mind started to give thought to the criminal side of things. "Do you think that Graziano was really the half good, half bad guy he says himself to be, or do you think maybe he buried lost a few bodies out here in the swamp"?

"I can't say one way or the other. He did a lot of bad things, and I can't believe that every single person he attempted to corrupt went along with it. I never even thought to ask if he had ever been brought up on charges, but I suspect that he has very good lawyers. In fact, I think that Oreski must have had as well, although both would have kept their distance to the extent possible if there was killing or maiming to be done. Certainly, Graziano appeared to be somewhat appalled by the type of crime involving the drug trade and the enslavement of people pouring into the world of Oreski and Alvarez. There was speculation that Graziano had an arrangement to pick the best of the people coming across the border or those being disenfranchised within the country. I have to think some of these people may have disappeared along the way, maybe Perez was the muscle.

"I don't really get the whole drug trade issue, why people use it or why Mexico is such a problem. I always thought we were just talking about marijuana and that it was a gateway drug to heroin. But people have used it for years and never got into hard drugs and now it's being legalized here and there. What can you tell me about this? You're an economist at heart".

"Well, I am not sure marijuana is the most difficult problem at this point in time. I saw this documentary called 'the Business of Drugs', on Netflix I think. Almost all I am about to say comes from this documentary. Like you say, it is slowly being legalized, although there are mistakes being made in that process. Government sometimes gets things wrong strategically, because the people enacting laws don't really understand black market enterprise. Cocaine has been a long-standing larger issue and the vast majority of it comes from Columbia and gets shipped around the world, but clearly the U.S. is the biggest consumer".

"This issue goes back centuries and it's really about the desire, or perhaps need, for humans to have an altered state of consciousness, to feel elation for a small period of time, maybe for ever-increasing periods of time, to escape the existence they find themselves living. If you think about it, the Egyptians made beer, the indigenous in Columbia chewed cocoa leaves as long back as we have history. Mankind has had a long-standing history with some form of drug-alcohol, tobacco, and so forth. We have drugs for recreation and drugs for therapy and as lots of it is legal and lots of it is illegal. The world is a big place with an ever-expanding population, much of it living in poverty, meaning the market continues to grow. And because of this there is a huge market to be capitalized. Because most of the drugs are considered harmful, and partly because they are not legalized, this is a black market which is therefore impossible to enforce and control".

"To date the federal government has spent billions on the war on drugs and has nothing to show for it. Moreover, it is estimated that the cartels' income is in excess of $20 billion annually. That enables them to buy ships, airplanes, trucks-whatever they need and whoever they need-to move the product".

"For a time, the main avenue for cocaine from Columbia was through Miami and was run by a guy named Pablo Escobar. At the height of his cartel, it is estimated that he controlled 80% of the cocaine shipped to the United States and had an estimated net worth of $30 billion and was one of the ten richest people on earth, presumably. It is rumoured that he had established a shipping base on an island in Bermuda and at the height of the cartel, it was estimated he shipped 15 tons to the U.S. every day and was earning $50 million every week. One of the reasons for lasting as long as he did, was that he spent millions to help poor neighborhoods in Columbia, building schools and roads, soccer fields, power lines and so forth. It was estimated that he killed thousands of people, politicians, civil servants, journalists, over 1000 police officers, but he was eventually killed by the police".

"During his time, he controlled all aspects of the cocaine trade, from production through to processing shipping and end point sales. From what I understand, when he was killed the drug trade changed, and the trade route through Miami was largely shut down through law enforcement efforts. When that happened, the black-market route was moved to Mexico where cartels control the territory through which the drugs pass, primarily through violence".

"So, the tv show Miami Vice has some basis in reality. I saw a documentary at one time that I think said Florida has a law that requires banks to notify the DEA if there is a deposit in excess of $10,000. As a result, apparently, the drug dealers had a whole warehouse full of money they couldn't bank".

"Yes, I think that was largely the case at the time. The problem today is that instead of one person controlling all aspects, a significant number of smaller actors filled the gaps at each stage of the process making it harder to find and locate because it begins in a large unpopulated area of the Columbian jungle. A drug industry, maybe any industry to survive, requires a stable supply and demand, and Columbia is able to provide the supply. People buying in the black market are willing to pay because they understand the risk, and they choose their dealer based on reliability of the supply and consistency in price".

"There are places in Columbia, remote places where the vast majority of people live in poverty, so the farmers harvest the cocoa leaves, take it to a lab for processing into cocaine, others transport it to ports, some are employed to hide the product, and then it is shipped, now mostly going through Mexico. A farmer harvesting the leaves gets a miniscule daily rate that has not changed in several decades. The price is set by a Columbian cartel which gets about 100 times more than they have paid for the product. A little over $2000 will hit ten times that on the streets in the United States".

"Why doesn't the Columbian Government enable the farmers to grow other crops, like coffee for instance?'

"The terrain is very mountainous, and the government doesn't have the wherewithal to build roads that would enable the product to get to market. Beyond that, coffee prices are very unstable and therefore there is no reliable income, plus it is subject to environmental fluctuation. Cocoa has the advantage of being produced once every three months whereas coffee is just an annual crop".

After thinking for a while, Sheila turned to marijuana. "You mentioned problems with legalization of marijuana. What kinds of issues are there"?

"I don't think the government policy makers have an adequate understanding of the issue because they did not take the time to understand how the economics work. I have a friend that has been a long-time user and along with millions of others has never reverted to harder drugs. Lucky, perhaps, that he didn't ever purchase from a dealer trying to get him hooked by lacing it with heroin. He doesn't buy from the government legalized shops for two reasons. First, he says the government licensed product is so mild he doesn't get high unless he buys and uses a large quantity at one time. That makes it expensive. Second, it's already expensive because a gram is still half as much on the street as it is from the licensed shops. Add to that in some cases the closest licensed shop may be a 40-minute drive".

"That's on the personal level. But in terms of licensing producers, in some states there is so much regulation that the only people that can afford to get into the market is to prove that you have huge cash reserves sitting around. As a result, in California, for example, I heard or read somewhere that 80 percent of marijuana sales are still through the black market".

W. D. Loewen

We were just coming up to Houston and had decided to take the Sam Houston Parkway around the outskirts. The overall loop around Houston is an 88-mile loop that enables you to get off the I-10 which otherwise takes you through downtown. Coming into Houston from the east you have a choice to take the south or the north loop. As we approached the road sign was in two halves, the left-hand sign indicated that the south was a toll road, so we chose to go around the north way, past the George W. Bush International Airport. That way turned out to be a toll road as well. As we drove around the north side the road turned south and there were lots of side roads where cars without toll stickers could exit out and then back on immediately. It indicated you would be billed by mail. The interesting thing was that on the east side of the parkway there were no such exit points and the signage clearly said violators would be prosecuted. Not very tourist friendly!!

Traffic was slowed to a crawl, but I was very impressed with how courteous the drivers were in Houston. I cannot say the same thing about Fort Lauderdale where people 10 cars back begin to blow their car horn as soon as the light changes color.

San Antonio

WE CONTINUED AROUND THE OUTSKIRTS and back onto the interstate towards San Antonio and the traffic thinned out nicely. There were small pockets of construction on the way into San Antonio, but nothing too serious. We had decided to stay the night in San Antonio and had booked a hotel about 5 blocks from the famous riverwalk area. The hotel was on the east side of highway 37 and we would have to walk under the freeway to get to the downtown area. We originally thought the location was great, but as it turned out, walking under the freeway later in the evening was not ideal. It was dark and a congregating place for the homeless and users.

I had another reason for choosing that hotel. The several hotels in the not so nice areas near the freeways were thought to be used by human traffickers as pickup and delivery points. There was signage in the elevators with respect to what human trafficking consisted of and to report if you came across it. Ironically, after we checked in and headed out the door to walk downtown, Three Sheriff SUVs stormed into the parking lot and right into the hotel's parkade. Obviously, something was going down.

"Maybe, this is what Michelle and her team are all about," commented Sheila as we walked under the freeway. "We might want to take a taxi back", she suggested, concerned about our safety. Under the freeway, there were two individuals, maybe homeless, hanging out, having a joint. We walked under the freeway, across a couple of streets and just like that we were in a great high end downtown mall right at the riverwalk.

There are small tourist boats that wander down the river, along the riverwalk. We decided it was the thing to do, and then, as restaurants line the riverwalk, we would pick one out for supper. A guide on the little boat tells you stories and history of the area. How much was true is open to interpretation. According to Wikipedia, the city was apparently founded in the late 1600s as a Spanish mission. Our river guide stated that when the Spanish came to the area, they were warmly greeted the 40,000 Payaya aboriginal living in the area. As the story goes, they were so welcoming that the Spanish priest sad that they would be good to convert as "they are just like us". He claimed that 5 Spanish missions were built, one of which was the Alamo.

An internet article I read stated that San Antonio entertains more 20 million tourists annually, many of which are from among the 35,000 air force recruits at Lockwood air force base. It is the seventh largest U.S. city and is home to 4 Fortune 500 companies. Unfortunately, it also has a downside, likely drug related. In 1993 there were 1200 drive by shootings, in 2016, 151 murders, the 4th largest number in the country. However, since then I understand the city is much safer, but like every other American city, still has a few issues.

Our guide had much to say about the settlement of the area and Texas generally. "Did you know", he asked, "that as a frontier area there were many outlaws and the local saloons and bars required patrons to leave their guns at the door. However, they were allowed to keep their ammunition. As their money ran out during the evening, the saloons allowed them to pay for their whiskey with a round of ammo. That is where the phrase, a shot of whiskey originated."

More stories followed, and the ride was well worth the small fee one pays to take the cruise along the river.

As the boat meandered slowly down the river, we picked out a Mexican-themed restaurant for supper to return to for supper. After getting off the tiny cruise, we walked back along the riverwalk to get some tacos and discusses our plan for the next couple of days. As we wandered along several horse drawn carriages came by, decked out in beautiful flowers, and stopped in front of a downtown hotel. In time, a wedding party came out and got into the carriages. A unique sight. Later, as the evening wore on, the horses and carriages came right into the compound behind our hotel. Downtown San Antonio!

The next morning, as we were about to leave for Phoenix, the phone rang. It was Michelle Savonne wanting to meet as she was in Austin, a short drive from San Antonio.

Michelle explained. "I had called Jeremy and he let me know that you are in San Antonio. I have some questions about my father and all that entails, but more importantly, Jeremy asked me to arrange for the rest of the team to meet with you and give you the lay of the land. We are close to being able to lay charges against a number of players and need you to know where the resources that you will be responsible for securing, and are willing to testify, will be on that day. Those that will be in Mexico when this goes down will need safe passage across the border. They have their own means of transportation, but we know that the cartel bosses track their workers through tracking devices on the vehicles. If they go off course or the tracking device goes dead, they are dealt with severely. We can meet you in Austin later this afternoon. I will text you an address for a local ranch outside Austin city limits on the west side, so you won't have to go into the city. We have been using this location for our own meetings for about three months now and both the ranch and the access points are regularly monitored and swept".

Michelle's Team

I AGREED TO THE MEETING and Sheila agreed to go on to Phoenix on her own, which meant we needed another vehicle. I called John to let him know Sheila and I were parting ways and the reasons for that. He said he would apprise Jeremy as well. I left around noon for Austin. The country outside of Austin is very treed, rolling hills and essentially green. I arrived at the meeting site and was met at the gate by a security guard, looked like a cowboy to me. He had been informed of my arrival and directed me to the large barn and said I should go up to the loft. Some loft! A nicely furnished office area complete with air conditioning, the best high-tech computers, software and communication capabilities. Michelle and her team were already there.

"Good afternoon," said Michelle. "I thought I should give you a brief explanation. The way this works is some of the team works for the cartel for minimum wages or less and are involved with repackaging the drug product and delivering it to local dealers in San Antonio, El Paso, Austin, and Houston. Drugs are also shipped across Louisiana to New Orleans, Mississippi and Alabama. Most of the product we are dealing with is cocaine from Columbia travelling through Mexico and into the U.S. As far as the cartel members are aware, the members of our team are just like any other illegal immigrant, some of us have falsified criminal records, false identities and so forth. When the charges are to be laid and cartel members in the states will be rounded up, the people that are not part of the

FBI, and who have agreed to be informants, will need safety. We anticipate that several of these people will be in Mexico when this all goes down. You are one of several people that will need to bring them back across the border".

"Okay", I said, it seems to me there is a lot I need to know. Where will I find these people when the time comes, what transportation will be available to me, and where do I get into Mexico and how do I return"?

"Michelle motioned me over to a large map on the wall. We have been able to identify several border crossing points, many of which are through tunnels under the ground. These tunnels are not short little passageways. Rather they travel about a mile into Texas and open near an old farmhouse, some of which are occasionally occupied by drug dealers posing as farmers. Some tunnels open into a barn or a garage on the properties. This side of the border, the DEA or FBI will look after. We will ensure that the locations on our side are secured, and the locals arrested and removed the day of the event. You will be assigned to one of the tunnel locations to bring our witnesses back from Mexico. This operation will occur on both sides of the border, but we want our people out before the Mexican authorities show up at the sites in Mexico. We need the witnesses on our side of the border to testify."

The team pointed out three farmhouses where tunnel exits and entrances were to exist, depending on which side of the border you were on. The tunnels were about 50 miles apart and the team had aerial photos of the properties on the Mexican side. "The entrances to the tunnels are generally in the garages or the barns where there is one on the property. The drugs are stored for a brief period of time in the buildings and shipments usually occur at night. The shipments are broken into parts. Some are moved across the border in trucks, hidden in cargo holds of semis, etc., and some are shipped through the tunnels. Your assignment will be to meet with and transport a group of witnesses through one of the tunnel accesses".

"Trucks going across the border are not our concern for this operation, although some of the individuals running the trucks have agreed to testify. Because we want them on our side of the border when this goes down, we are going to let them through the border crossing. With respect to the locations we have chosen, we were able to identify them because we have been able to piggy-back on the tracking devices the cartel uses to track their vehicles and mules. We have picked one location for all of the individuals, you will pick up, to meet you. They will dislodge the tracking devices and it will appear as though they are not moving. They will have about 30 minutes to reach your location before it is known something is amiss. At that time the Mexican authorities as well as us, will remotely, but temporarily take down the technical system at the locations from which the vehicles are being tracked. We have been causing occasional service interruptions at these sites so that the loss of service will seem normal at the time our operation goes down. You will leave the vehicle we provide you in the building at the tunnel entrance. When you are safely out on our side, you will decimate the vehicle as it will have been rigged to explode when you decide. We will provide you with a cell phone to enable that to occur".

"Just when is this likely to occur", I queried, and how will I know the people I am supposed to bring back and how will they know me"?

"I am providing you with a USB that includes photos, names, and code words that will identify them to you and vice versa. We have moved things up and will exercise this exactly one week from today. Jeremy and John provided me with your burner phone number and I am texting you the GPS coordinates for the tunnel access on both sides of the border. It may be in your best interest to check them out before, which means crossing into Mexico in advance. We suggest you keep some distance but scout things out in advance. Whatever you do, do not let the USB fall into the hands of the cartel members. As well, we are providing you with surveillance equipment, a spotting scope and you should feel free to take your handgun. This is open carry territory, so you won't need to hide it from anyone. It would be odd for a rancher to not have a weapon, given the reputation for outlaws and rattlesnakes".

We spent some time going through the plan and then Michelle asked if she could meet with me on another matter. Of course, I agreed, knowing it was about Graziano.

"Brock, I am astounded that this person could be any type of relation to me, but I have my mom to thank for keeping him at a safe distance and out of my life. I am equally surprised that a man such as this cared enough about a child that he watched over me all these years and set up legitimate businesses for my future. On one hand I would have liked to have met him, but on the other hand, it is probably best that I do not have to deal with his criminal activity like I would if he were still alive. I would have hated what he did to earn his living and would have likely wanted to bring him down. Of course, the FBI would never allow me into an operation that involved a relative. He has passed, murdered, no less, so now I am hoping that the information he turned over will go a long way to ending some corruption. I am glad he never sought to deal with the likes of Oreski and Alvarez".

"Let me just augment what you are saying, for a moment, Michelle. Graziano did not like Oreski and had spies in his organization, and right now it appears as though one of Graziano's own men took out Oreski at one of his brothels. This same individual may well have been behind the assassination of your father and is looking to take over his syndicate. At this point the special agents, your father was working with, have all the data that your father was turning over to the FBI. It details the people involved in various corrupt activities and approvals of contracts up and down the Atlantic coast and extending all the way into Texas. As well, we know that Alvarez was planning something with Oreski and wanted it to be kept quiet. Oreski's death will make Alvarez a bit skittish with respect to whatever that plan was. Also, this operation your team is involved with, if all goes off successfully, will also cause Alvarez to back away from the states, for a time at least. I guess I am saying all this to you because I am wondering if you or your team has any inkling, heard anything through your contacts as to what Alvarez was planning".

"Yes, as a matter of fact, we have heard rumblings about Alvarez working out an arrangement for shipping opium and fentanyl into the U.S. through the ports at New Orleans, West Palm Beach and Fort Lauderdale, as well as through the tunnels. The ports and inland waterways, with all the yachts and boats make it very difficult to police effectively. What is rumored is that a lot of this is making its way into the backwoods, the swamps and bayous from where it gets distributed. Even the use of drones doesn't make finding the sources any better".

"A while ago, while I was working for Parole Services, I had this client tell me about what can only be described as evil taking course in the bayous. He said that there were places where very rich men could go and commit unspeakable debauchery for a price. He said at the time that this was connected to Oreski and that he had seen Alvarez meeting with Oreski at one of these places. Apparently, Alvarez was looking to make these places his own, partly as a distribution center, a place to manufacture synthetic drugs, but also as a means to connect with people who feel they are above the law and able, in some ways to bend the law in their favor".

"When I joined the FBI, I shared this with Jeremy and asked if I could be appointed to whatever task force was dealing with issues of this nature. You see, my mom grew up as a swamp person and the bayou had a special place in her heart. But she knew how dangerous it was for young women in particular. Jeremy had the same opinion and wasn't willing to assign me to that kind of team. But I know there are a lot of really good people out there, many that have found a way of life in the bayous. They came in from slavery and from places like Haiti and they still carry on the old African traditions. Like Voodoo, for example, which is just part of the old religions brought from Africa during the slave trade. As a result, I know there are resources that can be tapped into, willing to look after what they consider their land".

"I have made contact with some of the people my mom had introduced me to over the years and have maintained contact with some of them. They are very concerned about some of the criminal activity that has been going down in the bayous and have identified a couple of large buildings where unsavory events seem to be taking place. They are willing to help hide, house and look after some of our witnesses if we, the government, can remove these, let's call them houses of ill repute. I spoke to Jeremy about this several weeks ago. He liked the idea, and he has a plan in place to eliminate those two threats.

"It seems like maybe we got off the path a bit Michelle. You wanted to talk to me about something other than just thanking me for information"?

"Yes, I am wondering if Graziano, that's what I am going to call him as I don't want to use the word father in his case any longer. "Where did he live, do you think the FBI would let me go there and just see what it was like? And I am still wondering how he picked you, how you just happened to be there".

"Everything is pretty much as I explained it, Michelle. I was just there at the time, and he needed help. So yes, I did go with him to his house and if the FBI clears it, I can take you there. With respect to being where I was at the time, I doubt very much if he would have chosen me to find you if he had had the opportunity to pick someone else. In fact, I suspect that that task would have been given to the CEO that runs all the business ventures he established in your name. I am sure that when the time comes, you will want to meet with him, and learn more. However, at this point we still are not certain who orchestrated Graziano's demise, so we still need to be cautious. I suspect that one or both of his lieutenants were involved, and it now appears that at least a man called Perez is in some way".

"Okay", said Michelle, "when this operation is finished, I will give you a call and maybe we can set a time. Despite everything I don't like about the man, I still want to see how he lived as it will now always somehow now be a part of who I am".

MY Tunnel

. . . .

I SAID MY GOODBYES TO the team, picked up the keys to my newly assigned vehicle, headed back to my hotel room in San Antonio and worked for the next few hours memorizing the names, faces, code words and location for the pickup in Mexico. I took some time to pull up the maps of the area, including the topographical, and then selected the pieces I needed. My plan was to head out a couple of hours before dark and pick an off-road location on the U.S. side of the border to scout out the Texas exit of the tunnel that I was to bring them through. When the pick-up and the arrests were to occur, this side of the tunnel would be covered by FBI swat personnel, and I was to pick up 6 passengers. My cover was as a local rancher, so I needed to dress a bit the part. Lots of local stores in San An sell that kind of gear, but it couldn't look new, so I had to find a thrift store and be choosey. Old cowboy hat, torn jeans, worn and scuffed boots, and the essential-a snap button plaid shirt.

When it was time, I headed out, drove across an open field in the desert to a spot I had picked in advance which provided a place to leave the vehicle hidden. I had to walk a bit to get a view of the farmyard/ranch and barn where the tunnel came out on the Texas side of the border. I stayed my distance and watched through the sniper scope they had provided. Odd, a sniper scope that gets taken off the rifle, instead of binoculars. The logic was sound though, a scope took up little room and was much clearer than binoculars. I watched for any signs of activity and didn't see anything going on.

This was not unexpected, the location was essentially abandoned except for the old run-down buildings, a perfect cover for a drug operation out in the middle of nowhere. As it seemed abandoned, I headed to the barn to get a firsthand look at the tunnel exit and maybe the distance to the other end. I figured there may be security cameras and expected the barn door to be locked up, so I wandered down the side to where an old window was located. I was able to force it open and crawl inside. The information, with which I had been provided, showed me where to look for the tunnel entrance-in one of the old horse stalls, under an aged pile of straw. I pushed the straw aside, lifted the hatch and climbed down into the tunnel.

To my surprise, this was no ordinary tunnel. It was large, obviously not dug by hand and the walls were well supported with cement structure. I was using a flashlight but noticed there was electrical infrastructure, not currently working and most likely operated from a generator on the Mexican side of the border, in order to stay off the grid. I wandered the entire distance to the other end of the tunnel, approximately a mile and a half based on the length of time it took. At the end of the tunnel sat two electrical golf carts with cargo boxes, ideal for transporting drugs through the tunnel. It occurred to me that they would also be ideal for transporting 6 men through the tunnel more quickly. I chose to end my excursion at that point as I had no idea what was above. The tunnel would provide a quick escape from the Mexican side. At least one or more of the men I was escorting would be familiar with the tunnel and the operation from the Mexican side, so that might come in handy. All in all, this was a good reconnoiter. The trip back to San Antonio took another couple of hours and when I hit the hotel room there was a message from John, asking me to call, but I decided to call Sheila first and see how things went in Phoenix.

She answered on the first ring. "Hi Sheila, it's good to hear your voice, but tell me, how was your meeting with Diane Atkinson"?

"Well, no small talk, eh? Right down to business. Okay then. Diane met me on her own, no family members present, and I shared the amended copy of the will with her. She was pleasantly surprised by the amount of money involved and I explained that the will still had to be executed. She was surprised that Graziano would have left money to her father but said that her dad had done a fair among of legal work for Graziano as it related to his estranged daughter Michelle, which she knew to exist from talking to her dad. She said that everything her dad did for Graziano was strictly on the up and up, no criminal activity was ever brought his way to deal with. Graziano kept that all separate from the work her father did. She said the money would be a real blessing. I said there were some legal matters to be resolved and that either I or a lawyer would be in contact with her. She asked what kind of legal issues, and I explained that I was informed that it might take a bit of time and that I was unaware of what they were. She asked if I could keep her informed of any progress".

"Are you then heading back here to San Antonio tomorrow"?

"Well, that depends. It's kind of nice here at the hotel. Great pool and all that. If you are still going to be tied up for a day or two, I think I'll just hang in here. Let me know when you are finished, and I'll head your way then".

"Sound like a great plan. I will let you know. We should touch base daily, maybe around 9:00 P.M. every night"?

"Great", she replied. We continued our conversation for a time and then parted ways. I then called John at his office and got no answer. Then I tried his personal cell, again no answer. Odd I thought, he always answers. I left messages and then decided to review the topographical data related to the tunnel's Mexican access. Eventually, I figured I had it memorized and planned to head into Mexico across the border at Laredo.

The next morning, the phone woke me at 6:00 A.M. It was John's number. When I answered he said a quick good morning and immediately started talking. "Brock, I believe you told me Sheila was heading out to Phoenix to meet Jeff Atkinson's daughter Diane. You need to get to Sheila right away and maybe pull her back from that trip. Jeremy, Hazel and Jimmy, based on all Graziano's information, decided to do a more detailed and thorough check of

Jeff Atkinson and John Sterling. Although everything up to now has indicated they were squeaky clean, Atkinson's daughter Diane was married to an FBI agent, the very agent found dead at the murder scene. She has been notified of his death and it now seems to me that she would have mentioned that to Sheila. It seems very odd for her to have kept that a secret from Sheila".

"And there is more. You had fake identities created by a gentleman you identified as just Jimron. Jeremy said his real name is James Ronaldo, and the FBI has had him on their watch list for some time. After Jeremy was cleared and I informed him of your going to see this man to create your identities, he was not surprised as he was known to the FBI. They were not overly concerned with Ronaldo's little operation because knowing who was coming and going from his place was an asset. Why this matters now is because Jimron was found shot to death in the back of his shop, this morning and his place was ransacked. It appears as though someone is cleaning house".

The news about Sheila hit me like a brick in the temple. I realized then, for the first time, how much she was becoming to mean to me. I responded to John's news, beginning with the news about Sheila and Diane Atkinson.

"Sheila has already been to Phoenix and met with Diane and has returned safely to her hotel. We had a good conversation last night. She said it all went just as we suspected it would for a living relative of Atkinson, but why would she not mention her deceased husband? There was no suggestion of anything untoward, and now I am wondering what her personal involvement is, how much does she know about Oreski and Graziano? The news about James Ronaldo's murder is equally disturbing. I would have thought he was considered a significant asset to Graziano's syndicate. Heck, any criminal. It is likely that whoever ransacked his place was looking for the identity of someone for whom Ronaldo did some work, maybe me".

"And that could very well be you", replied John. "Hazel and Jimmy are hot on that trail as we speak, in the meantime, I suggest you warn Sheila to be extra cautious. Maybe get her back to San Antonio".

With agreement we immediately ended the call, and I phoned Sheila. No answer, so I left a detailed message explaining what we had learned. I wasn't overly concerned she didn't answer because we had agreed to connect in the later evenings. I hoped for the best given there was no further plan for Sheila to again meet up with the person posing as Diane Atkinson. With that caution, I headed for Laredo and crossed into Mexico.

I followed along a small mountain ridge and took the 4-wheel drive, with which I was outfitted, off road. The vehicle was built with the best under-vehicle skid plates for rough terrain as well as a roll bar and it gave me some comfort knowing that it was also fitted with bullet-proof glass and bullet-proof metal panels. Not great on gas though, so I made a note to keep the top half of the tank full so I wouldn't have to worry about the bottom half. As per the FBI's special specs, the vehicle's gas tank was also shielded from bullets. I had no idea that the FBI had these kinds of resources but was thankful they did. I parked the vehicle some distance and out of sight from my destination. I took care to leave my phone with the vehicle as there were important contacts on the phone that could not fall into someone else's hands-like Michelle, John, and Sheila. I walked for half an hour before settling down at the top of a small knoll surrounded with brush. I took out the scope to survey the Mexican side of the tunnel entrance. There was no barn at this location, just a shed behind a run-down house. There were two old half-ton trucks parked in front of a veranda so surveying the tunnel was not likely today.

I knew from the data that the tunnel entrance was in the shed. I considered waiting until dark, hoping that the vehicles would leave. But that came to a quick end when I felt the searing hot steel of a rifle barrel pressed against the bone just behind my ear. "Maybe you come with me gringo", said the voice, as he reached down and took my spotting scope and tucked into his belt. "Let's see if you have any weapons", as he took my gun from the holster and tucked that into his belt as well. "Let's go see my friend down at the house so we can have a little conversation with you".

I considered my options as we walked towards the house. I was in no mood to be interrogated by a company of not so gentlemanly tough guys. Unfortunately, my captor kept his distance and there was no opportunity to dislodge him from his task. We walked in through the front door as he proudly announced that he had found a 'lizard' lounging about in the desert. The guy placed my scope and gun on the table, and I made a note that there was only one other guy in the house. My captor and his buddy sat me down in a chair, tied my hands behind the chair back and taped my legs together just above my ankles. They spent the next two hours trying to get me to open up about why I was there and what my plan was. This was accompanied by an occasional punch in the side of my head and threats to cut off a few of my fingers or maybe a toe or two. After no luck and a bit more discussion, they decided it could wait until after they moved the drugs from the shed through the tunnel and into Texas. In the meantime, they dragged me still tied to the chair, out to the shed to keep me away from my weapon and anything in the house, like a knife that might aid my escape and as well, to keep an eye on me while they started moving the drugs out.

Despite the ringing in my head, a swollen eye and difficulty hearing, I could make out the electrical circuitry when they switched everything on. They left me sitting while they started moving the drugs down and onto the golf carts.

Diane Atkinson

SHEILA WAS ENJOYING HER DAY in the shade by the pool when Diane Atkinson came along and sat beside her. Sheila was amused by the thought that entered her mind in that moment and was surprised to hear herself say it out loud- "along came a spider and sat down beside her". They both chuckled.

"I thought I would drop by for a visit since I have the day off. I must admit though, it took an hour to locate you. I told the hotels I phoned, several of them, that I was your sister, and would they put me through to your room? Easy as pie really, just took a little time. The reason I am here though is that my dad's work is archived at his old office which we still keep. It's in a strip mall that he owned. For tax reasons we just kept the office in the mall. How would you like to go with me to check into the files and see if there is any record of his creating a will of the nature you have shown me"?

Sheila thought for a moment before responding. She was concerned that if they found a copy of the original will, she would have to explain why Hans Goebel is not on the copy she showed to Diane. That would give rise to suspicions, and she needed to know what the story was. In the end, she decided to accept the invitation. On the way she could think of some explanation. The drive only took 15 minutes from the hotel, and they pulled into a parking spot at the back of the building. Other than their car, the lot was deserted.

Diane unlocked the door and motioned for Sheila to step inside. As she did, Diane turned and locked the door behind them. Diane sat down behind a desk and motioned for Sheila to sit across from her. "Just give me a few minutes to start up this desktop and we'll see what we can find". "You know, little miss Muffet", she said continuing the metaphor that Sheila had started, "you aren't the only one adept at using fake names and identities. I had been around the office a lot as my dad's legal assistant when he was drawing up things for Graziano. He spent a lot of time doing work for Graziano and was never really appreciated. Despite what I said earlier about my father, some of the work related to assisting a guy named James Ronaldo in creating fake identities for people Graziano wanted to protect because Graziano had corrupted them to the point they had to disappear to get away from the law. The truth is, my father convinced Graziano to leave something to those who deserved better than the straight life was ever able to give. That is where the will comes in. He managed to get Graziano to sign it along with the mortgage documents Graziano had to sign when he eventually sold his house in Phoenix".

"On top of everything else, I saw the toll his arrangement with Graziano was having-doing work for a man he knew to be evil, even though most of it was technically helping Graziano with only the legal side of things. In the end it drove him to his death, and I hated Graziano for it and decided I was owed. I knew about the penthouse in Puerto Vallarta, of course. One time while I was there, a man came up to me and asked if I wanted a drink. In the process of getting hammered, I shared my ill will towards the man known as Graziano. Graziano, he queried, well, well, it seems we have something in common. To make a long story short, he treated me very well, I fell in love and married that man. You see, I am the woman married to the FBI agent that was killed on Murder Street".

"When he met my dad, they had a long discussion about Graziano and eventually my dad arranged a meeting between them. At the time we were destitute financially and Graziano convinced my husband that he was not all that bad, especially when compared to Alvarez or Oreski. In the process, Graziano mentioned to my husband that there was an even greater threat to the U. S. than

Alvarez, apparently some European organization. He asked my husband to infiltrate that organization, without FBI approval, to find out who and what they were all about and what they were planning. At the time, Graziano had said he was planning to turn over substantial data about his syndicate to the FBI but wanted more evidence about this other organization. In exchange he agreed to pay us quite handsomely. However, he suggested for our own security that a false name and identity be used and gave us a contact to arrange this."

"We managed to get this man called Jimron, who Graziano had mentioned several times in conversation, to create a false identity for my husband, so he could be undercover surreptitiously. In exchange Graziano said he would arrange for substantial monies to be transferred to us when the time was right. In order to make all of this work, I also had to have a fake identity as his wife. When my husband was killed in Fort Lauderdale, I hightailed it back to Phoenix and resumed my original life. A fake identity had enabled the two of us to hang out at the penthouse without anyone knowing who my husband was, which was important because it worked as a refuge for him. Like when the FBI creates identities, I also filled in the background and posted on the internet as if I had two daughters and a different husband. You see, Google accepts fake news, identities, the whole ball of wax. As long as the person searching doesn't do a deep dive, the identity holds up".

"I am truly astounded", said Sheila. "It seems to me we should be friends. If you know Atkinson created a will to leave something to himself as well as my dad, then you must know about the third person named in the original will, someone named Hans Goebel, maybe, given you are in a position of advantage here, you can take the time to tell me about him".

"I know the name because that is the name Graziano asked my husband to use in order to infiltrate this organization. Graziano asked him to go to Munich and gave him an address for an office there.

"All I know is that Graziano, my husband and my father had serious concerns about the link between Oreski and Alvarez. Alvarez is the head of one of the largest cartels in Mexico and Graziano has always been a thorn in his side, largely preventing Alvarez from moving effectively into the U.S. Alvarez was planning to move against Graziano's syndicate, or maybe it is more correct to say he is planning. The thing is, someone took out Graziano before Alvarez had the chance to consolidate the areas around Fort Lauderdale and New Orleans, well, actually all of Louisiana. In the meantime, I understand Alvarez was in West Palm Beach when his newest partner, Tony Oreski was murdered, and a bolo was put out for Alvarez as a person of interest in the murder. Of course, it wasn't him. As a result, he is likely back in Juarez, looking after interests there".

"While he was concerned about Oreski and Alvarez and all related things, Graziano, however, was equally or more concerned with this other entity and now it seems to me they may have been responsible for Graziano's and in some way with my husband's murder".

The Desert Near Laredo, Mexican Side

I FIGURED THE GUYS TRANSPORTING the drugs over to the American side would take about 45 minutes to get to the other side, unload and get back. I knew that the FBI was monitoring the location on that side and wasn't about to allow the drugs to make it to their distribution point, but I doubted that they would arrest the two guys at this point in time as we were only two days away from everything unfolding. I knew I had to get out of my bonds, and as luck would have it, this wasn't my first rodeo tied to a wooden chair. While they had wrapped my feet together, they had not bound them to the chair. As a result, I was able to stand, walk over next to the wall and swing the chair against the shed wall, splintering it sufficiently that my hands and arms became free of the chair. The broken pieces of wood enabled me to slice through the ties on my hands, although it took a little longer and a bit more effort that I was comfortable with.

The next task was getting back to the house, picking up the gun and waiting for the two to make their way back. I considered just leaving but that would likely mean they would notify their boss that something was amiss. It was possible though, that they would keep quiet about it because they allowed me to escape. I decided against taking that risk as there was just too much at stake to allow them the opportunity to inform anyone that they had been spied on. I went back to the shed, picked up the broken pieces of the chair and tossed them behind the house. I then went back to the kitchen, got another chair and the tape, headed back to the shed and proceeded to loosely wrap my feet. I hid my arms and hands behind my back as if I were still tied and waited for their return. I needed both of them to come out of the tunnel before taking any action.

The wait was about 15 more minutes before I heard the sound of the golf carts. The guy who found me lurking around was the first to come out of the tunnel. I pretended to be semi-conscious. He smiled at me and asked if I was ready to share, a question I just ignored. A minute later his partner exited, and the first man turned his back to me. I stood and swung my gun across the back of his head with all my force. He slumped down, unconscious, and I pointed the gun at the second man and motioned for him to knee, hands behind his head. As he did, I performed the same knockout blow and he slumped onto the floor. I took my time at that point, to thoroughly tie and gag both of them. I didn't want them to be able to help each other get untied when they woke up, so I dragged my captor outside, around the back of the shed, in the afternoon shade, making sure he was not near anything that would allow him to get loose. I left them both in that state, knowing they would be found by the Mexican authorities in two days, when everything went down. I went back into the house, cleaned myself up, headed back to my vehicle, and crossed back into Texas at Laredo and turned my phone on. I noticed that there were a couple of phone calls and texts from various people, including Michelle and John.

As soon as I was safely back in the states, I headed to a restaurant and called Sheila, but there was no answer. I ordered a beer and enjoyed the sweet coolness of condensation as I pressed the bottle against my cheek and back of my neck. Two swallows later the entire thing was gone, after which I headed out to San Antonio. On the way I called John back. He answered on the first ring.

"Jeremy called today and said they are moving up the timeline, as Oreski's murder is causing concern that there may be a pause by the cartel in moving things. Everything will occur tomorrow night.

I was wondering if you had given any thought to how we might fund housing and protecting these people that are willing to testify. I understand there are a lot, both men and women, some with families".

"I have given it some thought but have not had any opportunity to think through an actual budget estimate for the expenses involved. Michelle had mentioned something about people in the bayou providing assistance and safe places as long as Oreski's bayou operations are eliminated. The idea of hiding witnesses in a dark and dreary swamp doesn't sound very nice, but on the other hand, it is likely safe. I was thinking the government could provide funds to those housing witnesses as well as the witnesses themselves. That would likely be more money than they would otherwise be able to make, at least until they testify. However, this also gave me another idea. A number of the people that Graziano corrupted are reasonably well off and live in beautiful homes. As long as the offenses committed are such that we could work out plea arrangements with severe penalties in the event of violating the agreements, these otherwise corrupted citizens could stave off jail time by providing housing and maybe even jobs with income for some migrants. Less cost for the government. How about a conversation with Jeremy, Hazel, Jimmy, Casandra and Timm to see if they can identify prospects that could work for us in this regard"?

"I can feel Jeremy and maybe Casandra and Timm out in that regard and see if they like the idea. They have already started working on arrest warrants and subpoenas. That will take some time, but in going through Graziano's materials, we have been able to identify judges and prosecutors in all 5 states that are willing to expedite matters and who are aware of the gravity associated with letting time slip away. We can offer our own legal people to provide assistance to the FBI team to draw up all the necessary legal papers. In the meantime, you should have a chat with Michelle and explore with her what she had in mind. I know they have arranged temporary places for these people to be kept, but that cannot be allowed to last very long. They will be at risk of being discovered, so movement of these people across state lines so they are some distance removed from where they have been operating would be a good idea and better if it can occur quickly. The other thing is that there will be fallout in communities when the drug supply dries up for a time. Regular users will be desperate to find new sources and there will be those willing to fill the gaps. Some violence is likely to ensue, and this will take the DEA and local police away from any protection details".

That ended the conversation with John, and we agreed to chat after things went down. I then dialed Michelle again and this time she answered immediately.

"Hello, Brock, we have been concerned that we haven't been able to reach you for a few hours and we have a concern about Sheila. First of all, are things still okay with you?

"Yes", I replied, though "I am a little worse for wear. "I had gone over to the Mexican side of the tunnel to check things out. A couple of guys found me and things got a little tense and rough for a few hours. However, they are confined and the tunnel access still available for the people you are to bring back. I am certain they will be no problem and we can likely bring them back across the border with us, still, tied up. But what about Sheila"?

"No, it is better to leave the Alvarez's bad guys on the Mexican side of the border. They will be picked up soon enough. In the meantime, you should know that when Jeremy advised our team lead that Jeff Atkinson's daughter was married to our deceased agent we thought it best to do two things-put a tail on Sheila and dig deeper into Diane Atkinson. Without going into the detail right now, you should know that Diane and Sheila are together at Jeff Atkinson's old office in a strip mall in Phoenix. What is more important, however, is that Diane was employed her father as a legal assistant for several years. The thing is, although we have a man in place at the location, we can't risk doing anything until after tonight is over. We are going to have to let Diane's plan play out or alternately hope that Sheila can figure her own way out. We pinged her phone and discovered it is in her purse, and still turned on. However, she hasn't yet answered".

That was the second shock in two days. I felt ill to my stomach as I thought about the possible danger Sheila was in. I was too far away from Phoenix to do anything about it myself and we were too close to the end of the operation for me to be able to leave. I decided to try another phone call. Again, no answer. I called Michelle back.

"Does the agent have eyes on her"? I asked.

"No, they moved into a back room, he can see into the front of the office, but neither woman is in the front. In addition, I can't leave the agent just sitting there with everything that is going down tonight. We need all our available manpower, so I have to pull him off right away. I just thought it best to let you know".

I Thanked Michelle for the heads up and got to San Antonio in the late evening and had less than 24 hours before I had to be back in Mexico. I was supposed to leave my vehicle on the Mexican side of the Border, at the tunnel entrance but decided to change that around. The tunnel could just as easily be destroyed from the Texas side and FBI agents would be waiting there in any event to transport my passengers. That would leave me a quicker drive to Phoenix if Sheila needed my help, or even just my support after the fact. I suspected that the tunnel or one like it would eventually be rebuilt in short order with a new set of players.

Sheila and Diane

"I DON'T QUITE UNDERSTAND WHY you brought me here", "said Sheila to Diane, "I have no idea who your husband is or why that matters".

"Getting you to come to Atkinson's old offices was the only way I could think of to have this conversation with you in a place I know to be soundproof and very secure. I did my research and knew you are John Sterling's daughter, that you kept the private investigator business that he started, and in fact, expanded it considerably. It's not as though I am in a position to just go to the police in New Orleans and ask them to prove my husband innocent, nor for that matter what his involvement was with Graziano's murder. The thing is, that doesn't matter to the authorities, they will just assume he was corrupt when he was just trying to get the goods on this other organization Graziano was worrying about. What I want is to hire you and your firm to prove that he was a good man with the best of intentions and clear his name. I am willing to enter into a very lucrative contract with your firm if you undertake this assignment".

"Other than the money, just why would I do that? Your husband was employed by Graziano as well as by some unknown organization and all the associated mayhem they may have created in the Gulf States. Certainly, if I were to agree to take this on, I would charge you a pretty penny and I would need to be pointed in some direction or another to get started".

"Surely, you are brighter than that", commented Diane. "Think about it. Graziano was not involved in the darker side of crime, well, maybe it depends how you look at it. There has to be a hundred or more very wealthy types that were corrupted by Graziano and his syndicate. Any one of them could have wanted him dead and out of the way. Anyone of them would have the wherewithal to hire a hitman. Or perhaps it was one of his two lieutenants-Perez or Martinez. On top of that, we didn't want anything to happen to Graziano because we were in a partnership with him, attempting to get the goods on whatever this other organization's involvement is. Why you and your firm? Because you can go where the police cannot and undertake things for which the police require warrants. What matters to me is that my husband must be cleared of criminal wrongdoing and have no criminal record".

Sheila mulled over the request and realized that whoever killed Graziano must have known he was going to the FBI and that implied that he wasn't about to enter into any kind of an arrangement with Oreski or Alvarez. If anything, maybe he was setting them up. Not only that, but it was also unlikely that any of the people he corrupted were at fault either. They would not have known about his turning documentation over to the authorities to end his syndicate. That made it more likely that someone internal to Graziano's syndicate was in some way responsible, and now with Diane making her request, it seemed even more likely that either Martinez or Perez, or both, were involved in Graziano's murder as well as her husband's murder, perhaps through a contract with this so-called secret organization. However, it was still not entirely clear that there was an internal struggle within Graziano's organization. Since the authorities were well into the investigation and about to move against the cartel, Sheila knew she couldn't say anything about any of that. To Sheila this looked like easy money.

"Okay, Diane. My agency will pick up this investigation, but I will need an iron clad contract and $50,000 up front money as I have no idea where this will lead and will need to assign more than one of my people to the investigation".

"Not a problem", replied Diane. I already have a contract drawn up, we can fill in the details and I will let you get on your way". She opened up the laptop, printed off the document and Sheila spent some time going through the details. When they were both satisfied with the changes the documents were signed. To Sheila, this all seemed very surreal -a seemingly corrupt but well-intentioned deceased FBI agent has a spouse signing an agreement with a private investigator to prove her husband innocent of entering into a contract with a corrupt and evil man, attempting to get inside information for yet another unknown evil entity.

Just East of Laredo a few hours later

· ·

STILL CONCERNED ABOUT SHEILA, I headed out to the tunnel site on the Texas side of the border. At the appointed time, when I knew everything was going down in several different places at the same time, I entered the barn, walked over to the stall and climbed down. I footed it across though the tunnel and climbed up the other side. I reached the electrical box and flipped on the power to light the tunnel. I checked on my first captor to ensure he was still tied, and to my pleasant surprise discovered he was none too happy. I went around the back of the shed to find the other still there and sound asleep. I doused them both with water and let them have a nice long drink. All I now had to do was wait for the men that were about to become federal witnesses, to arrive. It didn't take long. Six men from two different directions arrived by old half ton trucks and immediately got out. I took some time to separate them and then ensured the faces matched those I had been given to memorize and we exchanged the pre-arranged code words. All went well. Four of them spoke broken English and I explained that there were two bound men that I needed their help to move into the house to leave them in a slightly cooler place until Mexican authorities could pick them up.

With that accomplished, we climbed in the carts and headed through the tunnel to the Texas side. When we arrived and climbed out DEA agents were there waiting to move the men to safe houses. When they left, I removed the explosives from the truck and set them to blow inside the tunnel at various points throughout the tunnel length. With that done, I got in the truck and drove a safe distance, dialed the number given me and detonated the explosives, collapsing the tunnel. I did not lose the truck as originally requested because I wanted to immediately head out to Phoenix. I dialed Sheila's number and to my relief, she answered.

"You'll never guess what happened to me, or who Diane Atkinson really is", she suggested. I did not want to spoil her fun by telling her I knew what had happened. What I did not know was that Diane had hired her to look into Graziano's murder in order to clear her husband.

"It's an odd request", I stated, given that she knew he was taking money from a known criminal boss. I wonder why a clear record in the U.S. matters to her so much. Let's mull this over while you head back to San Antonio, and I head back to Austin to meet with Michelle and her team. I also need to talk to John, or maybe Jeremy to see if all went well at other points in the puzzle. Also, maybe you can tell me what you have in mind, given what the FBI and DEA are not doing or able to do with respect to Graziano when we get back together the day after tomorrow".

"Okay", replied Sheila, "I could see you back in San Antonio, or better yet, why don't I book a place in Austin and we can meet there. Maybe we will take a little break and spend a couple of nights visiting a blues bar or two".

"That sounds great", I replied, "the Austin part I mean. I'll look forward to a text letting me know where I can find you. I'm happy you are okay, truth is, I heard about you meeting with Diane. The FBI looked into her very closely and know all about who she is. They put a tail on both of you and let me know you were meeting with her. I thought you were in danger, but we couldn't do anything because of other events. We couldn't risk Diane finding out something else was happening and then they had to pull the agent away for the larger operation. You were on your own if something bad was about to happen. I wasn't too happy about that. Maybe we can prevent that as you go about your investigation, presumably involving something the Feds can't do above board". We agreed to think about it further and I put Laredo in my rear-view mirror.

Michelle's Plan

BEFORE CHECKING INTO THE HOTEL Sheila had booked for us in Austin, I met up with Michelle and her team for about half an hour. They were busy with a variety of legal issues and tasks and Michelle had very little time for the meeting.

"All went very well", she began, "we have already started taking statements and have placed all those willing to testify in temporary accommodation. We will begin moving them to new living quarters where most will have jobs as gardeners, maids, and so forth, but some are also educated and we intend to employ them as teachers where we can have a small community, as long as there is safety, likely in the bayou where we know they will be accepted and protected. Thanks for your help, it was a large operation and every man counted".

"How long will you remain at this location processing documents and people", I asked, I assume this ends your undercover assignment"?

"About two weeks if we work really long days. Combined with DEA agents this shouldn't take all that long. When I am finished here, I head back to New Orleans to see my friends and find a place to live. I think this assignment takes me, with some of these people, into the swamp areas where we can ensure their safety until after they testify, which may or may not be in person".

"I am curious though, you told me about your thought that people in the bayou would be willing to hide, feed and protect witnesses. Why would they be so willing to do that"?

"It's their adopted home and to an extent represents the only freedom they have ever known. Most are descendants of slavery or current conditions to this date in Haiti. There was a priest, apparently, according to a little pamphlet:

'A Brief History of Voodoo: Slavery and the Survival of the African Gods. A guide to Strange Gods, Strange Alters' -A. P. Antipas-published by Hemb Comex N.O. 1990

"The pamphlet is available at Marie Laveau's House of Voodoo in New Orleans. My grandmother and mother took me there several times, and sometimes deep into the bayou. Many people chose to live there because they are still nervous about the plight of blacks in America, as well as being worried about the fact that they still practice some of the ancient African religions. The pamphlet essentially outlines that much can be traced back to a priest named Bartolome de la Casa who feared that the enslaved Indian population on the island of Haiti would be exterminated in the hands of the Spanish. It is said he convinced Charles I of Spain to export blacks from Africa to Haiti and the Portuguese, who had footholds in Africa, accepted orders. By 1540, it is suggested that about 10,000 a year were transported to Haiti and the West Indies. By 1600, the Portuguese, French, Danish and English are thought to have shipped more than 900,000 blacks to the Caribbean, Mexico and South America. Many died being marched to the ships, on the ocean and eventually as slaves".

They continued to worship their own gods under the guise of worshipping catholic priests. For example, Legba is the Lord of the Crossroads and of all gates, the veil which separates men from gods. He is represented by Christ and John the Baptist. Sometimes he is depicted as a feeble old man, a sack on his back, leaning on a crutch, all of which hides his incredible strength. Those he possesses fall down as if struck by lightning. Another is a supreme and powerful voodoo god, Damballah-Wedo whose symbol is a snake. He is merged with the image of St. Patrick, because he too, is surrounded by snakes. His wife is Ayido-Wedo, he is the sun and she is the moon. Ayida is the magic principle of good fortune and prayed to by all who wish to become wealthy. She appears as the Virgin Mother".

"How did you become aware of the willingness of these people to aid those in trouble with the law, and why would they"?

"They see the laws, here in America, despite American history, as the most probable protector of freedoms. There was a slave revolt in Haiti, sometime around 1791 and it continued until 1804. At the time the then Governor of Louisiana forbade the importation of slaves from Haiti for fear that the revolt would spread to the Spanish controlled territory. Many plantation owners were forced to take refuge in Cuba, but when the Louisiana Purchase took place in 1804, the refugee plantation owners, with their household slaves and families arrived in New Orleans. Under Spanish and French rule, the slaves in Louisiana toiled under very repressive and constant supervision, but later, under American supervision the life of a slave became somewhat freer and New Orleans began to hear the beat of the African Drum in what, for a period of time, came to be called Congo Square. The pamphlet goes on to speculate that it was this that may have given rise to New Orleans Jazz".

"With respect to how I came to see these people as a possible aid to those in trouble and willing to testify, the history of Marie Laveau was a huge clue. One of my parolees told me about these places "of evil" in the bayous. The people living a life of what they considered to be a gift of freedom, saw the effect of drugs and the evil of the dealers and users being undertaken in those places. They consider the dealers and holders of these places to be no different than the plantation owners that enslaved their ancestors. They also see the refugees and immigrants as slaves themselves. There is an affinity of suffering that is understood and that is why they are willing to help".

"But that is only half of the story. The other half is the way Marie Laveau became wealthy. She developed a chain of household informants in some of the most prominent homes, as those former or current slaves regularly came to her to have their fortune told or to obtain a voodoo bag of herbs and roots to bring good fortune or ward off enemies. Having learned of this throughout my childhood, it ultimately occurred to me that the FBI could use the same context to learn about events taking place in certain households. As a result, we developed our own group of a different type of informant, as we set up presumably underground shops where such practices could still flourish and conversations of events occurring in certain households were brought into our sphere of knowledge without anyone suspecting. This is now an ongoing strategy and one we protect vigorously, in part by not using any of the information directly or asking any of these individuals to come forward to testify against those they work for. Rather, we simply use the information as an entry point to gain further knowledge. In some cases, the information we gain allows us to take a suspect right off the suspect list or add someone we didn't previously suspect of doing anything illegal".

"At some point though, I will want to come to West Palm Beach to visit the house where my father, Graziano, lived. I understand you have been inside with him and wonder if you would be so good as to go there with me. I just would feel better not being alone the first time in".

"I would be happy to do that. I will have to check with the FBI in West Palm Beach to ensure the house is no longer off limits and to find out if the house itself is being possessed by the government as a result of being used for illicit activities. I am not sure what the status of the murder investigation is at the moment, so I am not sure if I will be staying at my own house. We better remain in contact only through the burner cells for the time being. Whoever killed your father and Tony Oreski, or arranged for those events to happen, is still at large and may well be looking for me still".

"Okay", replied Michelle, "expect to hear from me in about two weeks and we'll go from there". We said our goodbyes, wished each other luck, and parted ways.

Austin and the Drive Home Recap

SHEILA ARRIVED IN AUSTIN THE next evening and decided to head to Maggie Mae's Blues Bar for a bit of fun. Austin is famous for its blues venue and there are several places in the downtown area that are close to each other. If you aren't liking the music at one, you can walk to another. We decided to stay a second night so we would have a full day in Austin as well as another evening. The next morning, we were back on the road to New Orleans, about an eight-hour drive from Austin. We planned to stay overnight and then drive to West Palm Beach the next day.

"Have you given any thought to how you will approach your investigation", I asked Sheila.

"Well, I made some notes, thinking along the line that we needed to have a refresher about what questions remain outstanding, and in the process our list of suspects. Then we could talk about whether my own investigators can get involved in something where the FBI is unlikely or less likely to venture".

That sounds like a good idea", I volunteered, "do you want to go through your whole list before I respond, or do you want me to react with each question"?

"With each question", but I am going to use my phone to record the conversation, I can't make notes in a moving vehicle without getting a headache, and I will never remember everything we talk about".

"Okay, I said, "shoot"! And she started.

"Number one: who killed Oreski and why?"

"That one seems answered already", I replied, "while it is not certain that Perez committed that murder, he was identified fleeing the scene. Whether or not he can be charged will depend upon whether the CSI team can place him in the room where Oreski died. Maybe there will be news for us when we get back. We don't have a motive for why Perez would personally kill Oreski, but there must have been something personal between them, or Perez would have just hired a hitman. A lot of police and law enforcement agencies are looking for Perez at the moment. So, we should leave that search to them. Diane Atkinson doesn't know about Perez being seen, so you could let her know that you have discovered that much. That gives her some hope that you are making progress not that we really want to support a spouse attempting to clear a corrupted FBI agent".

"Good idea", said Sheila, justifies my billing her a little bit, though I feel a little guilty passing it off as if I did the research".

"No need for you to feel guilty about billing her for passing information to her. It is part of private data to which you have access".

"Number 2 then: Diane made a comment to me that I just salted away. She said, 'you aren't the only one that can get a fake ID'. Why would she think that I was using or had used a fake ID"?

"It could be as simple as her thinking you are a private investigator and therefore must use them all the time. There doesn't seem to be any other visible explanation at the moment".

Sheila moved on. "Number 3: who killed Jimron or James Ronaldo and why was that necessary, did he know something critical to Graziano's murder"?

"He must have done so as he kept records of everyone that entered", I replied, thinking back to my visit and use of his services. "That would mean that he would have a record of some kind somewhere in the shop. The police and crime lab will have been through the place by now and confiscated records and videos of anyone entering the shop, if any were left. Whoever ransacked his place, as well as the police, may have missed something. He was a very careful person and kept video files of everything. I made sure he didn't keep any of me, but in retrospect, he likely had some form of protection beyond what was in the shop. He could have left something with a lawyer, a safety deposit box or even had something at his house. Diane used his services, Graziano knew and referred people to his services. Given that he was very cautious there may still be evidence out there. How about you check into Ronaldo's life, see if he was married, where he lived, and if possible, see what you can learn. Maybe create a fake will so you can inherit", I joked.

Sheila smiled sarcastically, "Number 4: What is going on with Hazel and Jimmy? They seem to have cleared almost everyone within the FBI, and neither they nor the FBI itself seem to have any evidence surrounding the viable suspects regarding who killed Graziano. It seems to me that Diane had information about which they have not learned-something about a secret organization her husband agreed to infiltrate on behalf of Graziano".

"Well, not exactly", I replied. Hazel and jimmy have been assigned to investigate this agent and Diane Atkinson herself. As far as the FBI is concerned, Oreski and Alvarez in some combination as well as Perez and perhaps Martinez as well are likely suspects re Graziano. Martinez and Perez could be in it together if one of them discovered Graziano was turning the entire syndicate over to the authorities and identifying all the people they corrupted. But it does seem to me that Hazel and Jimmy do not have any internal suspects within the FBI, or at least none they have shared with anyone. The behavior of Jeremy certainly suggests he and his team were not involved or they would have attempted to subvert the investigative efforts in some manner".

"Number 5, then, continuing on that same vein. What progress are Casandra and Timm making with respect to fully bringing down that syndicate. They have a ton of evidence, and of course, we still have copies of it all. Do you think we should do a deeper dive into the data on the hard drives to give them some help"?

"Maybe", I replied, "but I am inclined to let them do their work. There was so much detail and Casandra has a serious financial background. I will stop in at their secret place of work and see what they are looking at and what they are willing to share with me. It might be a good idea to do that with Jeremy and maybe John as well. Diane is correct on one point, there are some very senior people, senators, etc. that are implicated up to their eyeballs in that data. While it is possible one of them could have decided to try to prevent Graziano from going to the authorities, they would have had to know about his plan. I think it's far more likely that it was someone like Perez or Martinez that somehow got wind of his plan. Let's leave that aside until I can meet with Casandra and Timm."

"Okay for now, question number six: whose names have arisen in the Graziano murder that we have not had a close look at, really delved into"?

"Hmmm, weighty question", I replied. "Okay, here goes. I am beginning to think these two parallel investigations are somehow connected. The FBI team, Michelle's team, let's call it, is investigating drug and human trafficking that involve a cartel headed by Alvarez. Alvarez is connected to Oreski, who is now dead, apparently killed by the number 2 or 3 man inside Graziano's syndicate. Graziano sends me to James Ronaldo to get me fake names and IDs, and I find a will that involves your father, drawn up by a lawyer that knew Graziano, and his daughter turns out to be married to an FBI agent Graziano was essentially bribing to join, and work within, some secret, or at least an organization that is not known at the moment, and to use the name Hans Goebel to accomplish that. On top of that Michelle is Graziano's estranged daughter who just happens to be involved as part of the team investigating drug and human trafficking orchestrated by Alvarez who is connected to Oreski. It seems to me, at least in part, his daughter is part of the reason Graziano decides to go to the FBI and Interpol".

"At least one rogue FBI agent is killed in the shootout that killed Graziano, but Hazel and Jimmy, the agents external to the FBI, appointed to investigate the FBI itself, have found no linkage to a leak within the agency. Only that he was killed by the people he himself was involved with during the shootout. Further, he was using the name of the third person identified in the will. I presume the reason for that is so he could claim the inheritance mentioned in the will. However, the real Hans Goebel is presumably a deceased man in Germany. I have not been able to fathom why Graziano would ask him to use that name.

"To now answer your question. We have not really looked into several people. Graziano appointed a CEO to look after the legitimate businesses he created for Michelle. I think you should take that on. Michele has two close friends Jesse and Louise who were very protective of Michelle who is an FBI agent, so it is odd that they would see themselves as her protector, instead of the reverse. You could also check into those two more thoroughly. These three individuals all appear to be upstanding citizens and the authorities are not looking their way. As far as an investigation is concerned, this comes under the heading of leaving no stone unturned".

"Meanwhile, as you take on those tasks, I am heading to Europe. Someone gave up Graziano to someone. I intend to look into Casandra to some extent, given Graziano trusted both the FBI and Interpol and Hazel and Jimmy have apparently hit a dead end within the FBI. I am also going to track down one Hans Goebel and try to figure out who he was. When Ronaldo hooked me up with that ID, he said Goebel was deceased, but it would be good to know what his involvement was with Graziano. In addition, there is one other thing that is lurking in the back of my mind. Your father retired to France, another European connection, but the will leaves him a villa in Malaga. I think I may visit that little abode and see what's there".

"Wow", exclaimed Sheila, "that is quite a list. I am good with my agency taking on those "good guy" investigations, but I think I should be with you if you go to the villa, doesn't seem right that I am left out of that first visit".

"Tell you what, it depends on what I find with Hans and Casandra, if all is well, maybe I'll give you a call and you can hop on a plane, and we can meet in Malaga together. Sound okay"?

"Okay", replied Sheila, as we pulled off the freeway onto the Pontchartrain expressway and headed back to the Quarter House. We spent a great evening together and the next morning Sheila headed back to Atlanta to take care of some business while I headed back to Fort Lauderdale.

Spreadsheets

I CALLED JOHN ALONG THE way and briefed him on the success of the mission to take down a large chunk of the cartel operation, along with where things were at with Michelle. John suggested he would save his briefing to me until we could both meet with Jeremy, Casandra and Timm. There was no mention of Hazel and Jimmy. Once again, I found my way into a time share in the town of Weston, about 15 miles straight west of the airport. It is definitely a beautifully landscaped, fully manicured little city.

Jeremy, despite being immersed with his staff, the DEA and a number of staff pulled from other offices across the gulf states, agreed to join us in Fort Lauderdale. I asked permission to stop in to see Timm and Casandra before meeting John and Jeremy. Timm and Casandra were located within the confines of a company with ties to the U.S. military. The building was heavily secured as a result. The had been given an entire floor to work with and most of the walls and furniture had been removed. Casandra had posted spreadsheets all over the walls, related to various projects that Graziano had undertaken. The spreadsheets for specific projects were huge, with extensive rows and columns. We exchanged hellos and I asked them how things were going. Casandra responded first.

"We are just getting started really, but so far everything seems on the up and up re the construction aspects. The costs seem legitimate at least on the surface of things, but we haven't really delved into the detail. The spreadsheets appear to total correctly, but so far, I have just added the total column down and the total columns across and the totals match. Unfortunately, there are hundreds of these spreadsheets and I am just getting started".

"However, what I have found is that the spreadsheets Graziano identified as fraudulent contain multiple incorrect entries, and someone had gone to a great deal of trouble to arrange the numbers down each column and across each row in in such a way that the totals match order to hide cost bumps. However, when we compared the spreadsheet to the legitimate spreadsheet we were able to identify the differences. When we were done the number of altered entries totaled well over $3 million dollars on just a single spreadsheet. And, there were several such spreadsheets just for this one project.

"It is amazing", she said, "what I need to do now is connect those cost bumps to specific payments to individuals as there is corresponding data for each company that supplied materials or contributed as a subcontractor. If the payments don't align, then the next step is to see where the additional monies went. I suspect they went to individuals involved in the permitting process or some such place. Graziano kept amazing records and linked each of these spreadsheets to certain individuals involved along the way. We should be able to ultimately trace where the over-expenditures went, but that may take some time. I say 'we', because Interpol and the FBI have authorized a host of actuaries, many through private consulting companies, to assist".

"One thing is certain though; he had a genius of a financial guy. On the other hand, so am I. I should be able to develop an algorithm to assess these spreadsheets in the way we just started and link them to the invoices".

"As well, there are a lot of land purchases associated with several of the larger projects. It would be good to know what type of shell company, or partner company he was using to make those purchases quietly-purchases that occur, in some cases, over a couple of years, sometimes longer. Graziano had to have inside information to know what land to purchase, knowing that a project was being considered. It could be, or rather actually was likely, that he was bribing officials to build where he had already purchased or otherwise bribing officials to ascertain where to purchase the properties".

"I think both scenarios could be true", Timm piped in, depending on the project or state of government approvals. The other issue is that it may well be that these excess payments are being made through laundered money and if they are through a country that doesn't like to cooperate with our investigation, we may have difficulty connecting the dots. However, once Casandra and her future team uncover enough data it will be my job, along with another team of people to track down the individuals involved, perhaps confront, and ultimately lay charges against them".

"There is a lot of work ahead of you both", I empathized. "As far as getting cooperation from another country, it may be that John can help with that. If it's from a country that receives a lot of aid from the U.S., then we can put some pressure on that country to allow us to trace the transactions. Casandra, I assume you will be talking to your supervisor and that he is relatively highly placed within Interpol. I wonder if you could ask him if he would be willing to meet with me to help track down a missing piece of information from my other case, involving one Hans Goebel, which is taking me to Germany. I am of the opinion that that case is connected to this one very closely".

"Of course, she replied, but he is in Amsterdam. Maybe he can meet you in Munich. When will you be going"?

"I am meeting with John and Jeremy later this morning and then hopping on a plane. I will be available tomorrow, if such can be arranged".

"I will let you know, is there anything he can do in preparation for the meeting. Maybe it's possible a phone call would suffice, depending on what it is"?

"Maybe. I am interested in finding a man named Hans Goebel that has been identified in a will, leaving him some inheritance from

Graziano. I know that seems strange, but it seems to somehow be connected".

Casandra agreed to make the call and let him know and I gave Casandra my burner cell number to give to him. With that, we said goodbye and I headed over to John's office. Jeremy was already there once again. We went into the boardroom and after the usual pleasantries, Jeremy started right in.

CIA-FBI Update

. . . .

"TWO DAYS AGO, WE RAIDED the bayou buildings that Michelle's contacts had said were being used for all kinds of not very nice things by some very wealthy people. In the process of the swat team swarming one of the outposts, there was some exchange of gunplay, but the compound was not really well prepared and was not expecting the type of heavy assault we brought. Most importantly, amongst those we rounded up was Perez. He had chosen to go there to hide out, which somewhat brought into question whether Graziano was aware, or party to, these operations. In interviewing Perez, it became apparent very quickly that he was seriously afraid of being found by Alvarez. He asked for protection, of all things, and agreed to become states witness against the syndicate. As he talked, we got around to the question of whether he killed Tony Oreski and at that point he lawyered up. In the process however, he babbled on about how much hate he had for Oreski and Alvarez as he thought that one or the other had arranged Graziano's murder. Perez went on to say that he admired Graziano who had taken him out of the gutter, so to speak, and built a life for him within the syndicate. Then he said that neither Oreski or Alvarez would personally involve themselves in killing someone and, whoever they did hire, was someone to be very afraid of. Perez went on to explain that he had arranged to meet Oreski to delve into Graziano's murder, but that Oreski was already dead when he went into the prearranged meeting room. On top of that, we have interviewed all of the women who frequented the brothel, and none were willing to admit that they saw or heard anything connected to the murder".

John then added a bit more. "Jeremy also advised me that the forensic unit didn't find any evidence that Perez had actually been in the room where Oreski was killed. Of course, that doesn't necessarily mean it wasn't him. What it does mean though, is that at this point we don't have enough evidence to go to trial where the murder is concerned. However, there should be more than enough to hold him on multiple other charges as he starts to testify".

"With respect to James Ronaldo, or Jimron, the local police forensic unit also advised that there was no opportunity to confiscate any video tapes associated with his creation of false identities for various individuals. Whoever killed Ronaldo made sure there was no remaining evidence at his office. To date there is no indication of who committed that crime".

"I am curious", I piped in, was his home searched, was he married, family, all that stuff looked into"?

"Yes, he was married and living with his wife, no kids. We have not gotten a search warrant for his home as of yet. We'll see what information we get from the crime lab and go from there. It's possible that forensic evidence will turn up a clue or two as to who had been there recently".

I didn't share with John and Jeremy that Sheila was going to look into this as well. They would have seen that as a possible intrusion into their investigation. However, it is not unusual for a CIA operative to go about doing things behind the scenes, looking for his own avenues, and the same holds true for a private investigator.

"The other question I have regards Martinez. Throughout all of this investigation his name never seems to appear. What do we know about him and his whereabouts"?

"Martinez is an enigma", replied Jeremy. "We have difficulty keeping tabs on him, he comes around once in a while then just vanishes. It is rumored that he is responsible for Graziano's European operations, but Interpol have the same issue with him. On the one hand there are guys like Oreski, who like the limelight and reputation and then there are really bad guys like Martinez who is very secretive. No one knows where he actually lives, and he doesn't seem to hang out in nightclubs or places like that. Given we now have Perez, Hazel and Jimmy have turned their attention to him at this point, thinking that perhaps Martinez has an in with the FBI at some level. But so far, they have drawn a blank. Casandra suggested, that since you were on your way to Europe to check into Hans Goebel with her boss in Interpol, you might ask him about Martinez. Casandra said they have had a long-standing interest in Martinez, but she had not yet been able to determine is whereabouts when he came to Europe".

About that time Jeremy's phone pinged. It was the security firm that was monitoring Graziano's house, and they had sent through a video clip showing two men breaking through the gate and climbing out of their car. Neither man was known to me, but Jeremy speculated that they were there looking for the hard drives, which would have meant had known or been given information about the existence of the hard drives and had been told they might be at Graziano's house, hidden somewhere. Likely one was Martinez or perhaps both men worked for Martinez, because I couldn't think of anyone else who might have had access to the elevator codes inside the house. On the other hand, if they knew the elevator codes, then they would know the house was monitored by a security firm and that there were alarms. It was more likely that they had no idea about the codes and therefore were not likely connected to Martinez. I was thinking that this was a red herring, someone set this up as a distraction. But to what end?

"Whoever went in had to go through the police tape, thereby knowingly breaking at least that law", said Jeremy. "I suspect we can add break and enter to that as well. We should have a good chance of still catching the person in the house. As soon as the call comes through, I'll put it on the speaker. Hopefully, we can get some useful evidence from this".

While we were waiting for the call, I filled Jeremy in on my planned trip to Europe and my chat with Casandra and Timm, along with the evidence on the spreadsheets. He asked again if I had time to create a budget to house witnesses in the bayou but this time, I asked why the FBI itself didn't develop its own budget for this purpose. Jeremy figured that there was still an outside chance that there was still a senior FBI official or someone with access to FBI inside knowledge that could compromise the witnesses or worse, eliminate them. For now, they wanted to keep that portion of the operation separate from anyone within the agency. I agreed to spend some time on it before I left Fort Lauderdale, given that squirreling witnesses away in safe house was nothing new. It would not take me more than a few hours.

A few minutes later the phone rang, and Jeremy just talked to the person on the other end. When he hung up, he said that the men breaking in were caught, but unknown to the police or FBI. They claimed to have been paid some amount of money to do exactly what they had done. The best explanation for this was that someone was still wanting to know if Graziano's house was alarmed or monitored in some other way. The point is someone wanted access to the property. The question is, given the time passage, someone like Martinez would have known about the alarm system and by now, if he had been aware of the hard drives, would have disappeared. Whoever set this up was wanting to gain access for another reason. There had to be another motivation. At that point, Jeremy called Hazel and Jimmy advising them what had occurred and had the exact same discussion with them. As they were the ones to first search the house, it was logical for them to go back. At this point I continued to withhold my information about the secret room and the escape tunnel.

Also at this time, I figured the meeting was over and we all agreed to check in when I returned from overseas. I took my leave and went to the hotel to prepare a budget for Jeremy and emailed it in. Food and operating costs basically as the outposts in the swamp, now under FBI control, had adequate buildings to house the witnesses to be placed there. Transportation would be surreptitious and handled through Michelle and the people she knew. When done, I booked a flight to Munich for the next day, under my own identity. I then called Casandra and she advised that a senior Interpol official would meet me at the airport.

The next morning, I called Sheila to touch base. "Well, helloooo", she hummed on the phone, as bright and cheerful as ever. Now why would you be calling me"?

"Just wanted to say hello, hope you are missing me", I joked. I then filled her in on the meeting with John and Jeremy and the news about James Ronaldo. "Perfect," she said, "I have already determined where he lives, that his wife works during the day, and I should arrive in Miami tomorrow, early. I didn't call the wife to advise I wanted in because that would have alerted her to hide anything if she knew about it. Although I guess she may have done so as soon as she heard he had been killed, if she even knew about any of his underworld activity".

"I will make it into his house in good time, disable the security system and should have the full day to look for any evidence he may have hidden there. Especially video tapes and financial data. I am wondering, though, if the murderer cleaned house at his office, maybe they also cleaned office at his house, so to speak".

"It's possible", I volunteered, "or they, whoever they are, may have taken longer to determine where he lives, and you may need to be very careful going in as well as keeping an eye on the outside to ensure no one is already watching the premises. It would be good to reset the alarm after you are in and plan an escape route in case someone shows up while you are inside. Maybe we'll get lucky on this one".

"On the other fronts, have you had a chance to check into the CEO, and get more depth on Jesse and Louise"?

"With those three, she replied, I have assigned a team member to each of them. It may take a couple of days to get detailed information". And with that, I am just out the door", she said, "call me when you are on your way to Malaga and let me know what is happening".

"Shall do", I replied, "except for getting into Ronaldo's home, there is no real time urgency. The FBI will take a while to go through all the data and arrange for charges to be laid given the scope of the investigation. If all goes well maybe you can meet me in Malaga and we can spend a week together hanging out around there".

"Sounds wonderful, I will now expect that will happen, when do you think you will be there"?

"it's too early to say. It will depend on who Hans Goebel is and whether I can arrange to meet with him. As soon as I know more, I will call you". And with that said, I was out the door and off to the Airport.

Munich, Interpol and Hans Goebel

I ARRIVED IN THE LATE afternoon and was greeted by a man holding a sign with my name on it. I walked up to him and held out my hand. He didn't shake a paw! Rather he announced that he was the driver for one Mr. Van de Vries and would I please join him in the car? I followed him out and got in the back of a Mercedes e class sedan and was greeted by an elderly gentleman, with greying hair, about 3 inches taller than me, wearing a fedora and a topcoat which I must have obviously admired. "Do you like it he asked, made by Dries Van Noten, cost a pretty euro, but it is warm and classy"!

"It is very nice", I replied, "obviously a Dutch company, I am guessing"?

"Non", he replied, "Belgian. I am on my way to a meeting of some importance. I figured I could just catch you here for a few minutes and then be on my way. Can we give you a lift anywhere? My driver, just so you know, has top level security clearance and has been a Captain in the Police Nationale. We may speak freely with him, and he may have some insights as well. My understanding from Casandra is that you want to locate a German gentleman by the name of Hans Goebel. Is that correct"?

As glanced for just a moment to see our driver smile. "Yes, that is the case," I replied, "I assume Casandra briefed you on my search for Graziano's daughter, Michelle Savonne. As you are likely now aware, Michelle was undercover with the FBI working a case involving drugs and human trafficking. I believe there may be some connection between the search for Michelle and Graziano's murder itself. As for the ride somewhere, I guess I will just check into my hotel for now and drop off my luggage etc. Tell me what you can".

"Well", he began, "Graziano has been on our radar for some time and efforts to find substantial evidence had eluded us for quite some time as I am sure you know by now. In addition, he has, shall we call him a lieutenant, by the name of Martinez, a man we know to be a Spanish national. Martinez comes and goes, but he always uses assumed names and is obviously careful going through airports, if he even uses them, so we have never been able to get facial and body recognition software to catch him so that we could tail him. But the name Hans Goebel is very intriguing as it relates to Graziano, just how did you come across that name. We haven't really ever told anyone outside of our own little circle about that name".

"It was referred to in a will I found in Graziano's house. However, because of the possible leak within the FBI, I have kept that card close to my chest and have not shared this knowledge with anyone. Graziano is leaving a tidy sum to one Mr. Hans Goebel and because of all the connections in the case, I decided I should track him down. You see, Graziano left a nice sum to the private investigator he had hired to watch over his estranged daughter. As I mentioned, she now coincidently works for the FBI on a case that is at least partially linked to Graziano. Through my efforts and also the daughter of the private investigator, who now runs the detective agency, we were able to locate Graziano's daughter and inform her that Graziano has left her significant wealth thorough legitimate businesses, and that he had appointed a CEO to run those operations. The father of the private investigator, one John Sterling, retired to France and died shortly thereafter. The will left him a place in Malaga, where I intend to go next".

"In addition, the will also left proceeds to the lawyer who did work relating to Graziano's legal operations. As it turns out, however, this lawyer's daughter was married to an FBI agent that was killed at the same time and place as Graziano. It now turns out that Graziano himself had bribed the agent to infiltrate some secret or unknown organization in an attempt to discover who they were and what they were planning. There was a third person named in the will, Hans Goebel. Under the circumstances he could be a good guy or a bad guy. I have tried locating him in person but have been unsuccessful. That is where you come in. I have an address, but"....

Van de Vries held up his hand stopping my monologue. "I am sorry", he interjected, did you say you have an address? How did you come by that address"? he asked, as the driver abruptly pulled over to the curb.

"It was included in the will, or at least the reference to a flat in Munich is".

"Amazing", he said, "we have been looking to find Hans Goebel and have never been able to locate an address anywhere in Europe. It is as though the man never existed and does not currently exist. Van de Vries then took the time to explain to me what he knew about Hans Goebel.

I listened to his information, or shall I say, the lack thereof as it related to Hans Goebel. "There is one more question I wish to ask and that relates to Casandra. I am guessing she works for you directly, but I would still like your commentary regarding her ethics and legal integrity".

"Casandra is beyond reproach", Van de Vries responded, "she has been instrumental is salting away several high-profile criminals and we were all looking forward to end Graziano's work in Europe. She is very trusted by everyone in the legal community".

"That is great to hear", I responded, and thanked him for that information.

I salted away the information regarding Hans Goebel away for future reference, and they dropped me off at the hotel, reminding me to be very cautious. I went out for a beer, after all, it's Munich, a bite to eat, and back for a good night's rest. The next morning, I got a taxi, as I don't like Ubers, and headed to the address for the flat of the Hans Goebel.

As it turned out, this was no flat, but rather an office in a modern office building. There was a single receptionist behind a desk and a single door leading to an office or offices behind her.

"Good morning", I volunteered, I wonder if you could help me? I am looking to find a Mr. Hans Goebel. My name is Jeff Atkinson, and I am in possession of a will that leaves some significant funds to Mr. Goebel".

"Well", she replied, "we are always happy to receive monies. This office, however, is basically a place for our staff or clients to pick up emergent mail or deliveries or sometimes obtain directives for a new venture. Our facilities are actually out of town, and if you were to visit there, you may be introduced to Hans Goebel". As she gave me directions, she smiled, as if she had a secret she had no intention to share.

I left the building, hailed a taxi, and provided the directions she had given. The drive took 45 minutes and ended at a large estate bordering the edge of Munich. Entry to the estate was controlled by an electronic gate, giving the appearance of being very private. However, as the taxi pulled up the gates were opened without any security request. We drove up to the entrance to the front door of an impressive castle-like structure. The architecture was obviously medieval and very imposing, but above the front doors, the signage, in both English and German read: 'Huber Adventure Resort and Hotel".

I paid the taxi driver, went to the front desk and explained to the desk clerk that I was here to see Hans Goebel. The receptionist asked if I had a reservation and I replied that I had not, but that I had heard this was a good place to stay.

"Did someone refer you", she asked.

"Hans Goebel", was my reply, to which she just smiled.

She then asked if I had been made aware of the programs that they offered, to which I replied that I was not, only that it was a good place to have some fun while on a trip.

"Well, that is partly true", she said with a smile. "Only we take our fun very seriously. We provide recreational military training to begin with but if someone shines in the fun part, we sometimes offer that person actual employment in a somewhat military vein, as mercenaries, where we are hired to undertake things such as rescue missions. What we won't do is get involved in an actual war or we would never be able to replace our losses given this is a private operation".

"What does the fun part of the training involve", I asked.

"Well", she began, "all our training is small hand guns and hand to hand combat including some with knives and a few exotic means. The firearm training is limited to a week, but the hand-to-hand combat training can take much more time. Of course, if you are only interested in the recreational side of things, we also have a world class spa, swimming pools, a fully equipped gym, a couple of basketball courts, tennis courts, etc., everything you need to have a great vacation without leaving the premises. And, of course, three exceptional restaurants. The estate has a number of trails into the surrounding woods, so hiking is a great past time here".

"Sounds idyllic. What is the fee for a week's stay"?

"It is $750 euros a day, but if you choose to become a full-fledged member of our organization the fee will be returned. After that, the wages are truly exceptional. May I ask more about this Hans Goebel you mentioned"?

I chose to not share what I had learned from Van de Vries. "Actually, I have never met the man. Only that I was a lawyer, my name is Jeff Atkinson, and I am in possession of a will left by a man named Graziano which leaves some significant funds to Hans Goebel. The will has yet to be executed and I have had some issues finding all the people named. I was hoping someone here could assist me with that".

"We likely can", she offered, Hans often comes here so I am sure we can arrange something. We are very familiar with Graziano and were saddened when news of his death reached us. I believe Hans is currently living in the United States and if I am not mistaken, that would be in New Orleans. Given that Graziano was in West Palm Beach, I am somewhat surprised that he did not leave a New Orleans address for Hans. However, we can dig that out of our records and maybe text you the information".

"That would be very great", I responded, "but since I am here, could I get a tour of the rooms and the grounds. I might just decide to spend a bit more time here in the near future. I am a single man, at loose ends, if you will, and this sounds like a great retreat with some action and adventure".

"Sure thing", she replied, I will have one of our staff come out and join you shortly. Is there anything specific or would you like to see everything"?

"I think I am most interested in the military aspect. Is it possible to have someone show me that today, while people are performing"?

"Certainly, I will be right back". In a few minutes she came back out with a large, bulked up man in his late thirties, was my best guess. He took me through the grounds as men and women were practicing firearm training as well as another area of hand-to-hand combat training.

"With respect to the recruitment of people into the paramilitary side of the program, how do you choose who goes into that, does everyone actually get accepted"?

"Absolutely not. We develop a psychological profile. They must have a willingness to risk their own life with limited fear. We do recruit people that are married and may have a family, so their assignments tend to be in less risky areas of the world. As well they have to be willing and able to follow orders and not go around doing their own thing. It doesn't always work out, but we are pretty successful in identifying the right candidates. With that in mind and your expression of interest in the military side of things, I am guessing you have some military background. What do you think, would you be interested in looking at this"?

"Maybe in time I will consider this, depending on the type of assignment for which you might deem me qualified. I do have background with the U.S. military, as do many of our citizens, but it has never been a career. I am currently just finishing up a project and will look into it in a month or two. I like the concept of an organization that takes on rescue missions. Can you tell me anything about the type of rescue missions involved"?

"We undertake missions in a manner that the authorities cannot legally, such as if an event has occurred that crosses international boundaries. For example, a high profile kidnapping where the individual or child involved is spirited away and wealthy parents are involved and want us to chase it down. Our services in this regard are basically spread by word of mouth amongst wealthy people".

I left it at that and decided to head back to my hotel room. The operation I had just looked at was cleverly designed and now I was able to call Van de Vries back and let him know what he had asked me to do. When I got back, I called de Vries and filled him in and then called Sheila.

"Hi stranger", she said, it's been a whole two days and I was wondering if you had forgotten me".

"Well, you also have a phone with my number in it", I teased back. I then filled her in on my meeting with Van de Vries and asked what she had learned in the meantime.

"I spent the better part of the day in James Ronald's house looking for evidence from his identity scam operation. I found a wealth of data, most of it labelled with the names of what I believe may be false identities. I have not had a chance to review them in any detail and plan to have a couple of my staff go through them to see if they can identify the dates the videos were filmed. If that is possible, we should be able to see who enters his office on the day in question. I will then turn my attention to the CEO, Jesse and Louise, but I suspect they are all clean as a whistle, whatever that means. I have already assigned staff to look into these three and they will let me know what they find".

"Sounds about right", I said, "which means you are at loose ends, or at least don't need to be where you are. I am on my way to Malaga tomorrow, to see what will likely become your villa. Why don't you fly over and join me. I think you are looking at two days from now, so I will have already been there for a day when your plane lands. And, unless something odd happens, we have at least a week to spend together doing very little".

"I'm already on the internet booking a flight and should be there tomorrow", she said. "It will be nice to just let go of all this intrigue for a bit. There are things to see in Malaga, I know, but I also think we could take a trip up to Ronda, I hear it's a great spot".

"Sure", I replied, I will look into it and see if we can stay overnight somewhere, let me know when your plane lands and I will meet you at the airport".

Malaga

· ·

I ARRIVED BEFORE NOON AND rented a car. Rather than booking a hotel I went straight to the villa as the address was provided in the will. Not having a key, I managed to find a spare under a flowerpot, at the back of the house, having climbed over a gate to get into the garden. There was no alarm system. The villa was superb, two master suites, a large sitting room with a wood burning fireplace, a well-appointed kitchen, and a great patio and yard, and very private surrounded by a 10 foot high cement fence. The property was very dusty and had not been used for some time, probably not since John Sterling had passed. I unpacked, did a little research on the area and how to get to Ronda from Malaga, received a text from Sheila and noted that her plane was arriving after supper. I was curious as to why Graziano would have left this property alone after Sterling had passed away, and then thought that maybe Sterling used it to maintain or even hide materials from his life as a PI. That led to a comprehensive search and after some time, found a combination safe built into the wall in a closet, behind clothes that were still there, and in the room that was not the main suite. I decided it could, and maybe should, wait for Sheila and I went out for a bite and then off to the airport to pick her up. On the way I told her about the safe and suggested we should maybe get a cleaning service to bring the house back to ship shape. She agreed that would be a good idea. We arrived back at the house a little after eight. She unpacked and said the first thing she wanted to do was head to the shower.

"That sounds good to me, how about I join you in a few minutes"?

"Sure", she replied, with a bit of a smile. A few minutes later we were together without any clothes, because, after all, what good are clothes in a shower? We spent some time soaping each other thoroughly, I ensured certain spots received extra attention and turned her around so I could spend some time on her back, then my hands went around to her belly and down inside her thighs. "Let's go to the bedroom, I suggested, the shower is just too awkward".

Later she turned into me and nestled her head into my neck, in the space between my shoulder and my head, and laid quietly breathing in and out. Pure heaven!

The next morning, we laid together for a while cuddling and chatted about the safe. Sheila decided she wanted to leave it for now and just spend some time together, so we planned a couple of excursions around the city and then one out to Ronda, which is situated at the top of the Andalusian Mountain range. It was Sheila's turn to drive, lucky me, as the road up was a wee bit on the nerve-racking side given my fear of heights. Not being used to winding mountain roads, we were amazed at the motorcycles zooming by at well over the speed limit. Near the top we came across a restaurant, or maybe I should say a roadhouse, with all the bikes parked outside. We decided a break from the drive was in order and went in to order a coffee and settle our nerves-well, maybe just mine! A few miles further on we came across a leather store-way up here by itself and decided to stop on the way back. Yet another few miles on the road opened up to a huge valley, quite the surprise. It seemed surreal to me that there was a massive, flat valley at the very top of the mountain range.

We parked the vehicle just outside a castle wall and walked the rest of the way. At the town square is the bandolero museum, which was worth a visit. We also wondered to the bullfight arena, the oldest and touted as the original bullfighting arena in Spain and now a museum showing famous bulls, matadors, costumes and so forth and you can walk into the arena itself. Ronda has also influenced the likes of Hemingway and Orson Wells whose ashes are buried in a well of a retired bullfighter that was his friend. One of the bullfighting costumes was created by Giorgio Armani for an event in 2009, and the town served as the setting for a flower market in the movie, *Fredinand.*

"How about we go grab a bite to eat", Sheila suggested, I saw a restaurant with a balcony that looks out over the valley, maybe just desert". We walked in and were seated outside right on the edge of the balcony suspended above the canyon. The drop is about 300 feet. "I can't sit here", I winced, feeling vertigo setting in, "I get dizzy on the bathroom scale, so I'm moving to the far side of the table".

Sheila laughed and ordered a full meal and I decided to just have some kind of dessert I pointed at on the menu. When the meal came, I was presented with a full fish and other fixings. Way up here at the top of the mountain range! Later, when paying the bill, I asked how come I got a full meal. The gentleman taking the money simply said, "We only serve full meals at this time of the day, we selected that for you, hope you liked it"!

We wandered through the town for the rest of the day, taking a few pictures, stopping for a wine and enjoying the sun. On the drive back down the mountain, coming around a corner, a herd of donkeys were crossing the highway, and it was necessary to stop while they decided what to do. All in all, a great day with some adventure. We got back to the villa, decided on a light meal which we made ourselves and accompanied that with a nice bottle of dry red wine.

"Maybe we should intersperse our sightseeing with a look at what might be in the safe", Sheila suggested. "My dad used certain numbers for the safe we had at the office, and I knew the combination to that. It's likely the same combination. He wouldn't leave anything like this to chance".

"I like that idea", I responded, "if we find something to look at, we take a day or two seeing the sights and letting our brains digest it, if it is of value. At the very least it will have a sentimental value for you".

Shelia went to the closet and removed the clothing. The safe was large, about 18 inches by two feet, not a typical office safe. She plugged in some numbers and the safe opened on her first try. She reached in and pulled out several large envelopes. As she handed them to me, one by one I placed them on the bed. They were dated by year, for the 5 years prior to John Sterling's death. In addition, were several video CDs. We decided to watch the videos first.

At some point John Sterling must have decided to do his own investigation into Graziano, unrelated to the work that which Graziano had asked his agency to do to keep track of Michelle Savonne. One specific video showed entry into the Huber Adventure Resort and Hotel where he had filmed conversations with Perez and a man we believed to be Martinez, as well as others. There was ample evidence to bring cases forward with respect to financial irregularities shall we say. Much was augmented with photographs that identified specific individuals in the process of being bribed, money envelopes being exchanged and so forth.

"This is an absolute gold mine as it relates to our case. It is interesting who we find in these videos with Martinez. It is also fascinating that there doesn't seem to be any indication of Graziano".

"That is very telling to my way of thinking", responded Sheila. I am thinking that Graziano may have hired my father to investigate this Huber organization, and I now wonder if Graziano had this data himself. Certainly, if Graziano was unaware of the association between these individuals, it would cause him some concern. I wonder though if this is the only data, perhaps it never was shared with anyone, and my father passed away before it was sent anywhere. There is no mention in Graziano's tapes".

"I suspect you are correct Sheila", I responded. "I am thinking this is the organization that Graziano had the rogue FBI agent, Diane's husband, infiltrate. If that is the case, then Graziano must have been given some of that information. He knew about someone named Hans Goebel, who is definitely connected in some way to the Huber organization. In any event, this is the motherload and we need to bring Interpol, the FBI and the CIA all into the picture".

The next morning Sheila decided to check in with staff she had assigned to look into the CEO, Jesse and Louise. "Well, I think that part of our private investigation has come to a close, she said and given what we have, maybe you want to head back to the states and share this with the FBI"?

"Absolutely"!! Was my reply. "let's book our flights and then I will call John and have him arrange a meeting. I would also like to find out if anything more has been learned from Perez since he is in custody".

"You know", teased Sheila, when this is all said and done, I am going to sell my agency and come to the villa for an extended period of time. This is a beautiful setting and I think you should come and live with me and see how it goes. The way I look at your past is it just made you what you are today, and I kind of like that."

"You've never married or lived with anyone for any length of time, so are you asking if I want to have an extended fling, or maybe something more long term"?

"Definitely more long term. I am not a spring chicken anymore and think it might be nice to settle down with someone I enjoy having a good time with. Not only that, but if you think about it, we have a lot of investigation stories we could share with each other. That could go on for a long time".

"Well, a good relationship is hard to find, believe me I have had my share of failures. Are you sure you want to risk a guy like me, or am I the one taking the risk? Maybe you'll just tire of me quickly as well. Anyway, I am willing to give it a try. But before we do that, let's see what we can accomplish with the whole Graziano, Oreski, Alvarez, Ronaldo thing".

And with that said, I phoned John and asked him to set up the meeting with Jeremy, Casandra, Timm, Hazel, and Jimmy so that we could share what we had discovered, both in Malaga and in Munich. I also phoned Van de Vries and briefed him. He inquired as to whether he could come to the U.S. and join that meeting. I phoned John back and asked. A few hours later he returned that call and said that Jeremy was okay with all of that, and that Jeremy, given the relationship to Michelle, had called Michelle and arranged that we would meet at Graziano's house in a very grand great room. Apparently, Jeremy decided to ask Michelle to invite Louise and Jesse as well. I expressed that I did not think that to be a good idea and John explained his reasoning. I then asked John to bring me up to speed on the status of the Oreski murder and the interrogation of Perez, as well as what was known or not about the Ronaldo murder.

"Well," John began, "Jeremy said that Perez, despite his terrible past was terrified of both Martinez and Alvarez. Perez had said that he would be willing to become states witness but that in exchange for testimony, he wanted witness protection and freedom. Jeremy agreed to the protection, freedom, change of identity piece, plastic surgery included at government expense, as Perez apparently has significant information and data on the operation of the Alvarez cartel. The deal is predicated on the evidence being sufficient to put Alvarez and Martinez away for a long time, if not for the murder itself. That would mean bringing the Mexican authorities into the picture. Perez went into some depth to explain how much he admired Graziano, as Graziano had picked him up at a young age, when he was having all sorts of teenage troubles. Perez virtually thinks that Graziano is like a father to him and gave him a new beginning and what has, up to today, amounted to a pretty great life. He believes that either Alvarez or Martinez arranged for Oreski to kill Graziano. He said he had followed Oreski to the brothel, to confront him, but instead, at least this is his story, yet to be verified somehow, is that Oreski was already dead when he went into the room. Despite this, Jeremy agreed to the plea deal because of the wealth of other evidence regarding Martinez, Alvarez and Graziano himself".

"As for Ronaldo he continued, Hazel and Jimmy seem to think that Ronaldo was murdered because he had information that would be incriminating to Graziano's murderer, which would imply fake identification and passports accompanied with pictures and videos. Given that Hazel and jimmy have basically finished their investigation of the FBI itself, the Ronaldo investigation has now been turned over to them".

"Well, John", I said, "Sheila and I are likely to be able to fill in most of the blanks, but we would like to see the video surveillance of Murder Street as well as Oreski's murder to round out our suspicions, although I believe they are relatively accurate".

Graziano's House

WHEN I GOT BACK TO the states, I phoned Michelle and asked if she had time to meet with me and go see Graziano's home, her father's home. She agreed to meet me at the FBI offices in West Palm Beach and travel with me over to the house. Jeremy had arranged to give me access as the security codes had all been changed, with the one exception of tunnel access. We went in through the front gate and entered the house using the front door as opposed to the garage. We spent some time going through the 'normal' parts of the house-kitchen, den, and the great room which housed a board room sized table and chairs, all rich maroon leather and oak wood.

"This is where we will have the meeting", I explained to Michelle. "When we are here, all the serving staff will be trained agents". I then took Michelle up the elevator to the exterior office and the secret office as well. But I did not show her the tunnel access. I went through an explanation of bringing her father here and his handing me the files and also how I found the will. I explained that his dying wish was that I find her and provide her with the information needed to access your businesses and the monies they have generated for you.

Michelle's reaction to being in the house where he died, as well as the kind of man she now knew him to be was very mixed. She asked if she could have some time alone, wandering through the house, and I agreed that would be a good thing for her to do. I excused myself and went back to the grand room and waited for her.

When she got back and was ready to leave, I explained to her that we wanted to use the grand room as a place to discuss the murders and indicated the range of people we intended to be present in the house. The idea of identifying, or developing a plan to identify her father's murder in his own home, appealed to her.

I wondered out loud if Jesse and Louise might be persuaded to help out and suggested as well that she invite them over right away the next day, show them the house and obtain their help in setting up the food and beverages, be there during the event to be hosts, and set up the meeting room, given all the people that will be here. Michelle thought maybe it was a little odd, but replied that she would love to do that and would look after it all. Twenty days later everyone arrived within 10 minutes of each other.

Jeremy began. "We have gathered you all here today so we can all share our respective knowledge of the Graziano murder as well as those of Tony Oreski and James Ronaldo as they are all connected. By the end of the meeting, we should have a plan to move forward and hopefully resolve these cases. Graziano, your father, as you now know Michelle, was planning to turn over a significant amount of evidence to the FBI and Interpol regarding his operations. Unfortunately, as he was travelling to hand over this information he was murdered, and in a very public way, and in a way that took a lot of coordination. We have considered a number of possibilities, including even the possibility that Brock, who happened upon the crime scene by accident may have been involved. Brock, do you want to jump in here and explain what occurred as you took a wounded Graziano back to this estate"?

"Sure", I piped in. "As I watched the event unfold on what is now known as Murder Street, I saw that everyone involved was dead with the exception of a wounded Graziano. He had with him a briefcase with several hard drives, explained he was turning states evidence and insisted I take him back to this house where he turned over the hard drives. He provided me with funds and gave me the name of someone to provide me with fake identities. He implored the necessity of this as he did not trust anyone other than the agents he was working with-Casandra and Timm here. What he first wanted me to do however, was to find his daughter Michelle, and provide her with knowledge of a set of legal businesses created with her as owner. Graziano had employed a private investigation firm, which was owned by Shelia's father, to keep track of Michelle as she was growing up as he had committed to Michelle's mother to keep his distance and stay out of their lives. He continued to receive updates until Michelle was in her thirties, when she joined the FBI. She then disappeared from surveillance as she had gone undercover, along with several other agents to investigate drug and human trafficking that turned out to involve Alvarez as well as Oreski. At this time, I had no idea where to find Casandra and Timm and it was much later that I was able to turn the hard drives over. Best to hand this back over to you Jeremy".

"No, I think Hazel should outline her investigative outcomes at this point".

Hazel began. "The death of a rogue FBI agent at the scene, killed by one of his own compatriots at the scene, led us to believe that someone high up in the FBI itself may have been involved. As a result, we were hired as outside investigators, known only as Jimmy and Hazel, to look into the FBI itself. We concluded the agent had been corrupted by someone and was now considered a possible liability that needed to be eliminated. Our theory was that Tony Oreski was planning something large with respect to taking over some of Graziano's territory and we now know that he had formed an association with a Mexican cartel led by a man named Alvarez. As time went on, we were able to eliminate senior FBI officials as suspects and turned our attention to possible connections within Oreski's and Alvarez's organizations. We combined our efforts with the FBI at that point, given that one of the deceased was an FBI agent involved without authority to be there. We were able to connect the agent in question to Graziano's own organization but were unable to identify the group of assassins he was working with. As a result of eventually working with Casandra, we were able to trace his bank deposits of somewhat large amounts which were then used to pay off gambling debts. The funds came from one of Graziano's illegitimate businesses, but until recently we weren't able to determine what organization Graziano was attempting to infiltrate".

"Brock, back to you".

"Thanks. I followed Graziano's advice and visited his contact in Miami, to arrange fake IDs, a man who called himself Jimron, whose name is actually James Ronaldo. I collected the hard drives and headed to New Orleans to honor the request to find Graziano's daughter. I had not yet met Casandra and Timm so was not willing to turn the hard drives over to anyone else in the FBI or Interpol. As a result of the FBI identifying me, John and the CIA were brought into the mix of people and I provided him with knowledge of events. While arranging the IDs I had forgotten to take the monies from Graziano and went back to his place. In the process I discovered a will leaving funds to three people-someone named jeff Atkinson, a lawyer, a John Sterling, the private investigator hired by Graziano to keep him apprised of his daughter, and which is how I met Sheila who now owns the investigator business. The third name on the list was Hans Goebel, who was apparently from Munich. Oddly, these three names were the names Ronaldo provided to me to use as fake identities. At first we thought Graziano must have always had these identities for himself as a backup plan in case something went awry with his becoming states witness. As it turned out, my appearance was coincidently similar to the rogue FBI agent Graziano had corrupted so we ultimately figured the will and planned IDs were originally intended for that agent. Graziano must have recognized this possibility when I came to his rescue".

Sheila"?

"When I arranged to meet with Jeff Atkinson's daughter, Diane, it turned out that she was married to the FBI agent in question, killed at the murder scene. Graziano had been using Diane's father as lawyer for his legitimate businesses and in the process, he discovered that Diane's husband worked for the FBI. Graziano had convinced them he was going to go straight and turn states evidence".

"Graziano learned that they were having financial troubles and met with the agent in question, Diane's husband, and bribed him to go under cover in this other somewhat secret organization. We believe the agent was also motivated, not just by money, but the possibility of enhancing his career within the FBI, since he believed he was helping Graziano to turn states evidence. When I met with Diane, sometime after her husband had been killed at Murder Street, she contracted with me, asking me to prove her husband's innocence. Hazel"?

"Yes, when Jimmy and I joined forces with the FBI we attended at the morgue and discovered that the agent looked a great deal like Brock. Up until then we were not sure whether Brock's involvement was just a coincidence or something more sinister. It did turn out that the agent in question and Brock are of similar age, height, body build and looks. We now also believe the identities in the will were intended for the agent, but that went south when the agent was killed, Graziano was wounded, and Brock just happened to be there. We believe Graziano saw the resemblance and knowing he was dying, took the risk of asking Brock to find Michelle, a task he was originally going to ask the agent to perform. At that point we concluded that Brock's involvement was truly a coincidence. Mr. Van de Vries?"

"Jeremy contacted me as it turned out that the majority of the deceased assassins at Murder Street were European. At that point, I then turned our attention, along with the FBI to the remaining deceased at Graziano's murder scene to see if we could establish any connections. As we at Interpol were already involved with Graziano and as Martinez is Spanish, we felt that there was a likely connection, and that perhaps Martinez was responsible. We were able to identify most but not all of the suspects. Unfortunately, no further connections were made at the time".

"Weeks later, Brock came to see me asking about this person named Hans Goebel, and said he had an address given to him by Graziano. The name Hans Goebel was known to us, but we were never able to find him. Brock agreed to keep us informed and he then reported back a few days later. Brock"?

"The address given for Hans Goebel was in the will and was an office staffed with a single receptionist, although there were empty offices in the back. The office was simply identified as an employment agency, dedicated to hiring temps. She stated that their regular staff used the offices from time to time and just came back to the office location to pick up mail and assignments. When I said I was looking for Hans Goebel, she gave me an address on the outskirts of Munich. I got the impression that she would not have done so had I not used the name. She gave me instructions and I visited what turned out to be a large, castled estate which provided a range of what were called adventure experiences, including military style training. I am convinced that this was not a hotel at all, and admission was granted to me only through the use of the name Hans Goebel. I asked and received a tour but when I inquired about meeting Hans Goebel was told that he was currently, she believed, in the U.S., maybe New Orleans. I then reported all this back to Van who said he would take the investigation in Germany from there. At his time, I went to Malaga where Sheila and I spent some time and made more discoveries. Sheila"?

"In the will mentioned earlier, Graziano left a villa in Malaga to my father in recognition, we believe, for the work done in keeping him apprised of his daughter. It turns out that my father was both investigating Graziano himself and also working on behalf of Graziano to investigate the Huber estate and Hans Goebel. He had accumulated a significant amount of evidence. In the villa that my father spent his vacation time, we discovered a large safe which was filled with video, tapes, photos etc".

"With my father's passing the investigation into Huber continued as my father had employed additional European investigators, with funds from Graziano. When we discovered this at the villa, Brock and I contacted the investigators still involved. When Graziano was murdered they ceased the investigation and had planned to turn over the evidence they collected to Interpol. We just happened to contact them a few days before they were about to do just that".

Sheila added to the sequence of events. "When brock and I contacted the investigators, I was able to prove that I was my father's daughter and owner of the agency. They accepted our explanation, given we had access to the villa and all the evidence my father had accumulated up to that point. They indicated that they occasionally met with Graziano to fill him in on events and shared certain videos with us. At this point we all concluded it was time to bring what we had to Interpol".

These recent videos included a significant number of surreptitiously recorded meetings between Martinez, Perez and others, complete with audio. Unfortunately, he died suddenly, form a heart attack and none of his work came to light until now. That is, until Brock and I discovered the safe and had a chance to go through it. We, and the other investigators involved, have turned all this over to the FBI and Interpol. However, amongst the findings were startling pieces of information. Van"?

"Brock and Sheila brought me up to date on what they had discovered. Amongst the findings was data on Hans Goebel from which we were able to piece together enough to know who Hans Goebel is. Rather, perhaps I should say who and what. To begin with the estate on the outskirts of Munich as well as the office in Munich is a large wealthy enterprise constituted in Saudi Arabia. You see, Hans Goebel, first and foremost, is a business and it is a business that supplies mercenaries, usually to business enterprises in, for example, African countries where security or more aggressive action is deemed required by companies requiring security. However, in addition, we believe that they also supply assassins in the event someone wants someone taken out. In this latter case, the assassin travels as a representative of a business enterprise called Hanss Goebel which is actually as subsidiary of the Huber estate. So, you see, Hans Goebel can be anyone, and likely anyone who is a member of the Huber Adventure organization. At this point we do not have enough evidence to take down the resort, given its international construct, but maybe certain individuals can be apprehended. Casandara"?

"Large donations go to the Huber enterprise from Graziano's syndicate. It was largely funding a significant part of the Huber resort. Moreover, from the video data supplied from the vault in Sheila's villa, Martinez was a regular visitor, and his name appears on the Board of Directors as constituted in Saudi Arabia. We now theorize that Graziano was unaware of the Huber enterprise and the funds going there from his syndicate until just recently. We have been able to ascertain that Martinez was siphoning funds from the Graziano syndicate. We were also able to ascertain, from the data supplied by Sheila, that the FBI agent with whom Graziano had contracted, i.e., Diane Atkinson's husband, was placed inside Huber to get information on Martinez for Graziano. We theorize that Graziano had discovered Martinez was planning a coup".

"We were also able to track funds going from the Huber estate to James Ronaldo's bank account, to finance an alternate identity for someone to murder Oreski and maybe Perez. It now appears that eliminating Ronaldo was also important as a loose end. As his office was ransacked, he must have had records of some type. We were able to trace funds through offshore shell corporations, in order to determine several missing puzzle pieces. Jeremy"?

"I am very sorry to do this Michelle, but I am placing both Jesse and Louise under arrest for their part in Graziano's criminal actions".

As he spoke, agents moved across the room and secured both women in handcuffs.

Jeremy continued. "You see, Jesse is a real estate agent and although she lives modestly, she has been the brain trust in the purchase of lands and resources for the crime syndicate. And Louise, in a similar vein, is the financial guru behind the secrecy of funding the transactions that enable Graziano to corrupt a range of officials and fund criminal operations. They were both recruited long ago and learned their craft from older stalwarts no longer alive. Amongst the charges that we will be levying, is conspiracy to commit murder. All of this is documented in the hard drives supplied by Brock, that were given to him by Graziano and the other investigators in Europe. We have been able to keep a rather long chain of events intact. In fact, there will be more than one such charge of murder where Louise in concerned".

A hush fell across the room as everyone turned to see Michelle's reaction. For more than a few moments she stood speechless, as if frozen in time. Then I could see her anger swell. Her body tensed, her fists clenched and her eyes narrowed as she stood and moved towards Louise and Jesse.

"This, this is the utmost betrayal", she screamed at them. "How could you, just how could you? Both of you. You played this game, a game of deceit knowing how I felt, knowing who my father was this entire time"?

"No Michelle", responded Jesse. "We never knew Graziano was related to you in any way until Brock and Sheila unknowing of our involvement, brought it to our attention. Graziano knew, of course, that we were life-long friends to you. It now seems likely he wanted to use us to bring you into the syndicate. But somewhere along the way something happened to change his mind".

"He went to the Huber estate for the first time, in an attempt to find out who Hans Goebel was", said Louise. "He had discovered that I was bleeding funds from the syndicate to fund a large chunk of that enterprise. Martinez had originally come to me to explain the need for such an organization, in part to deal with events he planned to undertake in Europe, but he insisted it was going to be necessary to address the Mexican cartel problems. It's no secret that crime syndicates sometimes need to take out opposition syndicate leaders. At the time I was unaware that Graziano knew nothing of Martinez's plans. On top of that Graziano also discovered that Perez had partnered secretly with Oreski to set up the debauchery brothels in the Louisiana swamp where some of the male clients could do virtually anything they wanted to and with trafficked women".

"As a result of a different undercover agent that Graziano placed within Oreski's organization, Graziano discovered that

Perez was receiving large funds from these clients and videotaping and blackmailing them on his own, without Graziano's knowledge. Graziano asked me to trail the money to see if it made its way back into our books. After I explained that there were no records of any such transactions, in a meeting where we were all present, Graziano and Martinez confronted him, and Martinez said he would take care of it

Sheila stepped into the conversation. "Except that everyone knows that when the second in command of a crime syndicate says he 'will take care' of it, I expect you both knew exactly what he meant. The photographs and videos that my father took included meetings that Martinez had at the Huber estate. These videos clearly show Martinez discussing the hit on Graziano, as he saw this as an opportunity to take over, eliminating his boss from the picture".

"Just a minute", I interjected, "Jeremy, you said the charges were conspiracy to commit murder. Just which murder or murders are we talking about. Who killed Graziano, Ronaldo, Oreski? Are you saying the same person is responsible for all three murders?"

Jeremy responded. "New Orleans was key to this investigation. Casandra and her team of forensic accountants were able to trace funds from your books, Louise, to James Ronaldo who was used in many ways to assist Martinez to come and go into and out of the United States and Europe without the FBI or Interpol tracking him. In turns out that Ronald kept significant video records of all his transactions which Sheila uncovered in the house. She realized the significance of her findings and informed us immediately. The local police in Miami already had a search warrant for the property and secured the data. What was most interesting about Ronaldo's records- an account with a New Orleans Mardi Gras company that produces masks, masks which can replicate anyone' features. Perhaps you have seen the movie "Face Off". That is the principle involved. Masks can be created to almost identically replicate another person. Basically, they are a silicone/latex blend that can move with your facial features. The trick though, is that the process requires the person being replicated, so to speak, has to be a cooperative member of the plan in order to sit to have a mold of their face taken. The search warrant turned up a set of keys, and as with all good investigators they uncovered a warehouse that had all of Ronaldo's molds. That means that Alverez and Martinez, et al were all originally in this together.

With different identities, fake passports, and multiple different companies, Ronaldo enabled Martinez, and likely others, to come and go across the globe. The records and videos also show you, Louise, procuring a mask that looks exactly like Perez. We cannot prove you killed Oreski yourself, but we can prove that you were in on the conspiracy to have him killed and frame Perez for the murder. Unfortunately for you, that is one of the discussions videotaped by at Huber where Martinez outlines in some detail that you would procure such a mask for exactly that purpose".

"Okay" said John, that takes care of who arranged the hit on Graziano and Oreski, so what was the follow up with Ronaldo. Surely, he was seen as a loose end, but is there any evidence of who was involved with taking out Ronaldo"?

"At the moment", responded Jeremy, "we have no evidence that implicates any one individual in Ronaldo's murder. The data Sheila provided from her father's investigation does not show any conversations that involve killing Ronaldo. That investigation is ongoing".

"What is happening with Hans Goebel, the man who doesn't exist"? I asked.

"We have Huber under further investigation", replied Van. "We know that the Huber entity is complicit in the murders of Graziano and Oreski, but there are issues with how they are constituted, being registered external to Germany. We will be conducting a very thorough investigation of the organization and will likely be able to secure at least a portion of their client list. One of the issues will be to separate those who legitimately attend for recreational reasons from the criminal element. In the meantime, we know that Martinez heads up a large chunk of crime in Europe and we have ample evidence to charge him with at least conspiracy to commit murder. However, we have no idea where he is, yet again".

As Jesse and Louise were escorted out of the building, Michelle sank back into an easy chair. "I can't believe that I have known these two women my entire life and they knew I wanted to find my father, and then to have them turn out to be in his employ, committing crime after crime, knowing I am in the FBI. I cannot believe this went on for such a long time without me having any inclination".

"They kept a very low profile, humble homes, no extravagant spending to draw attention to themselves". I offered. "Jeremy, it seems you have a solid conspiracy case against Louise, but you haven't said anything that implicates Jesse in any murder plot. Is there something I missed"?

"No, we have no evidence in that regard. However, she was clearly involved in a number of criminal activities in terms of purchases and bribery. We will try to make the case that she must have been well aware. It's likely she will get a lengthy prison term in any event".

With that said our little party broke up and Sheila and I headed back to my place.

"There is still the outstanding issue of Diane Atkinson's wife and her desire to clear her husband. However, based on what we heard today, I am convinced that is not possible. It seems he was truly guilty of involvement in a criminal conspiracy and attended Graziano's murder as a participant. That seems to sum most things up although I am still left wondering what the attempted phony break-in at Graziano's house was all about. I wonder if we'll ever know".

"I think that there must be some kind of information outstanding of which we are not aware. It may come out in the fullness of time. Meanwhile your thoughts regarding Diane and her husband are about right", I responded," it's time to let her know what we know about his actions and just leave it to her to see if she wants to pursue it further. In the meantime, there is this little matter of a will to expedite. She will receive monies from that, as will you, as well as a property in Malaga. I will arrange a lawyer first thing tomorrow and get that process of transferring the properties started. Let's order in and spend a quiet night together, maybe go for a walk".

"Sounds great". Sheila agreed. After supper we hit the sack and spent a time making love. "I have a question for you", she started. "What happens to us now. I seem to recall that we agreed to spend some time in Malaga together. Are you still up for that, and how do you feel about me. I don't want to continue with one off attempts at relationships and would like something more permanent, and I would like the next phase of my life, my retirement, in essence, to be with you. Where are you at Brock"?

"I am in the same place, though I don't want to get married again. The thing is Sheila, I do love you. In my past, I have used that word too freely without really knowing what I was saying. Heck, I suspect most people don't really know what it means when they say it. But that is not me anymore. I think the word is just a short-cut. What I mean when I use the word is a lot of other things. So, if I let it slip out, what I am really saying is this:

"You are very attractive to me. You are intelligent, notoriously funny, classy, independent, creative, wise, affectionate, and exceptionally kind".

"So yes, let's see if we can make a go of it. Does that mean I move to Atlanta?"

"No Brock"' I am going to sell my agency and move to Malaga, and am hoping, since you have no ties, that you would be agreeable to that".

"Of course", I responded, "I will sell my house as well, as you are selling your home and business. I am ready to start a new chapter and doing so with you is perfect. We have the weekend together and on Monday I will see a lawyer and a real estate agency and get these processes started."

"Great," she replied. "I will do the same, meaning that I have to head back to Atlanta and make those arrangements. I am sure there are individuals on my staff that would love to purchase the business".

On Monday, I arranged a meeting with a lawyer and handed him the original will. He indicated that it would be necessary to attempt to trace the real Hans Goebel if such a person existed. Given the Munich address and the circumstances involved he suspected the business itself and maybe more than one individual might come forward to claim the funds. In the meantime, however, he said he could arrange a full payment of the funds to Diane and Sheila and also expedite the Puerta Vallarta penthouse and Malaga villa transfers with some ease.

A week later, John phoned. "Good morning, Brock", he began. "Some things have transpired. Jeremy phoned to say that in the arraignment, that Louise was held to be a flight risk, but that Jesse was granted bail, which was immediately posted through her lawyer. She headed to her home, and then vanished. The FBI managed to track her to a flight to Spain. Meanwhile Van de Vries called to say that in Interpol's investigation, they have uncovered a marriage certificate in Spain. It seems that Martinez and Jesse are man and wife. Both Jeremy and de Vries have asked if you would be willing to go to Spain assist in their investigation, both into the corruption aspects associated with Hans Goebel as well as hunting down our happy couple. As well, Interpol will place both you and Sheila on Interpol payroll during this time. Would the two of you be up for that"?

I called Sheila, explained the events and the offer and she agreed to become involved. I phoned John back and let he and Jeremy know, as they were together at that moment. John said he would call Van de Vries and let him know so that arrangements could begin. It was to be an exciting new chapter. A love interest, a great job, and a villa in Malaga!

Printed in the United States
by Baker & Taylor Publisher Services